SECRETS ON SATURDAY

ANN PURSER

BERKLEY PRIME CRIME, NEW YORK

THE BERKLEY PUBLISHING GROUP
Published by the Penguin Group
Penguin Group (USA) Inc.
375 Hudson Street, New York, New York 10014, USA
Penguin Group (Canada), 90 Eglinton Avenue East, Suite 700, Toronto, Ontario M4P 2Y3, Canada
(a division of Pearson Penguin Canada Inc.)
Penguin Books Ltd., 80 Strand, London WC2R 0RL, England
Penguin Group Ireland, 25 St. Stephen's Green, Dublin 2, Ireland (a division of Penguin Books Ltd.)
Penguin Group (Australia), 250 Camberwell Road, Camberwell, Victoria 3124, Australia
(a division of Pearson Australia Group Pty. Ltd.)
Penguin Books India Pvt. Ltd., 11 Community Centre, Panchsheel Park, New Delhi—110 017, India
Penguin Group (NZ), 67 Apollo Drive, Mairangi Bay, Auckland 1311, New Zealand
(a division of Pearson New Zealand Ltd.)
Penguin Books (South Africa) (Pty.) Ltd., 24 Sturdee Avenue, Rosebank, Johannesburg 2196,
South Africa

Penguin Books Ltd., Registered Offices: 80 Strand, London WC2R 0RL, England

SECRETS ON SATURDAY

A Berkley Prime Crime Book / published by arrangement with Severn House

PRINTING HISTORY
Severn House hardcover edition / 2006
Berkley Prime Crime mass-market edition / April 2007

Copyright © 2006 by Ann Purser.
Cover art by Griesbach and Martucci.
Cover design by Leslie Worrell.
Interior text design by Kristin del Rosario.

ISBN: 978-0-425-21451-0

BERKLEY® PRIME CRIME
Berkley Prime Crime Books are published by The Berkley Publishing Group,
a division of Penguin Group (USA) Inc.,
375 Hudson Street, New York, New York 10014.
The name BERKLEY PRIME CRME and the BERKLEY PRIME CRIME design are trademarks belonging to Penguin Group (USA) Inc.

PRINTED IN THE UNITED STATES OF AMERICA

10 9 8 7 6 5 4 3 2 1

The Lois Meade Mysteries by Ann Purser

MURDER ON MONDAY
TERROR ON TUESDAY
WEEPING ON WEDNESDAY
THEFT ON THURSDAY
FEAR ON FRIDAY
SECRETS ON SATURDAY

For Philip

ONE

꒳

Lois Meade, boss of cleaning business New Brooms and experienced amateur sleuth, looked out of her window along Long Farnden's main street, idly thinking about nothing very much. A car drew up and stopped outside her house, and a man—tall, thin, nondescript-looking except for a slight limp—made his way up to her front door.

She dodged behind the curtains in time-honoured village fashion, and waited until she heard the bell. Then she waited some more until her mother came from the back of the house and opened up. "Good morning." Gran paused, and Lois heard a soft voice asking for New Brooms.

Time to make an appearance. "Can I help you?" she said, and Gran looked at her crossly. Gran liked to know who people were, and to glean as much of their business as she could before handing them over to Lois.

"I wanted to ask about cleaning," he said politely, looking from one to the other.

"Then you've come to the right place," said Lois, ushering him in firmly. "Our main office is in Tresham, but I'm happy to see you here. Come through."

Not to be beaten, Gran followed with an offer of coffee, which the man accepted with alacrity. "It's a cold morning," he said, "and the heater in my car is on the blink."

Lois sat behind her desk and picked up a pen. "Now," she said. "First of all, where's your house? Got to make sure you are on our patch. People have rung me from Dorset and Yorkshire, but we stick to a radius of about thirty miles around Farnden." As Long Farnden was in the Midlands, the heart of England, this took in a nice mix of town and country for Lois's team of cleaners, and had worked well for a number of years.

"Oh, well, that's fine," the man said. "The house is right here in Long Farnden. In the new estate off the High Street. Used to be Tollervey-Jones land. All the nobs are selling off their birthright these days!" The man smiled a wintry smile, and accepted a steaming cup of coffee from Gran with obvious gratitude.

"Oh, right. Have you just moved in, then?" Both Gran and Lois knew who lived in every house in the village, but neither had known that any of the Blackberry Gardens lot were up for sale.

"No, no," he replied. "It was my uncle's house, but he's too old to live by himself now, and we've moved him away to a nice comfortable old folks' home."

"What?" said Gran. "You mean Mr. Everitt? That nice old chap who used to take his terrier for a walk every morning and evening?"

The man nodded, and Lois said evenly, "We had no idea he needed help. The village is usually very good about looking after its oldies. Now," she added, "could I have your name, please?"

"Abthorpe," he said, "Reg Abthorpe. He had no children, his wife died, and there's just us cousins to be responsible for him. I'm the only one left in England. The rest emigrated to Australia."

"So how can we help you?" Lois asked. She looked Reg Abthorpe up and down, and decided for no reason at all that she didn't like him. She didn't like his soft, smarmy voice, or his thin, mousy hair carefully trained over a bald patch. She didn't like his soft suede shoes with quiet rubbery soles, and most of all she didn't like his smile, his cold, one-sided smile.

He settled into his seat, and spoke with more confidence now. "We promised Uncle Herbert that we'd keep the house in a good state for him. Aired and cleaned, that sort of thing. He thinks he'll be back when he's better, poor old lad, but that won't happen. We just go along with it to please him. After all, it's his money paying for it! So I wondered if you'd take on the job? Once every couple of weeks should be enough. I'm afraid nobody's been in for a while, so you may need to do a bit extra at first. We'll pay, of course." He smiled at her, and she shivered. "Can you take it on?" he said.

"Yes, of course." For all her shrinking feeling, she wouldn't turn away good business, and it sounded like a doddle, once they'd got the place shipshape.

She took down all the necessary information, and said she'd be in touch when she'd worked out her schedules. He gave her an address in Suffolk, and limped softly away down the path to his car. Lois watched him go.

"What a nice man!" said Gran, coming up behind her. "Nice job for Sheila, that one."

"Hey, who's cleaning business is this, anyway?" said Lois. "Back to the kitchen, woman, and get busy with the lunch."

Gran laughed. She and Lois were very alike, and sometimes sparks flew, but on the whole it was a very comfortable arrangement.

REG ABTHORPE PULLED UP HIS COAT COLLAR AND started his engine. It was reluctant, but he coaxed it slowly down the street, turning off to cruise into Blackberry Gardens. He sat for a minute outside the deserted house, and then quickly walked up to the front door, unlocked it and went in, shutting the door firmly behind him. An inventory was needed. After all, he'd never seen the Meade woman before, and for all he knew she might specialize in light-fingered staff who were adept at removing small objects which nobody would notice. There was nothing really valuable in Uncle Herbert's house, but people flogged the most extraordinary rubbish at car boot sales these days. Seems there's always a customer for everything, he thought to himself. He took a notebook from his pocket and began to make a list, room by room. He paid particular attention to the freezer.

The task was a tedious one, and it took Reg a good hour before he had finished. He looked at his watch. Half past one, and he was hungry. He'd noticed a pub on his way into the village, and decided on a snack before he returned—not to Suffolk, but to his real home, which was not nearly so far away.

He looked around, checking that he had turned off lights and shut doors. The central heating was turned down low, but left on continuously to keep damp at bay. It would be better once the cleaner was coming in regularly, if only to stir the air. He locked the front door and glanced around at the garden. It must be kept trim, and he made a mental note to check on this. Then he was back in his car and driving down the street towards the pub.

"Morning," said the publican, Doug. He and his wife were new in the business, and very good at it. They had quickly become popular in the village. Now he welcomed his customer and said, "A bit parky out there this morning! What can I get you, sir?"

"Pint of Best, and what've you got to eat? Something hot, if possible." Reg Abthorpe smiled at Doug behind the bar, his one-sided, chilly smile.

Doug wondered why he felt a draught of cold air. The log fire was burning well, and doors were shut. He drew up the pint, and then went out to order food. "Who's in?" said his wife, Meggie. "One of the locals?"

Doug shook his head. "Not seen him before," he said. "Seems all right. Here," he added. "Did you have the back door open just now?"

"Nope, not the day for it."

Doug shrugged, and decided he'd imagined it—or someone had walked over his grave . . .

"Not very busy today," remarked Reg, as a plateful of steaming fish and chips was placed in front of him.

"Weekdays, not many about," Doug said. "The occasional travelling salesman, or the weekly lunch for the Darby and Joan club—highlight of the week, that is."

"So weekends is your busy time?" The fish and chips were disappearing fast.

"Yep," Doug replied with a smile. "We get the regulars then. Darts and bar skittles, husbands and wives come in then, and we do well on the food. Food's where the money is in pubs these days. Leastways, until we have the smoking ban." Doug returned to his usual spot behind the bar and leaned on the counter. "You're not local, are you?" he said, his curiosity getting the better of him.

Reg shook his head. "Just passing through," he said. "I'm one of your travelling salesmen," he added, and Doug asked quickly what he was selling.

"Don't worry," Reg said, thinking rapidly. "Nothing that you'd be likely to want. It's stuff for computers and office systems. That kind of thing." He was rather proud of this sudden inspiration. It sounded convincing, and Doug was unlikely to question him further.

"Oh, yeah," said Doug, sounding relieved. "All double-Dutch to me, I'm afraid. Now then, can I get you another pint?"

Reg refused, saying he was driving, and it would be just his luck to meet a policeman with nothing better to do than to breathalyze him.

"Far to go, then?" Doug asked.

"Mmm," Reg replied, getting to his feet and feeling for his wallet. "How much do I owe you then? It was very nice, just the job."

After Reg Abthorpe had left, Doug cleared away the plate and glass and went out to his wife. "He's gone. Might as well close up. We'll not get anybody else now."

"What did you find out about him?" Meggie said. It was a big part of the fun in running a pub to ask questions and discuss the answers. Meggie came from a family of publicans, and would not have been happy in any other job. Long hours on her feet were no problem, and her cheery smile and delight in small talk had made her many friends in the locality.

"Not a lot." Doug busied himself stacking the dishwasher. Then a thought struck him, and he turned to Meggie with a frown. "You don't think he could've been some kind of inspector?" he said.

"I didn't see him. What did he look like?" Meggie regretted she had not gone through to the bar to see for herself.

"That's the funny thing," Doug said slowly. "I can't think of anything much—just a nondescript sort of bloke. I think he had a bit of a limp, but hardly noticeable. Nothing you'd remember him by. Except . . ."

"Except what?"

"His smile," said Doug. "It was sort of one-sided, and very chilly. His eyes stayed cold. I like a bloke who smiles with his eyes."

"Well, we'll probably not see him again. Unless he's an inspector and makes a bad report. But those fish and chips were fresh as a daisy, and his plate looks as if he licked it clean. So let's get on with the work, and then we'll have a sandwich and a nice cup of tea."

Doug did as he was told, but for the rest of the day that chilly smile returned to make him shiver.

Two

MONDAY MIDDAY, AND THE NEW BROOMS TEAM assembled in Lois's office in Long Farnden: Hazel Thornbull, nee Reading, and her mother Bridle; Enid Abraham from the mill; and Sheila Stratford, farmworker's wife and Waltonby born and bred. Jean Slater was the most recent member of the team. She had been involved in a very unpleasant episode that had all but destroyed her life, and Lois had been not at all sure about employing her. But she had given Jean a probationary period, and so far she had been an exemplary worker.

Bill Stockbridge had not yet arrived. He had telephoned to say he was held up at the vet's, where he worked part-time. Lois had wondered if, now that he was a married man, he would give up cleaning and get a more lucrative job. But his wife Rebecca was still teaching in Waltonby village school, and he had declared he had no intention of giving up a job he enjoyed. Lois had been pleased. Bill was a steady young Yorkshireman, and she relied on his good common sense.

"Shall we start? Bill can catch up when he arrives." Lois began to go through the schedules, and then came to the new client. "There's this house in Blackberry Close," she said. "It's empty—well, nobody's living there—and we have to keep it clean and tidy. It was old Mr. Everitt's house. He's gone into a home somewhere."

"What? Old Herbert? Why on earth . . . ? It's a bit sudden, isn't it, Mrs. M?" Enid Abraham was usually the quiet one. Steady and reliable, she ran her mill house as a bed and breakfast, and fitted in all her jobs with characteristic efficiency.

"Did you know him, Enid?" Lois was surprised at her outburst, and frowned. "Wasn't he getting a bit past looking after himself?"

Enid shook her head vigorously. "Right as rain. Certainly had all his marbles, and his house was clean as a new pin. And his garden well looked after."

Sheila Stratford nodded. "Old Herbert was fine," she said. "Walked that little dog morning and evening every day, and he'd go quite a long way. My Sam used to meet him in the woods sometimes. He was in really good shape for his age. Did he have a stroke or something?"

Lois shrugged. "I really don't know," she said, and told them about her interview with Reg Abthorpe. "Anyway," she added, "it's not our business to know the client's personal circumstances. We just go in there and do what we're told. I'm going in myself at first, and then I'll probably send you, Enid, if you've got time."

The door opened and Bill came in. "Morning all," he said cheerfully. "What have I missed, Mrs. M?"

"Not a lot, Bill," said Lois, and gave him instructions for the coming week. Then she mentioned Herbert Everitt, and he showed no reaction. "Good," he said. "Another client in the village cuts down travelling time! Blackberry Gardens, did you say? Who's going to do it?" He looked round the team, and they all looked at Lois.

"I am, at first," she said. "Then Enid, probably. She knew Mr. Everitt. His nephew said the old boy expects to come back to the house, but there's no prospect of that."

"Why don't they put it on the market, then?" Bill said.

"That's their business," said Lois, sharply now. "Anyway, let's get on."

"Um, before we do, could I just ask where Mr. Everitt has gone?" Enid flushed. "I'd like to visit the old boy, if possible."

Lois sighed. "I've no idea," she said, "but I'll try to find out from Mr. Abthorpe. He lives in Suffolk, but I've got his number. I'll let you know, Enid. Now, can we change the subject, else Hazel'll never get back to Tresham."

Hazel manned the office in Tresham, which was always shut on Monday mornings because of the team meeting. She should open it up at two thirty, and Lois could see time slipping by. "Any questions or suggestions?" she said. Nobody said anything. They had known Lois for a long time, most of them, and were well aware that she was ready to wind up the meeting.

"I saw the new woman from Hornton House in the shop," Sheila ventured after a pause. "She said her daughter is looking for a part-time job, and I said I'd mention it to you."

Lois nodded. "Fine," she said. "I've made a note." She looked around the familiar faces, and said, "Thanks a lot everybody. Any problems, let me know. Have a good week."

After they'd gone, Lois went into the kitchen where Gran was making a sandwich. "I'm just going out for a few minutes," she said, and Gran looked mutinous. "What about this sandwich, then? You can't go without something to eat."

"I'll not be more than a few minutes," Lois said. "Just going to see Josie in the shop." Josie was her daughter, who had run the village shop successfully for some while.

"Can't it wait?"

"No. Back soon."

Lois set off down the street towards the shop, but she did not go in. She carried on and branched off into a close of detached modern houses—Blackberry Close. As she approached the one for which she had the key, she stopped and looked around. Nobody about. She walked up the path and disappeared into Herbert Everitt's empty house, unaware that although there was not a soul to be seen, behind net curtains there were watching eyes.

"HI, MUM." JOSIE WAS STANDING AT THE OPEN DOOR of the shop. "I saw you go by. D'you want a cuppa? It's a slack time, and we can keep an eye open for customers."

Lois shook her head. "Love to," she said, "but Gran will kill me if I don't eat the sandwich she cut for me half an hour ago. But I'll come down after closing time this afternoon—I want to ask you about old Mr. Everitt."

"Old Herbert? Haven't seen him for a while . . ."

"Right, well, I'll be down later." Lois hurried away up the street to face Gran's wrath. But when she greeted her bravely in the kitchen, Gran's mind was on something else.

"I've been thinking," she said.

"Oh, no," groaned Lois.

"Thinking about Herbert Everitt," Gran continued.

"Don't you think it's a bit odd that none of us knew he was ill and couldn't manage? I wouldn't swear to it, but I'm sure he looked very sprightly last time I saw him out walking."

"I suppose you don't remember when that was?"

"No, but it was quite recently. Why don't you ask Josie? He was a regular at the shop."

"I will," Lois said. "But it isn't really any of our business. Still, Enid wants to visit him, so I'll try to find out where he's gone. I hardly dare ask," she continued, "but is my sandwich . . . ?"

"I ate it," Gran said shortly.

THREE

It was cosy in the stockroom at the back of the shop. Josie and Lois sat on stools either side of an electric fire, insulated by boxes and packages on shelves that reached to the ceiling. A small sink and electric kettle served for quick snacks during the day, and now with mugs in hand, mother and daughter chatted comfortably about the day's events—which were small and unsurprising, and part of the everyday life of Long Farnden.

But there was one episode not so easily absorbed and forgotten by Lois. Her visit to Blackberry Gardens and Herbert Everitt's house returned naggingly, and she finally opened the subject with Josie. "So what can you tell me about Herbert?"

Josie thought for a moment, and then said, "Not a lot. His name was Herbert and he never allowed anyone to shorten it to Bert. He had been married years ago, but his wife died early. They had no children, and he was sad about that. But he had his little dog and I think he was happy. No, not happy, more resigned to being old and alone except for Spot. He liked it in the village, because people were friendly."

"Did he go to the pub?" Lois could see that in fact Josie knew quite a lot about Herbert Everitt. Most village people liked Josie, and told her their life stories given half a chance. It had come in useful to Lois in the past, and now looked like being so again. Not, she told herself, that she suspected anything sinister in his going away, but some background information would be useful in the cleaning job. She deceived herself, of course, but it was early days.

"Oh yes, he liked a pint." Josie smiled. "I think Spot had a sip or two. The old boys in the dominoes school welcomed him in, which, as you know, is the seal of approval in Long Farnden. He had some stories to tell, so he said. His dad had been a bit of a dodgy character, apparently. Not always the right side of the law. He seemed quite proud of him."

"Did he ever talk about the rest of his family—sisters, brothers, cousins?"

Josie shook her head. "Nope. Always said he was alone in the world, and when he was depressed he'd say nobody cared whether he lived or died. I used to point to Spot outside the shop with his lead on the dog hook, waiting patiently. 'He'd care,' I'd say, and that'd cheer him up nine times out of ten."

"He must have some relations," said Lois, frowning. "That Mr. Abthorpe is his nephew, which means he had or has a brother or sister. Still, they're all in Australia, apparently. Only Reg Abthorpe left here."

Josie looked at her curiously. "Are you worried, Mum? Sniffed out something wrong?"

Lois stood up and took her mug to the sink. "Well, I went to Herbert's house this morning. You saw me passing by. It was creepy, Josie. Not cold or damp or anything. In fact it was quite pleasantly warm, and everything tidy and clean. Well, a bit of dust here and there, but nothing to speak of. There's magazines on the table, and a newspaper folded neatly by the bed. The bed's still made up with clean sheets. And the fridge! Still stocked up with instant meals, milk—sour, of course—and wrinkled apples."

"What were the sell-by dates?" asked Josie the shopkeeper.

"Good girl," said Lois approvingly. "I looked at those. All out of date about three weeks ago. And the newspaper dated around the same time. So that's when he went . . ." Lois reached for her jacket. "I must be getting back. Nice having a chat. It's closing time now, so you can lock up. See you tomorrow, love."

Josie watched her mother disappearing up the street. She had that purposeful walk that meant only one thing. She suspected something out of kilter, and wouldn't rest until she'd discovered what it was. Josie sighed. Poor old Dad! That cop Cowgill would be nosing around again. Oh, well, there was nothing they could do about it, except to help her mother and hope she didn't end up at the receiving end of a gun . . . like last time.

"HELLO? IS MR. ABTHORPE THERE?" LOIS HAD DIalled the Suffolk number he had given her, and a woman's voice answered.

"Who?"

"Mr. Reg Abthorpe. He gave me this number to contact him."

"Never heard of him," said the woman, and rang off.

Lois sat frowning for a minute, then checked the number she had written down and tried again. "Hello, please don't ring off. It's Mrs. Meade from Long Farnden. Could you kindly tell me whereabouts you are? Is it a town or . . . ?"

"What d'you want with this bloke? You after him or some thing?"

"No," said Lois patiently. She explained about the cleaning job and Abthorpe's uncle.

After a pause, the woman said, "Oh well, I suppose it won't do no harm to tell you. This is Sudbury in Suffolk. An' I still don't know no Mr. Abthorpe. G'bye."

Sudbury. Lois dialled enquiries, and asked for a Mr. R. Abthorpe of Sudbury, Suffolk. The helpful young man could find no trace. "No R. Abthorpe in the Sudbury area," he said. "No Abthorpes at all. Sorry I can't help you." Lois felt a growing sense of unease. She was also irritated at wasting so much of her time. Then she heard Derek's van outside, and shut her office door with a bang and went through to the kitchen.

"Hello, me duck," Derek said, giving her a hug, and leaving dirty smudges on her face. "Good day?"

"Not bad," Lois lied. Derek musn't suspect she was even thinking of ferretin' about. He was a man who liked a quiet life. And much as he loved her, he dreaded her involvement with another of her mysteries—and even more, a renewed acquaintance with that bugger Cowgill!

He pecked Gran's cheek and started towards the door. "Got a surprise for you, Lois," he said. "And don't say anything 'til you've thought about it." He disappeared out to his van, and when he returned he was carrying something small and white and furry. "Here," he said. "In need of a good home. Named Jemima at the moment. Mother a pedigree Cairn, and father an old farm terrier who should have known better. I said we'd have her . . ."

Lois closed her eyes and took a deep breath. They had no pet animals now. The cat, Melvyn, had died a couple of months ago, and old Cyril's dog that they'd taken in temporarily, had been claimed by his sister in Tresham. Lois opened her eyes again, and Derek advanced and held out his bundle. Lois reluctantly cupped her hands, and the small, shivering puppy fitted exactly. She was not entirely white, but had grey ears and patches on her cheeks. Her enormous brown eyes looked up anxiously at Lois, who hesitated, then melted and buried her face in the soft fur.

"Oh God," said Gran. "Another job for me, no doubt. And isn't it dirty, Lois? You don't want to catch anything."

Lois shook her head. "Smells of disinfectant and

puppy," she said. "Still, I think I'll just take her outside and see if she'll perform." On her way to the door, she kissed Derek's chilly cheek, and said, "Thanks, love. She'll fit in nicely. Jemima? Bit much for a tiny thing . . . I think I'll call her Jeems until she's bigger."

Derek looked across at Gran, and she stared back at him. "All right, Gran?" he said, when Lois had gone into the garden.

She shrugged. "Nobody asked my opinion," she said, and then added, "still, it's quite a pretty little dog. Our Lois'll make a fool of it, I daresay, but we'll manage." She sniffed, and returned to the oven.

Four

THE NEW PEOPLE IN HORNTON HOUSE WERE FOR-eigners, according to the village. A family with two children in their late teens had arrived not so long ago, and were, of course, treated as foreigners, though they were as English as Mrs. T-J.

"What's their name again, Mum?" Lois asked, finishing her toast and marmalade.

"Pickering. Why d'you want to know?"

"Sheila said their daughter was looking for a part-time job, and had asked about New Brooms. I thought I'd call and see what she's like. I need a willing girl for a few more hours."

"Willing to do what?" said Derek from behind the morning paper.

"Ignore him," Lois said.

"Know anything about them, Mum?" Gran was a WI

member, went to church, and belonged to the Darby and Joan Club. Not much in the village escaped her notice.

"They're townies," she said. "Come from Birmingham, apparently. He works at the brewery in Tresham, and she's an ancillary at a school there. The boy's going to university, and the girl doesn't know yet what she wants to do. I expect that's why she wants a little job."

"Blimey," said Derek. "You don't really need to call on them, me duck. Gran's covered everything!" He got up and shouldered his canvas bag.

"Cheese and pickle in there," Gran said fondly. "Your favourite."

"Right-o, then," he said, and blew Lois a kiss. "See you later." And as he went out of the door they heard him mutter, "Wish *I* worked in a brewery."

Lois stood outside Hornton House and looked up and down the street. Nobody in sight, except a car approaching slowly. Then, quite suddenly, it quickened up with a rasp of acceleration, and she instinctively drew back. As it sped past her, she noticed that the driver had turned his head away, as if to look at the shop opposite, but Lois knew there was something familiar about him. And the car: she had seen it before. But where? She shrugged, and walked up to the Pickering's front door. Her finger had scarcely left the bell when the door opened and a pleasant-faced woman appeared.

"Good morning," Lois said. "I am Mrs. Meade from New Brooms . . ."

"I know you are," the woman said with a smile. "We've been telling Floss to come and see you for weeks! Did Sheila mention her?"

Lois nodded, and followed the woman in to a room where the atmosphere was warm and smelled pleasantly of polish and flowers.

"I'll just call her," Mrs. Pickering said. "She's upstairs. Spends a lot of time at her computer, like they all do."

She disappeared and Lois heard her call. Then both she and her daughter came in, and Floss was introduced. She was conservatively dressed for her generation, thought Lois. Jeans, of course, but with a cheerful red jersey that showed no hint of bare midriff. That was a point in her favour! Her blonde hair was cut in a long bob, parted in the middle and tucked smoothly behind her ears. In all, she made a good impression, and Lois smiled.

"Perhaps I could have a word with Floss?" she said. Mrs. Pickering left tactfully, and Lois said, "Now then, just a few questions. First of all, why do you want to work for us?"

"I'll be honest, shall I?" Floss offered.

Lois looked surprised, and said, "Of course."

"Well, I can't say I've always wanted to be a cleaner, or that I'd do it for ever. But I didn't get very good GCSEs, and can't decide at the moment what I really want to do next."

"So you'd just be filling in time?"

Floss nodded. "But I'd take it seriousiy, and work hard," she said. "Mum'll tell you I'm good around the house. And I'd give you plenty of notice if I finally decide what my career is going to be," she added ruefully. "Dad is a bit fed up with me," she continued, "but Mum understands."

Do I really want a pleasant but dim girl with a pushy father? Lois asked herself. Well, why not? She wouldn't need starred As to clean Mrs. T-J's mansion, or tidy up behind the vet's totally spoilt brats.

They chatted for a few more minutes, and then Lois got up to go. "I'll let you know tomorrow," she said. "You'll not have references yet, but perhaps I could see your last school report. That'll do for the moment."

Mrs. Pickering and Floss showed her out, and she walked home thinking the girl could well be a useful addition to the team. Halfway there, she stopped suddenly. That car! It was Reg Abthorpe's, of course. And it had been the back of his head she recognized. Thinning hair, something one-sided about his shoulders. Yes, that was

Reg Abthorpe. So why was he in Farnden, a long way from Suffolk? Had he been to Blackberry Close? And if so, what for? He had said he wouldn't need to be back, but would leave everything to Lois.

"That man," Lois said, as she met Gran coming down the pavement on her way to the shop, "that Reg Abthorpe . . . has he called on us?"

Gran shook her head. "There's been no callers this morning," she said. She looked curiously at her daughter. "You all right, Lois? You look as if you've seen a ghost."

"I'm fine," Lois replied. Before Gran could ask more questions, she said she had a couple of phone calls to make, and continued on her way. She was absolutely certain it had been Abthorpe, and decided she would start work on Herbert Everitt's house tomorrow.

THERE WAS A MESSAGE ON LOIS'S ANSWER PHONE. A man's voice, asking her to call a familiar number. Chief Inspector Hunter Cowgill. What did he want? There was only one way to find out, but Lois was well aware of Derek's mild objection to her ever working for that cop again. She hesitated. It wouldn't necessarily mean another job for her. He might have some small enquiry, a point to clear up from last time. She dialled the number.

"Lois? Thanks for ringing back."

"Well, what d'you want?"

"And very nice to hear from you, too," said Cowgill good humouredly.

"Well, get on with it. I've got work to do."

She hasn't mellowed, thought Cowgill fondly. "I just wondered if you've noticed anything amiss in the village lately," he continued. "Any strangers moving in, or residents moving out unexpectedly . . . that sort of thing?"

Lois frowned. She knew how Cowgill felt about her. After all this time, she would have had to be blind and deaf not to notice. And, although she would never admit it, even to herself, she quite liked the old fool. He never gave up, and on many occasions had turned out to be a very good policeman indeed. But she never gave him any encouragement, remembering how Derek had once decided the pair of them were having an affair, and her marriage had teetered unsteadily for a while.

"Of course people have moved in and out of the village," she said. "That's what people do."

"Yes, Lois, but don't pretend you don't know what I mean. Has anything about the usual course of things seemed to you slightly askew? What about the new people in Homton House? Or rumours of lonely old people being taken advantage of?"

"Ah," said Lois. "So you know about that."

"About what?" Cowgill failed to make the question sound innocent.

"Old Herbert Everitt from Blackbeny Close. That's what. Gone away, and nobody knows where. Except a so-called nephew came round and said he'd taken Mr. Everitt to a very nice residential home, where he could be properly looked after. He engaged my cleaning services until it was decided what to do with the house. Oh, and he gave me a false telephone contact. Any use?"

"As always," replied Cowgill. "The empty house has come to our notice. At least, it's not empty of furniture, but the old boy seems to have gone missing. Neighbours informed us. Worried about him and his little dog. Still, if he's safe in an old folks' home, that's fine. Know anything else about it, Lois?"

"Nothing, really," she said. "The nephew is Reg Abthorpe—at least, that's what he said his name was. Could be as phoney as the telephone number, I suppose. I'm going to do the cleaning myself for a bit. I'll let you know if I find anything. Must go now. Bye."

"Sheila?" Lois had dialled Sheila Stratford straight away. Sheila was one of her original cleaners, and although an incurable gossip, she was absolutely reliable. Her reliability was vital, but her knowledge of local goings-on was even more useful to Lois.

"Do you want to change my schedule?" Sheila was also the most immediately available, and always ready to swap duties.

"No, not at the moment," Lois replied. "I'm still wondering about Mr. Everitt . . . can't get him out of my mind and I'm going to work there tomorrow. I was . . . well, I remembered you said Sam used to meet him in the woods with his little dog. Did he talk to him or anything?"

"I thought you were getting his nephew to tell you where he'd gone—for Enid?" Sheila said.

"I tried. It was a wrong number. A woman answered, and she'd never heard of him. But she did say she was a Sudbury number." Lois told her about the blank result from directory enquiries, and then paused. Sometimes Sheila had a sudden recall. She was getting on in years, was a granny several times over, and her memory sometimes needed a prompt.

"Let me think . . ." Sheila said. "Oh, yes, wait a minute, it's coming back. Sam said the old boy loved birds and often had binoculars with him. He knew a lot about nature of all sorts. Liked to talk to Sam about farming an' that. But I tell you what, Mrs. M," she added confidingly, "he never mentioned no nephew. And nobody I know ever saw him with anyone who wasn't from the villages. You'd have thought if this nephew was his only relative in this country, he'd visit him now and then. Seems a rum do to me, Mrs. M." There was a pause, and then Sheila added, "And I know one or two of his neighbours are worried. My granddaughter's at school with little Donna from Blackberry Close, and her mother told my daughter and my daughter told me that they were worried about Mr. Everitt. It were so sudden, she said."

"Yes, well, maybe I'll find out more when I go in tomorrow. But ask around, Sheila. 1 don't like working on a job that's not straightforward."

"What about money?" Sheila was a crafty countrywoman, with her priorities firmly in order.

"Oh, that's all right," Lois said. "Reg Abthorpe paid four weeks in advance, and said he'd set up a direct debit to come straight to me. No, it's not the money I worry about. It's the old man. Anyway," she added in a brisker tone, "I won't keep you. You're at the vicar's this afternoon, aren't you?"

"Yep. Better be off. Always does me good to go the vicarage," Sheila said, and Lois could hear the smile in her voice. "Almost as good as going to church," she said, and the conversation ended there.

FIVE

"TIME YOU TOOK THAT DOG FOR A WALK, LOIS." Gran was throwing bread to the birds, and at the same time trying to stop the puppy eating it.

"She's too young to go for a walk," said Lois. "Here, I'll get her out of your way." She picked her up and stroked her velvety ears.

"What about that puppy lead Derek gave you?" Gran wasn't to be silenced so easily. "Why do you think they sell puppy leads, if not to take puppies for walks?"

"Oh, I give in." Lois turned around and made for the house. "I'll take her to the shop, on the lead, and see how she gets on."

"Good." It was spitting with rain, and Gran began to take in the washing. "We need apples," she shouted. "And baked beans!" she yelled. Sausages, baked beans and mash were a regular, and Derek said stoutly that baked beans were good for you, and, what's more, great for emptying a room.

Progress to the shop was slow. Jeems had little idea about walking in a straight line, but finally they stood at the open door of the shop, and Lois peered in. "Can I

bring her in if I pick her up?" she said, but Josie replied
that she couldn't break the "no dogs" rule, not even for
her soppy mother. "There's a dog hook out there," she
said. "She won't run away."

"It's her first walk," Lois said.

"So what? Am I supposed to put down the red carpet?
Come on, Mum, this ain't like you!" Lois hadn't the
courage to persist, and so duly hooked up Jeems, who immediately tangled her lead into knots and began to whine.

"Um, I'll just have some apples and a couple of tins of
baked beans," Lois said quickly, hovering at the door.

"Well, come in, for God's sake!" Josie was losing patience. "You're just as bad as old Herbert. When his dog
was a pup, he used to tuck her inside his jacket when he
came in, hoping I wouldn't notice."

"And did you?"

"Of course I did."

"And did you turn him out?"

"Well . . . not every time," Josie admitted, and her
mother pounced.

"There you are then," she said, unhooked Jeems and
tucked her under her arm.

The apples and baked beans were produced in record
time, and Lois and Jeems retreated triumphantly. On the
way home, the little dog seemed suddenly to get the hang
of going for a walk, and in five minutes they were back
in the garden, where to Gran's irritation, Jeems squatted
down and performed, with a look of anguish on her hairy
face. Looking at her abstractedly, Lois thought of Herbert
Everitt and his beloved dog, and wondered if, wherever
he was, he'd been allowed to keep it.

LOIS WAS IN BLACKBERRY CLOSE FIRST THING NEXT
morning. As she stood in Herbert's porch, fumbling for
the key, a sudden shiver made her look back to the street.
There was nobody about, and she shrugged. But just as
she was about to turn back, a movement in the window of
the house opposite caught her eye. Net curtains were

twitching, and she had a glimpse of a face. It was pale, with dark eyes staring at her. She could see the upper part of the person, but could not tell whether it was a man or woman.

Inside, the house was exactly as Lois had left it, except for a small pile of junk mail on the mat. Reg Abthorpe had said that all Herbert's post would be redirected to the residential home, but some had slipped through the net. She would ask Josie about that. There was no point in her delivering rubbish to Herbert's house. And it occurred to her that Josie might have been given instructions to re-direct mail, in which case she would know where he had gone. But she would have said, surely? She couldn't treat her own mother as a security risk, could she? Answer: Yes, she could.

She walked around the house, glancing in all rooms and seeing nothing different from before. Back in the sitting room, she began to dust and polish. It was strange, cleaning a house for nobody. With all her other clients, there was always a person, man or woman, for whom she did as good a job as possible. Here, nobody was going to run a finger along the surfaces, testing for dust. Nobody would have a chat while they had coffee, or look at the clock as she packed up and said goodbye until next week. Herbert Everiitt was not coming back, and there was no-body else to care. It was weird, she decided, and won-dered whether she should have refused the job. But no, if she was honest with herself she had to admit that a mys-tery was more to her taste than the best kept house with the pleasantest of employers.

She moved on to a small Victorian desk, where years ago genteel ladies had sat and written notes to their friends. It was a good piece, with pretty graining and a vase of flowers inlaid in different woods decorating the front. Lois noticed that direct sunlight had taken colour from one side, and considered moving it away from the window. But her instructions were to leave everything as it was, and so she polished it until it shone, and then idly tried the lid. It had a keyhole, but was not locked. She

opened the lid, which formed a writing surface, and then
decided a quick look in the small drawers would do no
harm. They contained old postcards and paper clips, rubber bands and pieces of string, and an old fountain pen.
Nothing interesting there. Lois shut the drawers, feeling
a creeping unease, as if she was being watched. She
looked around, but of course there was nobody there.
Then she realized she was standing in front of the window looking out on the street. And, yes, the net curtains
in the house opposite were moving slightly, as if in a
breeze, but none of the windows were open.

She shook herself. Imagination working overtime,
Derek would say. She began to close the desk, but noticed
a small hollow in the wood which, when pushed along,
moved a sliding panel. At first she thought there was
nothing there, but then she saw something white in a dark
corner. It was a tiny piece of blotting paper, and she
pulled it out. Holding it up to the mirror over the fireplace, she read, ". . . such cru . . ." She could make out
nothing else. Herbert's ink had obviously run out. She
took out the ink pen and tried it on another scrap of paper.
It was empty, and made no mark.

The curtains twitched again, quite obviously this time,
and Lois quickly put both scraps of paper in her pocket
and shut the desk. Just the usual nosey neighbour over the
road, she reassured herself, and continued with her work.
She left the kitchen until last, so that she could wash the
floor and not have to walk over it again. The fridge was
small, and still as empty as she had left it. She turned it
off and left the door ajar. Was there a freezer somewhere,
in a similar state? She finally located it, a large chest
freezer in the utility room, but it was locked. Reg must
have emptied it and taken the contents home. It occurred
to her briefly that it was odd for an old bachelor to have
such a large freezer, but she supposed he lived on frozen
ready-meals, and had prepared for a siege.

She finished the kitchen, and locked up carefully. The
street was still empty, and she walked quickly down the
path to the pavement, noticing that the garden was neat

and tidy. Useful to find out who was doing that job. Her mind being elsewhere, a sudden outbreak of sharp barking from across the road made her stop dead. Two frantic terriers had appeared behind a slatted wooden gate, and were encouraging each other in a frenzy of noise. As she watched, a woman, small and thin, with mousy hair falling over her face, grabbed the terriers' collars and dragged them into the house. It was all over in seconds, but Lois had caught sight of the woman's face: pale and narrow, with rimless glasses. And somehow familiar. Well, why not? She could have passed her in the street many times in the village.

"I've had enough of this place," Lois said aloud to herself, and marched off down Blackberry Close and into the High Street. She intended to call on Josie with one or two questions, and was rounding the corner when a car cruised slowly to a halt beside her. The window opened and Hunter Cowgill looked up at her.

"Morning, Lois," he said breezily. "Been to old Herbert's house?"

Lois glared at him, and said, "None of your business. And no, I haven't got anything to tell you. So if you'll excuse me, I've got work to do."

"Oops," said Cowgill, with a fond smile, watching her walk briskly away. "Not the right time." But he had known Lois a long time, and was convinced that something had upset her. Something not quite right in Blackbeny Gardens. "I'll be in touch later, Lois," he said under his breath, and drove on.

SIX

∽

"I KNOW WHO *SHE* IS," JEAN SLATER SAID. SHE AND Lois were sitting in New Brooms' office in Sebastopol Street, Tresham, with Hazel Thornbull at the desk, discussing business. Business, of course, was concerned with clients, good and bad, old and new, and the exchange of miscellaneous information which might be useful to Lois.

Jean was the latest cleaner to join the team, and Hazel one of the originals. They were talking about Herbert Everitt's house, and the nosey neighbour Josie hadn't been much help to Lois, and had said she couldn't place her, probably, she had added bitterly, because she did all her shopping at the nearest supermarket. But now Jean Slater seemed to recognize Lois's description.

"They haven't been there long," she said. "Came from London . . . somewhere in the East End, somebody said . . . and there's just her and her husband, who's away a lot of the time. She's a dim sort of creature, apparently."

"No wonder she's got those two nasty terriers," said Lois. "She's probably scared of being on her own a lot of the time." She paused, and then said, "What's her husband look like?" A thought had struck her, but was immediately dispelled.

"Big bloke, bald as a coot—you know the sort. Drives an HGV and annoys the other residents of Blackbeny Close by parking it in front of their houses."

"How do you know all this, Jean?" Hazel said. Hazel's husband farmed close to Long Famden, and she was

distinctly put out that a Treshamite should know more
than she did about the village. She was also hesitant, as
were the rest of the team, about being instant buddies
with Jean, whose husband Ken was serving a long prison
sentence for a nasty murder. Lois had been involved in
sorting out a tangle of suspects, and most of the team considered amongst themselves that Lois's judgement in
employing Jean had not been as sharp as usual.

Now Jean laughed. "It just so happens," she said, "that
an old friend of mine lives in the same road. I pop in to
see her now and then, and we gossip."

"Not about New Brooms' business, I hope," Lois said
quickly. She knew she was fighting a losing battle, but at
every opportunity she stressed the need for the team's
vow of confidentiality. "But it is interesting, Jean," she
continued, "that nobody seems to know much about
them. Josie usually has stuff on everyone. The shop's the
centre of what goes on in the village. Nothing much
passes her by. And why should that woman be so interested in me?"

"Not enough to do," Hazel said. "We know her sort
only too well, don't we, Mrs. M? They complain to their
husbands that they can't keep up with housework, and
then spend the day watching the telly . . . or go to stupid
coffee mornings to chew over the latest husband having
it off with somebody else's wife. Classic."

Jean nodded in agreement. "But in this case, I don't
think there'd be much interest in Mrs. Wimp . . . A
bloke'd have to be pretty hard up!"

"Any idea of her real name?" Lois said, but Jean shook
her head. Lois stood up. "Well," she said, "I must be
going. And Jean's in Farnden this afternoon." She left
Hazel answering the telephone, and watched Jean drive
off towards Long Farnden. I need to think, she said to
herself, and set off on foot up the street towards the pet
shop to buy puppy biscuits. "Big bloke, bald as a coot,"
Jean had said. So she's not Mrs. Abthorpe. She walked
on, frowning deeply, and failed to see a man waving to
her from a dark-coloured car.

Definitely something up with Lois, thought Cowgill, feeling a jolt of disappointment that she did not wave back. I must arrange to see her. He was still being pestered by the neighbours of Everitt.

DEREK HAD COME HOME FOR LUNCH, AND GRAN dished up a nicely browned cottage pie with carrots and peas. "Huh," Lois said grumpily. "If it was just me and Mum, we'd be sitting down to a bacon sandwich. You must come home for lunch more often . . ."

Derek saw Gran's face fall, and reached across the table to take Lois's hand. "Somethin' wrong, gel?" he said. She snatched her hand away, and said she was perfectly all right.

Silence fell, and then she sighed deeply and put down her knife and fork. "All right," she said. "I'm in a bad mood and I'm sorry, Mum. Whatever you make is always delicious, and your bacon sarnies are the best."

"So why the bad mood?" said Derek. He had a sinking feeling that he knew why. All the signs were there. Lois abstracted, spending longer than usual in her office, being irritable with poor old Gran. She was up to something again, and no doubt that bugger Cowgill was part of it. Sod it! Why couldn't she be happy with her business and family? He corrected himself. She was happy with her business and family, but she couldn't resist a mystery. There was no doubt she was good at her ferretin' around. Several times she had played a big part in solving nasty cases, and more than once put herself in danger.

"It'll pass," said Lois. "Maybe I'll send someone else into that Everitt house. It is sort of creepy. Nothing changes, except for a layer of dust. Magazines the same, some clothes still in the cupboards. Shoes in a neat row in the bedroom. It's like time's stopped."

"Surely it won't be for long?" Gran said. "After all, if Herbert's not coming back, they'll sell it, won't they?" She scratched her head and continued, "I wish I knew where he's gone. Don't like to think of the old boy on his own in some nursing home with a load of ga-ga old people. And no visitors, very likely. Can't you find out, Lois?"

"I've tried. That Reg Abthorpe seems to have disappeared too. Nobody round here has heard of him, his telephone number is wrong, and he never gave me an address. My fault—I slipped up there."

Derek was reluctant to encourage her, but said, "Have you seen any letters left lying about in the house? Might give you a clue . . . Or an address book . . . Is the telephone still working?"

Lois shook her head. "Nope. And there's no letters, no address book, not even a message pad. There's only this," she added, fishing in her pocket for the tiny piece of blotting paper.

Derek took it, holding it as if it would explode in his hand. ". . . such cru . . ." he read, peering at the smudged writing. "That ain't much help, me duck," he said, and passed it to Gran.

But she shook her head and wouldn't take it. "No," she said firmly. "I don't want anything to do with it. Just leave the cooking and washing and ironing to me, and you two can get on with playing at detectives."

"It's not playing, Mum. Could be serious," Lois said shortly, and left the room.

Derek looked at Gran. "So she's at it again," he said sadly. "Best do what we can to help, and hope it'll be over quickly."

"For Herbert's sake, if nobody else's," snorted Gran. She took a jam sponge pudding out of the oven and yelled loudly that if Lois wanted any she'd better come back straight away. "There's some nice custard here," she added, pushing a jug towards Derek. "Help yourself."

"Crude . . . crucify . . . crux . . ." Derek muttered, and Gran looked at him witheringly.

"Cruelty," she said. "What else?"

SEVEN

❧

"RIGHT, TEAM," LOIS said, in her best football manager's voice, "we have a new member today. Some of you may know her . . . Floss Pickering, welcome."

Sheila nodded, and spoke up. "We'll give you any help you need," she said encouragingly to the girl sitting at the end of the row in Lois's office.

"Thanks," Floss said, not looking in the least nervous. She'd set off up the street this morning, her head full of strictures from her mother not to be too know-all or casual. "Cleaning is Mrs. Meade's business," she had said, "and she runs it very efficiently. Got a good reputation. So mind you don't besmirch it . . ."

"Be-what?" Floss had answered, and left for work.

Now she listened to the team discussing schedules and giving reports, and realized the whole thing was not quite such a doddle as she'd thought. Lois suggested Floss should accompany Sheila Stratford for a couple of weeks, and help out while learning what she needed to know. "More than you thought, probably," said Lois, reading Floss's mind. "But you'll be fine. And think how useful it will be when you've a home of your own!"

There was a general laugh, while Floss protested that that was a very long way off in the future. "Mmm," said Lois, "that's what they all say. Mind you, our Bill here took his time. And how's Rebecca this week?" she added to the reddening Bill.

"Fine," he said, and then hesitated. "Um, that is, she's really fine, but . . . er . . ."

There was a pause, and then Hazel said with a delighted shout, "She's sick in the mornings? Come on, Bill, tell us—are you going to be a dad?"

Bill nodded proudly. "It's quite a way on," he said. "We thought we'd leave it before telling people, what with Becky being at the school and all the children getting excited. She'll be stopping work soon."

After that, not much more business was achieved, and Lois disappeared to open a bottle. "Wonderful news," she said, returning with a tray of glasses. "Here's to you both," she smiled, "and to the little Stockbridge on the way."

THE AFTERNOON WAS FINE AND SUNNY, AND LOIS HAD no urgent calls to make. She looked at Jeems chasing her tail in the garden, and thought maybe a short walk might be a good idea. After all the excitement of Bill's announcement, she needed to quieten down and let her thoughts settle. She found the lead and went to call the puppy. Growing bigger already, she noted. But it was a terrier, mostly, and wouldn't get huge, she hoped.

Gran had gone into Tresham on the bus, and Derek was at work, so Lois locked up the house and set off up the road out of the village. The countryside around was undulating, with smallish fields and occasional prairie-like vistas where in the past a modern-thinking farmer had decided to grub up hedges. Now several new hedges had been planted, and Lois recalled Derek grumbling about subsidies for farmers. "They get paid for going to the bog," he'd said tetchily.

She strolled on, and on a quiet stretch of road, unfastened Jeems's lead and let her run on. Then she called her back, and was delighted when the puppy obeyed. Once more she gave her a free run, and called—and this time the dog did not come back. She was hunched over something big and dark lying at the roadside. Lois began to run. As she reached the pup, she yelled, "Jeems! Come here at once!" On closer inspection she saw the dark heap was a badger, familiarly striped, and with its jaws open in a silent scream, showing its long, sharp teeth and a lolling tongue.

"Ye Gods!" Lois felt sick, and quickly fastened the lead. She walked to the other side of the road, pulling the puppy behind her. Then she stopped. Her nausea had subsided, and she was curious. Picking up Jeems, she went back for another look. The badger must have been run over by a vehicle, but she could see no marks on it. Perhaps it had a glancing blow on the head. Flies were beginning their demolition work, starting on the eyes, and she shuddered. Poor thing, she thought. Maybe I should tell someone. She walked on now, still dragging the reluctant puppy. A large tractor and trailer came in sight, fast towards her in the middle of the narrow road, and she hopped on to the verge. It slowed down to pass her, and she waved at the driver. He pulled up, and looked at her enquiringly. "Down there," she said, pointing back along the road. "There's a dead badger. It's big, and it's beginning to rot. Can you get rid of it?"

The driver was young, dark and handsome. She recognized him as the son of a farmer who owned land a mile or so away. He laughed at her unpleasantly. "Let it rot!" he said, and drove off before she could reply.

Lois walked on into a different landscape, with overgrown hedges, choked ditches and patched-up gateways. She passed a rundown farmhouse with a sheep dog straining at its chain and barking sharply at Jeems. The puppy stared at it, and then released a stream of sharp yelps. "Good gel!" Lois bent down to pat her head, and at that moment the sheepdog's chain broke and it charged full pelt towards them. Lois snatched up the puppy and faced it. A couple of feet away from her it suddenly stopped and looked back to where an old man with a stick hobbled towards them, cursing and swearing at the top of his voice. "Come 'ere, y' bugger!" he yelled, and the dog turned and slunk off into a barn.

"You should get a new chain!" Lois said angrily. "It could have done some real damage, that thing!" She could feel Jeems trembling, and did not feel so good herself.

The old man glared at her. "No good you talkin' to me, missus," he said, pointing to his ear. "Deaf as post." Then he cackled like a decrepit cockerel and hobbled away back to the house.

"THIS GOING FOR A WALK LARK IS NOT ALL IT'S cracked up to be," Lois said to Derek at teatime. She had told him and Gran about the badger and the sheepdog, and said for two pins she'd move back to the safety of a council estate in Tresham.

"Walks'll do you good, me duck," Derek said cheerfully. "You spend too much time in that office, or driving about to clients. A walk in the fresh air is the best thing for good health."

Lois stood up and walked quickly to the kitchen door. She opened it, and stood back, as if letting in a visitor. A powerful smell of well-rotted cow muck and slurry filled the kitchen. It was muck-spreading time on all the farms. "Fresh air?" she said. "You can keep it."

Later that evening, Derek was reading the local paper, Gran watching television and Lois talking on the telephone in her office to Josie. When she came back into the sitting room, Derek looked up. "Have you seen this, Lois?" he said. "Isn't this your cop chum?" He handed her the newspaper, pointing to a photograph of two people, the man in police uniform and the woman in an old-style wedding dress. Lois looked more closely, and then read the text. "Local Police Detective Inspector's wife dies in road accident. Two youths detained."

"Oh my Lord," she said. "That's Cowgill . . ." She felt dizzy and sat down heavily on the sofa.

Derek looked at her, and then at Gran, who said, "I think I'll make a cup of tea for us."

"Are you all right, me duck?" he said quietly, and went

to sit beside Lois, putting his arm around her shoulders. "Bit of a shock?"

"I met her once," Lois said in a flat voice. "At a school concert evening. She was very smart, and a bit fearsome. They'd been married a long time. She looked after him well."

"Then I expect he'll miss her a lot," Gran said, returning with the tea. "Poor bloke. He'll probably retire and go and live near his daughter."

"With any luck . . ." Derek muttered to himself.

But Lois heard, and rounded on him. "I don't want to hear no more of that!" she said, half in tears. "We've bin through all that before, an' it's put behind us. So can we change the subject and get back to the telly? You're missing your favourite show, Mum." She stood up, leaving Derek huddled on the sofa, and said, "I need to go to the loo, then I'll come back for me tea."

"I wonder if the youths were local?" Gran said.

"They don't stand much of a chance, wherever they come from," Derek replied. "Only one thing worse than killing a policeman—snuffing out his wife."

EIGHT

꒜

NEXT MORNING, SHEILA AND FLOSS WERE MAKING their way to Farnden Hall for a morning's work for Mrs. Tollervey-Jones, generally accepted as the squire's lady. Her husband had died some years ago, but she had stepped into his shoes with as much, if not more, efficiency as the head of a sizeable estate, and with an inherited sense of responsibility for her village.

"Don't be put off by her manner, Floss," Sheila said.

"She's not a bad old stick at heart." Sheila had no evidence for this, having never seen any indication that Mrs. T-J's heart was anything but stony. Still, the girl's first job was in at the deep end, and she wanted to help her to stay afloat. They parked around the back of the Hall in the stable yard, under the steady gaze of a large horse.

"He's lovely," Floss said enthusiastically.

"Do you ride, then?" Sheila said.

Floss nodded. "When I was young," she said, and Sheila laughed.

"So you've given it up, now you are the great age of seventeen?" Floss's reply was aborted by the kitchen door opening and an elegant elderly lady walking briskly towards them.

"Morning, Sheila." Mrs. T-J looked at Floss enquiringly, and Sheila introduced her as the new apprentice cleaner.

"I shall be teaching her exactly how you like things done," she said diplomatically.

"Shall I be paying double for this?" Mrs. T-J said brutally.

Sheila shook her head. "Of course not! Mrs. M just thought it would be good for Floss to begin with the nicest and most rewarding client we have." Dear Lord, forgive me, she said to herself. I mean it for the best.

"So long as I am not expected to reward you with cash, " Mrs. T-J said acidly. "You'd better come on in, then. We've wasted enough time already."

Floss was a good pupil. She had a natural aptitude for things domestic, and also a healthy curiosity stimulated by the splendour of the Hall's furnishings. "Mrs. Stratford," she said, "have you ever broken anything valuable?"

Sheila put her finger to her lips. "Ssshh . . . only once," she replied, "and that was not here, luckily!"

In the large front hall, Floss looked up at stags' heads mounted on the wall, and frowned. "Ugh!" she whispered. "Were they shot in the park?"

Sheila shrugged. "Sboudn't think so . . . more likely in

Scotland. Mrs. T-J goes up every year for several weeks. Got a house in Sutherland, I think. In the far north."

"But what's that? That thing with tusks?"

"Some kind of pig," Sheila whispered. "Wild boar, probably. I think it came from France. They shoot anything that moves there. Anyway," she continued, "we'd better get on and stop talking. Mrs. T-J will have her ears pinned back, you bet."

When Floss arrived home full of her first day with New Brooms, her mother asked her what it was like up at the Hall, and received a detailed account. "I wouldn't mind us living there!" Floss enthused. "Except them stuffed animals . . . I'd take them to the dump straight away. I reckon shooting them's cruel enough, but stuffing them to hang on the walls is grim. They're moth-eaten, too. Ugh!"

Her father came in at that moment, and was updated with Floss's day. "Ah, well," he said when she described the trophies, "that's the upper classes for you. What's grim to you and me is a day's good sport to them. Now then, Mother, what's for supper?" he added. "Your favourite—venison casserole," she replied.

After her parents had settled down in front of the television, Floss appeared at the door saying she was going round to her friend Charlotte for a while. "Righto, dear, said her father, without looking round. She was not, of course, going to see Charlotte, she had an assignation with young Ben Cullen, only son of a Scottish family who were the first to move in to Blackbeny Close. They referred to themselves as the oldest inhabitants, and were much liked in the village. Organizers of an event needing help could rely on Ben's family, and his mother sang in the church choir, belonged to the WI, and helped at the Darby and Joan Club once a month.

Floss's mother knew of the friendship, and approved, but her father had a heavy hand with boyfriends who turned up. Not that he was discouraging. It was the opposite, with the lad being welcomed with a friendly thump on the back, and offers of drinks, meals, books to borrow, family outings to join. By this time, the boy was thoroughly put off, deciding that there must be something seriously wrong with Floss if she needed such a sales promotion.

Ben was new on the scene, and of course it would not be long before Floss's father would hear of it. But by that time, Floss and her mother hoped the boy would be hooked sufficiently to ride out the welcome.

"So how did it go, Flossie?" Ben was waiting for her in the bus shelter near the pub.

"Good," she said. "Let's walk, shall we? Lovers' stroll through the woods?"

Ben laughed. "So tell me about your first day as a skivvy," he said.

Floss scowled at him, and was silent for a minute. Then she said, "I really enjoyed it, most of it. Mrs. Stratford was very kind to me. Which was just as well, because old Mrs. T-J is a dragon! Not surprising she has all those gruesome stuffed things on her walls . . ."

"Tell me more," Ben said. They were out of the village now, heading towards the woods. It was twilight, and Floss said she shouldn't be long, as she had once more lied to her parents. "But you're a working girl now! You can do what you want. Stay out as late as you like . . . with whoever you like . . . except that it has to be me," he added.

"Yukky, Ben," Floss said, and took her hand out of his. Ben was a couple of years older than her, and had been around. "Anyway, do you want to hear about the trophies? There was one," she continued, without waiting for an answer, "that looked like a hairy pig, and Mrs. Stratford said it was a wild boar and probably came from France. She said the French shoot everything that moves."

"Glad I don't live in France, then," Ben said. They climbed the stile into the edge of the wood, and Floss stopped suddenly, a few steps along the track. "Listen!"

she whispered. Ben looked at her enquiringly, and she put a finger to her lips. They stood motionless, listening. Voices, men's voices from deep in the wood, trickled through to them. It was dark now, and they could see nothing. Then Ben grabbed her arm and pointed along the track. Far along it, a small light, as if from a torch being carried, moved up and down, getting closer.

"Come on!" Floss said, and turning around, dragged Ben back to the stile. They were over it in seconds and running back down the road to the village. "What the hell was going on?" Floss said, when they were safely in sight of comfortingly lit houses.

Ben shrugged. "Don't know," he said. "Maybe alien visitors from another planet, or a secret coven of witches . . ."

"Witches are female. Those were men's voices," said Floss. "An' I'm not stupid, you know. Not a child any more. So you can forget the aliens. I didn't like it, because men in a wood in the dark must be up to something. But they weren't little green men with antennae coming out of their heads."

"Could've been Green Men, though," said Ben smugly. "Haven't you heard of them? Legendary ghostly characters who look a bit like trees and come at you in the dark. Then you're never seen again."

"OK, you've done it now. I'm off home. You can ring me, but don't be at all sure I shall speak to you." And Floss was off, running down the street and disappearing into Hornton House.

Ben laughed to himself. "She'll be back," he said, and turned into Blackberry Close. As he came to his house, his eye was caught by something moving in the garden of old Mr. Everitt's house. Then a car started in the road outside, and drove off, much too fast. Funny, that, he thought. Still, perhaps the old boy is back. Ben opened his front door and forgot all about it.

NINE

❧

POOR OLD BLOKE, THOUGHT LOIS. SHE WAS SHOP-
ping in Tresham, and passed the police station, looking up—as always—to Cowgill's office window. But
there was no stiff figure raising a hand in greeting.
Compassionate leave, guessed Lois. There was so much to
do in organizing a funeral. But he had a daughter living
somewhere over Waltonby way, so wouldn't be completely
on his own. She knew there wasn't much warmth in the
marriage, but they had stuck together and even a rather
chilly wife was a companion. Someone who was there all
the time, made the meals, talked about this and that.

"Hey, steady on!" It was Cowgill, and Lois had nearly
sent him flying. "Good heavens, it's you, Lois," he continued. "Not looking where you were going. I could book
you for a traffic offence!"

"S-s-sorry." Lois was nonplussed for a moment, and
Cowgill jumped in while she rapidly collected her
thoughts.

"Got time for a coffee?" he said, and a small smile
flickered across his face. Lois hesitated. Probably a bad
idea for them to be seen together, if she was to go on
working for him. On the other hand, it would seem churl-
ish and hard-hearted to refuse. He read her thoughts. "I
know a nice little café, dark corners and private. Mind
you," he added hastily, "I only mean . . ."

"I know what you mean," Lois said. "And yes, I'd
love a coffee. Lead on, and I'll follow a few paces
behind."

He led her through the market place and into an alley down by the Gloucester Arms. She waited a few minutes after he'd disappeared into a small café tucked into a corner next to the churchyard, and then went in to join him. In the Stygian gloom, she couldn't see him at first, but then saw a hand wave from the corner and went quickly to sit down.

"I'm really sorry. What happened?" she said.

"Thanks. It was so unfair." He looked down at his hands. "She was driving along at thirty, coming back from the daughter's down a narrow lane, and these kids in a stolen car hit her head-on. Drunk, high, God knows what else. Stolen car. They weren't touched, but she was killed instantly." He picked up his cup of coffee and his hand shook, so that some spilled on to the table. Lois quickly wiped it up with a paper napkin and put a hand on his arm.

"Don't say any more if you don't want to," she said.

"It's just to be got through," he replied dully. "Daughter and her family are very good, considering they're shattered too. We've all just got to get through it."

They sat in silence for a minute or two, and then Cowgill said, "It's good to see you, Lois. Thanks for coming here. How's your family?"

Lois smiled. "Oh, the usual, you know. Derek's still struggling to be head of the family, Gran is a tower of strength and a bit of an irritation at the same time, Josie and her bloke are doing as well as can be expected in the shop, and the boys are away and I've no idea what they're up to."

"Not much change, then," said Cowgill, with a touch of envy. "Any news of old Herbert Everitt?"

Lois looked up in surprise. "Are you sure you want to talk about it?" she said.

"Yep," he said. "Keeps my mind off graveyards."

Lois shivered, and thought hard. Surely there must be something useful she could tell him? "I still haven't got hold of Reg Abthorpe," she said, "but I think I saw him again, driving quickly through the village. I'm certain it was his old car." Then she remembered the woman and the terriers, and described what had happened. "She was definitely watching me," she said. "And those terriers were killers, I reckon. When she came out and dragged them into the house, I caught sight of her, and though she seemed a bit familiar, I couldn't place her. But Jean Slater . . ." And then she told him about that, too, and for a few moments he was the old Cowgill, coldly concentrating and registering everything she said. Then he sank into a silent heap, his face closed, and she judged it time to go.

"Must get to the fish stall before they sell out," she said. "I'll go first. And . . ." She hesitated. "And if there's anything I can do—even if you just want a chat—you know where I am." She felt her eyes smart, turned away and made for the door.

THE AFTERNOON WAS FINE, AND, SEEING THE SUNLIT garden, Lois decided to take Jeems for a walk. Which way should she go? Down the concrete road and across the stream, then back across a muddy pasture? Or up one bridle path and back down another? Or the same way as she went the other day, and risk confronting the sheepdog? She hadn't decided when she saw Floss walking by, on her way to meet Sheila at the vicarage. "Hi, Floss!" she shouted from the window. "How are you getting on? Come in for a minute."

The girl was smiling broadly as she walked up the path. She had liked Mrs. M. straight away. You knew exactly where you were with her. "Fine, thanks," she said. "I am enjoying it, and Sheila is very helpful. We went to the Hall . . ."

"And?" said Lois.

"It was OK, except for the stuffed animals. I could do without those!"

"They've bin dead a long time," said Lois cheerfully. "Nothing you can do about them now. Anything else?"

The girl hesitated. "Not to do with work," she said,

"but me and Ben—oops! Still everybody'll know sooner or later—we're an item at the moment."

"Nice boy," said Lois approvingly. "But what about him?"

"Well, we were going for a walk in the twilight—very romantic—and it got dark and we were on the edge of the woods, and we heard these voices . . ." Then the rest of it tumbled out, and she ended, "Just wondered if you knew who they were? And what they were doing there?"

Lois shook her head. "Advance party from Mars?" she said, and was surprised at the vehemence of Floss's reply. "Not you too!" she said, and then added quickly, "Ben said much the same thing. Sorry, Mrs. M. It's just that he does treat me like a child at times."

"Don't worry," Lois laughed. "Now, you'd better get on to the vicarage, else Sheila will be out looking for you." After Floss had gone, Lois stared out of the window, thinking about men's voices in the woods. She wished she'd asked her if they'd seen or heard dogs.

"Mum," she said, going to the kitchen to collect Jeems. "I think I'll go out with this pest here, work off some of her energy."

"Where are you going?"

"Probably up the hill as far as the woods. I'll see how she goes." She attached the lead with difficulty and set out, stumbling here and there as the puppy entangled herself in Lois's legs.

IN A CLEARING IN THE WOODS, REG ABTHORPE, with a battered hat pulled down over his eyes, stood talking to two men. One was tall and thin, with rounded shoulders and a shifty look. He never once looked at Reg, nor at his companion, who was short and rotund, with a completely bald head. "You must be bloody stupid," Reg said, glaring at them. "You know the rules! What are you trying to do? Scupper the whole business? Get the bloody thing straight away, and bugger off. Vanish, until I tell you to come back. And keep your traps shut, or else."

In seconds the men had gone. Reg lingered for a moment, his eyes closed, composing himself. Then he too disappeared from the clearing, following a well-beaten path to the thicket where he had hidden his car. "Sod it!" he said loudly, as he drove down the lane at speed. A woman and small dog were coming towards him, still some way in the distance, but he recognized her. It was that cleaner woman, and the last person he wanted to meet.

He made a quick decision. No chance of passing her so quickly that she wouldn't have time to see him. Couldn't run her down, though in his fury he would have liked to. One damn thing after another! He put the car into reverse, and backed as fast as it would go to an entry into the woods, turned and sped off in the opposite direction.

Lois had seen the car. What on earth was it doing? Some stranger lost his way, she guessed, and once more encouraged Jeems to walk in a straight line. "Surely that isn't so difficult?" she said, looking down at the hairy face. Then she walked on until she came to the entry. Not much point in going in there, she thought, not in broad daylight. She walked on, and came to the neglected fields, with the old house in the distance. No sign of the sheepdog, but she was brought to a halt by the puppy stopping, tugging at the lead and whimpering. "It's not around," she said. "Come on, silly." She tried pulling, but with no success. Then her eye was caught by something hanging from a farm gate a few steps ahead. "Ye Gods!" No wonder Jeems was terrified. A large, very dead badger had been tied by the neck to the top bar of the gate. She felt her gorge rise, and swallowed hard. At that moment she caught sight of the old farmer hobbling towards her, the sheepdog at his heels. If she retreated quickly there would be time to prevent another attack.

"'Ere, missus!" The old man quickened his pace. "I want a word with you!" His voice sounded distressed, and Lois hesitated. Perhaps he was in trouble. The dog seemed to be sticking close behind him, so perhaps . . . She picked up Jeems and held her tight. The old man had reached the

badger now, and stopped suddenly. Lois saw him sway and
lean on his stick. She rushed forward, and, tucking Jeems
under one arm, managed to help him away from the grisly
sight and on to a grassy bank the other side of the road.

"Can you sit down for a minute?" she asked. "You've
had a shock." Now what? She thought. No brandy, no hot
sweet tea . . . and no mobile telephone. Left it at home
the one time I really need it, she cursed.

But the old man seemed to be recovering. He sat down
gently, and his dog crouched beside him, its eyes fixed on
the puppy. "What did you want me for?" Lois said, hoping to take his mind off the corpse.

"I forget," he said, rubbing his eyes. "Anyways, I don't
suppose you did *that*, did you. Even a stupid old fool like
me knows that."

"Who did, then? D'you know?"

The old man looked at her. "No!" he said with force.
"No idea." But Lois could see that he knew and was not
going to tell. They sat in silence for a few minutes, and
then he began to struggle to his feet. "All right now," he
muttered, and walked shakily towards the badger. Lois
followed, worried that he might collapse again. "Look at
that," he said, pointing to where she could not help seeing that there were cuts all over its body and the skin was
pulled from its legs.

"I think I have to go," she said faintly.

He looked at her. "Right-o," he said quietly. "Thanks
for your help. Don't say anything about this. A secret between us, heh?" His voice was pleading now, and Lois
nodded. Anything to get away from here.

"Are you sure you'll be all right?" He nodded, and
watched her walk away down the hill. Halfway down she
turned around. He was still standing there, with the dog
immobile at his feet, and she raised her hand. He did the
same, and she went quickly on without looking back.

TEN

❧

By the time Lois reached home, Derek's van stood in the drive. He must have come home early, and Lois had never been so glad to see him. "Hey! What's wrong, gel?" he said, as she flung her arms around him and hugged hard. "Mind you," he continued, kissing her hot cheek, "I'm not complainin'."

"Looks like a cuppa is needed," Gran said, and put on the kettle. "Where's the pup?" she added. A scratching at the door answered her question, and Jeems bounced in, dragging her lead.

Derek detached her, and turned again to Lois. "Sit down, me duck," he said, "and tell me all about it."

Lois took a deep breath and sat down at the table. "I went for a walk," she said. "Unaccustomed as I am to going for walks, I looked at Jeems rushing round in small circles in the garden and decided to give her a change of scene."

"So which way did you go?" Gran said. "What did you see?"

Derek sent her a look that said "have patience," and she turned back to her tea-making, her shoulders huffy.

"I went up to the woods, up the narrow hill. And just past the wood, coming up to the old farmhouse, I saw this . . ." She gathered herself together, gulped, and described what had been hanging from the farm gate. Gran gripped the rail of the Rayburn, and Derek's face darkened.

"So it's all started up again," he said angrily. "No wonder you look like you'd seen a ghost," he said.

"But that's not all," Lois said, and sighed with relief that she was through the worst bit. Then she told them about the old man, and his reaction at seeing the badger. "Who is he, Derek?" she said.

Derek knew most people, either from his travels as an electrician, or from cronies in the pub. "It's old William Cox," he said. "His family have farmed there for generations. Now there's just him. His wife's dead, and they never had no kids. He works that farm—in a manner of speaking—by himself, with an old tractor and a bit of help at harvest. He can't possibly do it much longer. The whole place, as you've noticed, is fallin' down."

"Do the woods belong to him?" Lois knew that a large acreage on the hill was owned by a big estate and farmed by contractors.

"Not sure," Derek said. "He don't do much woodin', so it's all thicket and brambles. One or two clearings, but mostly too dense to get through."

"Clearings?" Lois remembered Floss's tale of voices and a torchlight. "You mean grassy bits where people can picnic?"

"And the rest," said Derek grimly. "All kinds of mischief got up to in those woods. I thought it was in the past, but now . . ."

"Badger-baiting," said Gran, fed up with all this pussy-footing around. "We had a talk about it at the WI. It's terribly cruel, and we're supposed to be on the lookout . . . tell the police, an' that."

"So should I tell them about the corpse?" Lois looked at Derek, who shook his head violently.

"Don't tell nobody," he said. "That's why old William pretended not to know. They'll take revenge. Could be nasty."

"How will they know it's me?"

"Oh, they'll know. Spies and lookouts everywhere. Half the village was at it at one time. And the farmers don't say anything, partly for fear of revenge, and partly because they don't want badgers on their land, giving the cattle TB. No, forget you saw it, me duck."

Lois said nothing more, and changed the subject to pleasanter matters. "WI tonight, Mum?" she said. "Who's the speaker?"

"Some woman telling us about being a magistrate. Another of the Mrs. Tollervey-Jones variety, if you ask me. I was talking to Ivy Beasley at Ringford on the phone this morning she's still very pleased with Bill, by the way—and she said it'd be that bossy Phyllis Franklin from Waltonby. They had her at Ringford WI, and she was as boring as—"

"Yes, right, well, I must get on. Thanks for the tea. I'll be in my office for half an hour or so. Thanks, Derek," she added, and patted his shoulder. "Now, don't you forget, me duck," he said. "No telling your pal Cowgill about that badger, else I shall end up looking for you in the woods one of these dark nights."

In her office, Lois sat down at her desk and shut her eyes. At once, a perfectly detailed picture of the badger formed in glorious technicolor, and she opened her eyes quickly. She had to get the horror out of her head somehow, and tried to concentrate on New Brooms matters. Sheila and Floss seemed to be getting on fine, and Hazel was as efficient as ever in the Tresham office. Enid was happy at the vet's house and an elderly lady's tidy cottage in Fletching. And Gran had said Miss Beasley was still pleased with Bill.

Miss Ivy Beasley: one of Lois's most tricky clients. She lived alone in Round Ringford, had lived there all her life, and very much resented being old and not capable any more of keeping her house up to the spotless standard she required. She had stipulated that Bill Stockbridge was to be her cleaner. He had a way with sheep and cows, and the vet valued his assistance, but, more importantly, he also had a kindly charm which went down very well with old ladies. Ivy Beasley considered herself proof against such wiles, but lately Bill had been asked to sit down for a minute or two after he'd finished. "Just for a quick chat," Ivy had said, and half an hour later he'd had to ease himself politely out of the front door.

It might be worth calling on old Ivy, Lois thought. She's bound to know something about the Cox farming family. And possibly about Herbert Everitt. She was reputed to have second sight, but Lois knew that she was just a nosey old woman who had spent her life disapproving of what went on around her. "Meat and drink to Ivy," her friend Doris had said.

"Going over to Ringford to check all's well with Miss Beasley," she said to Gran, as she went through the kitchen to her van.

"I just told you she's very pleased!" Gran was irritated, sure that Lois was up to something again. "There's no need for you to go out now."

Lois stopped. "Mum," she said, "I run my own business, and it's doing well. And that's because I know what I'm doing. So don't worry—shan't be long. Bye."

"That's put me in my place," muttered Gran. But she knew she was right. Lois was telling the truth, she was sure, but only so far. She got that from her dad. He'd been a genius at it.

MISS BEASLEY'S DOOR WAS SHUT AND LOCKED FIRMLY, as usual, and Lois walked round to the back door. The old thing was quite deaf now, though she hotly denied it, and did not always hear the door bell. Lois could see her in her usual chair, next to the range, her back to the window. A tap on the glass pane might make her jump, so Lois knocked lightly on the door.

She could see Ivy struggling to her feet, reaching for her stick, and advancing towards the door. "Who is it?" Her voice was harsh and peremptory.

Lois moved to the window and shouted, "It's Mrs. Meade. Can I come in for a few minutes?"

After bolts were drawn and the lock turned, Ivy Beasley stood looking at her. "Oh, it's you," she said. "You'd better come in, now you're here. Though I've no complaints. Bill is doing very well, now I've got him trained. You're not going to take him away from me, are you?" she added with a touch of anxiety.

Lois shook her head. "No, no, Miss Beasley, nothing like that. I've really come to ask for your help, you being the most knowledgeable person on local history and that."

Ivy frowned. "I'm not a gossip, Mrs. Meade," she said, and Lois gulped. Ivy Beasley, in her time, had been the biggest and cruellest gossip for miles around, and though somewhat mellowed in old age, her wits were still razor-sharp. "What is it you want to know?" Ivy asked grudgingly.

"It's to do with my business," lied Lois. "There's been talk of old Mr. Cox—William Cox—who farms in Farnden. Seems he's getting too old to manage, and I wondered if I should call on him and offer some help. I give a very reduced rate to people who really cannot cope, but want to stay living in their own home."

Ivy Beasley was on her in a second. "So why don't *I* get a reduced rate?" she snapped, and added, "Not that I would accept it. I can still pay my way, and don't want no favours. Anyway, you want to know about the Coxes?" Lois nodded. "You'd better sit down, then," Ivy began, settling back in her chair. "I know quite a bit about that family. My mother and old Grandmother Cox were good friends. Mother didn't have many friends, but Ethel Cox seemed to like her. They were two out of the same basket. William was older than me, but sometimes we were left to play together while the women put the world to rights over a cup of tea."

"Was he an only?" Lois said, and Ivy glared at her.

"If you're going to interrupt all the time, you might as well get going. My time is precious, you know."

Doing what? thought Lois, but apologized, and promised to be quiet.

"And, since you asked, yes, he was the only one. And thoroughly spoilt, as a result. He got the farm in due course, and worked it well. Always had a bit of a chip on his shoulder, and married beneath him. No children turned up, and his wife died a long while ago, never having made much of a mark on the rest of us. He's a tetchy old man now, and he'll probably set the dog on you. If you ask me, it'd be best to stay away and let him get on with it." She paused, and Lois judged it would be safe to ask a question.

"How'd he get on with other farmers? Couldn't some of them give him a hand?"

"Hah! Not them!" Ivy replied. "Especially them that go hunting. And that's most of them. Why? Because he banned the hunt from his land. Every year the Master would go and see him, butter him up and hope to change his mind. But he'd just smile and shake his head. If you ask me, he got a kick out of banning 'em. Claimed he was fond of foxes, and used to sit in his old Land Rover in the woods, watching the cubs play around in the evenings. Foxes got used to him, I reckon." Ivy's head drooped back on her cushion, and she closed her eyes.

Old bag! thought Lois, who knew perfectly well that this was an unsubtle way of getting rid of her. But she was happy with what had been said, and got up quietly. Ivy's eyes shot open. "You going?" she said. "I'll shut up behind you. And mind you look after that Bill. He's a good lad." Lois assured her she would, and walked quickly away.

As she drove off, she realized nothing had been said about Herbert Everitt. Ah well, another time. She knew Ivy too well to hope for anything more today.

ELEVEN

ॐ

"MORNING, MUM. AND YOU CAN LEAVE THAT DOG outside on the hook. It's what it's there for."

Lois marvelled at how like herself Josie had become. "Less of the sharp tongue, Josie," Lois said, picking up Jeems. "Or I shall be taking my custom elsewhere."

"There is nowhere else," said Josie. "Unless you get in your van and go off to Tesco for a box of matches."

"I haven't come for a box of matches. Look, here's a list, and I'll pick up the stuff at lunchtime." It was a long list, and Josie blew her mother a kiss.

"I love you really," she said.

"Ditto." Lois laughed and left the shop. She put down Jeems, and they set off at a cracking pace towards the edge of the village. Some way past the last of the council houses, Lois turned into a footpath across a field and released the puppy from her lead. She tore off at speed towards what Lois could now see was a bunch of sheep up ahead. "Damn!" Lois yelled after Jeems, but she was deaf to everything but the call of her instinct to chase anything that ran. Lois set off, running as fast as she could, and caught up as the sheep began to panic. "Come here, y' little devil!" Lois put on a final spurt and caught the runty tail just in time.

"Bad dog!" said Lois sternly, and re-fixed the lead. "Phew, I'm knackered," she told the unrepentant dog, and perched on the edge of a dilapidated brick edifice sunk into the ground. It was not very comfortable, and Lois looked at the rusty pipe coming from one end, guessing that it contained a water tank. Well, I'm more than glad to see it, uncomfortable or not, she thought, and after getting her breath back, she walked on.

"That's your walk for today," she cautioned Jeems, as they reached home. "I've got an errand this afternoon and it definitely does not include you."

LOIS PARKED HER VAN AT THE ENTRANCE TO WILLIAM Cox's house, and cautiously opened the gate. At once, the sheepdog sped towards her, barking frantically. She stood her ground, and it stopped, grovelling towards her on its haunches.

"Come 'ere, y' bugger!" It was Cox, hobbling across the muddy yard, scowling at Lois.

"Afternoon, Mr. Cox," Lois said, holding out her hand. "Mrs. Meade, from the village. Can I have a word?"

"Have as many as you like, s' long as you don't bother me," he grunted, and turned away.

"I shan't keep you long," persisted Lois. She followed him towards the house and into the kitchen, where she got a surprise. It was clean, tidy, and smelt of bleach. A saucepan simmered on the old range, and the kettle steamed gently beside it.

"Don't remember asking you to come in," Cox muttered. "Still, now you're here, you'd better have a cup o' tea. Sit down."

Lois wondered how she could refuse, but decided that if the mugs were as clean as the rest of the kitchen, she'd come to no harm. She chatted about the weather, and the sheepdog, and received grunts in reply. He made the tea, and set a large, clean mug in front of her and sat down opposite. "So what d'you want?" he said. "I ain't having one of them home helps."

Lois shook her head. "No, no. I'm not from Social Services," she said. "I run a cleaning business, but I can see you don't need me and my team. No, I wondered if you could help *me*," she added, and smiled appealingly at him.

"Get on with it, then," he said.

She turned to look out of the window, also clean and clear. "Those are your woods, aren't they?" she said. "D' you often go into them? My Derek could come and help you with wooding, if you like. Must be a bit much for you now. He could come at the weekend . . .

William Cox did not answer her questions. "That's not asking me for help," he said. "You're offering, not asking."

Lois laughed. "I'm getting there," she said. "I really want to know about the woods, because they'd be great for taking my dog for walks. She's a terrier—"

"I know, I've seen her," he interrupted as his eyes narrowed. "Plenty of open space for walking dogs. Why d' you want to take her in the woods?"

"Oh, you know," Lois said lightly. "Terriers love woods, rootin' about, picking up scents and chasing rabbits. But if it's not convenient . . ."

"Who says it's not? If you want t' take the little blighter in there, you're welcome. But just watch out," he added. "Don't go too far in. Stick to the edges, and if the dog goes off, wait until she comes back. They always do, unless they get stuck down a rabbit hole, which ain't likely."

"That's very kind of you," Lois said, draining her cup of tea. "Better be getting back, now. And don't forget, if you need help, New Brooms is always ready with the mop and bucket."

Suddenly a broad smile crossed Cox's face. "Right y' are, then," he said. "And if you're walking in the woods, call in for a cuppa. Any time. And don't worry about Rosie. I'll chain her up." He hobbled after her to the gate, and as she drove off she could see his hand was raised in farewell.

"Well, that was a doddle," Lois said, coasting down the hill into the village. "Tomorrow, to the woods!"

TWELVE

‰

THE NEXT DAY, A MONSOON SEEMED TO HAVE SET-
tled over Long Farnden. Nobody in their right
minds would take a puppy for a walk in the downpour. A
break in the rain halfway through the afternoon looked
promising, but Lois was keeping an appointment with old
Ellen Biggs, who lived in the small Victorian lodge at the
gates of Ringford Hall. The now frail ex-cook at the big
house had no cleaning complaints, but she was another
one reluctant to accept help, and had finally been persuaded by a deal with Lois. Ellen would allow a cleaner
to call, provided that once a month she baked a rich
chocolate cake, and Lois called for a generous slice with
a cup of tea. Although Ellen was well-liked in the village,
and Ivy Beasley and Doris Ashbourne came to see her
most days, there were still hours and hours when nothing
happened and she had no one to talk to. She missed the
hustle and bustle up at Ringford Hall, and loved to talk to
Lois, who always arrived well-primed with gossip from
the other villages to entertain her.

The rain began again, and Lois looked out of Ellen's
small, arched window with irritation. "Damn!" she said.
"I'd hoped to take the dog for a walk in the woods, but
now look at it!"

"Never mind, dear," Ellen said sympathetically. "The
forecast is good for tomorrow. Anyway, what woods were
you talking about?"

"Up on the hill behind Farnden." Lois finished the last
of the cake crumbs and licked her lips. "Very good cake,"

she said, getting to her feet, as always. "Thanks a lot, Ellen."

"You mean old Cox's woods?" Ellen was suddenly serious, and Lois sat down again.

"Did you know him?" she said. "O' course I did," Ellen said. "He married my sister Martha. She was a fair bit younger than him, but died first, poor gel."

"Was he a good husband?" Lois saw that Ellen was tired, and felt bad about asking her questions when the old lady should have been settling down for a nap. But this was important. It was very likely that Cox had seen Herbert Everitt walking his dog in the woods, and could well know something about his disappearance. Something connected with the past?

"Not what I'd call a good husband," Ellen said flatly. "If I'd had the chance, I reckon I'd have said no, but she was mad keen. His family weren't so enthusiastic, as I remember. Reckoned their William was marrying beneath him."

"Were they nasty to her?"

"Not exactly nasty . . . They just ignored her. Never sought her out for comin' to tea. Blamed her for not havin' children. But she were quite happy on the farm at first. Liked the animals and them woods you were talking about. Bluebells and primroses in there in the spring, y' know. Loads of 'em."

"And what else was in the woods?" Lois said.

Ellen turned her head sharply and stared at Lois. "What d' you mean? D' you know something about them woods?" Lois shook her head, unwilling to lie, and Ellen continued, "Because if you do, Lois Meade, and they're still at it, you'd do well to stay clear. I reckon it was something in them woods that frightened my sister into the state she was in. Never really got better, and faded away."

"What *were* they at? And who's they?"

"No need for you to know, if you don't know already. Just stay well away, that's my advice. Now, my dear, if you don't mind, I'd like to have a little shut-eye. It's about my usual time. Thanks for coming, and take care of that family of yours."

LOIS PONDERED ON ELLEN'S SUDDEN INTEREST IN HER walking in the woods. So her sister had been Cox's wife. The sister of a servant would not have gone down well as William's future bride, and the family were clearly not very kind to her. Was it them that turned the middle of the woods into a prohibited area? Only the clan allowed to watch a traditional sport? But William hadn't seemed too keen on badger-baiting. Lois had seen the result of his position with her own eyes. Derek had said most of the village was involved at one time. An exaggeration, she was sure, but clearly it had not been a minority sport in Farnden in young Martha's day.

Anyway, why am I so interested? she asked herself. It was not as if she was a seasoned campaigner against cruelty to wildlife. Not her thing at all. No, she was more than ever convinced that the disappearance of Herbert Everitt and the secrets in Cox's woods were in some way connected. And that shadowy woman with her killer terriers—fighting terriers?—why was she so curious about Lois's mundane cleaning visits? Tomorrow was cleaning day at Herbert's, so perhaps an excuse would occur to her for a call on the woman behind the curtains.

WHEN LOIS ARRIVED HOME, A LARGE AND SHINING motorbike stood in the drive. Jamie! Her heart leapt. Her youngest son had given no warning that he would be coming, but then that was quite usual. She suppressed the thought that he only came home when he wanted something, often money, and rushed in to greet him. He was sitting at the kitchen table with Jeems on his lap, his grandmother's eyes fixed fondly upon him.

He stood up, handed the puppy to Lois, and then hugged them both. "Hey! You're squeezing her!"

Lois kissed his rough cheek warmly, and turned to Gran. "So when did the prodigal return, Mum?"

"When I was in the middle of hanging out the washing," Gran said.

"So I helped her," Jamie said. "Shall I pour you a cuppa, Mum? I bet you've had a hard day, scrubbin' and polishin' and looking after the old ladies . . ."

"That's quite enough of that. It's true I've been to see old Ellen at Ringford, but that's more a social call."

"Nice cake?" said Gran.

Lois ignored her, and sat down to fire questions at Jamie. How was he getting on with his music studies? Did he like his new mentor, one of the best-known concert pianists in the country? And was he eating properly?

"Everything's fine, Mum. I know Dad thinks I'll never get a proper job, but I'm so lucky to be studying with Alf, and he thinks I stand a good chance of success . . . some day!"

"Never mind about Dad," Lois said. "Why are you here? Or have you been missing your old folks?" She knew this was the last thing that would bring him home, and waited.

"Well, it's like this," he said. "I've got this girl—I've told you about Helen—and we are planning on sharing a flat . . . It's quite expensive, but really nice."

"What do you mean 'sharing a flat'? Does that include sharing a bed?" Gran had reacted quickly and disapprovingly.

Jamie looked at his mother. "Yes, it does," he said. "Of course, Helen would pay half the rent, but I'd still need a bit more money. What d' you think, Mum?"

Lois was silent for a few seconds, then she said, "Well, if you've enough time to stay here overnight, I'll discuss it with your father." She was very serious, and Gran rounded on her.

"Why don't you say 'No' straight away, Lois!" she said, her voice rising in alarm. "Surely you're not having him living with a girl when he's still so young and a student?"

Not for the first time, Lois gently explained to her mother that this was a matter for Jamie and his mother and father, and nobody else. Gran at once retreated into a huff, and went out into the garden to check the washing.

After that, Jamie and Lois chatted amiably and did not mention the matter until Derek came home. Then the discussion became heated, with Lois on Jamie's side, and Derek unsure of what his attitude should be. He remembered so well the blissful times he and Lois had had before they were married, and the sleeping together didn't bother him. He and Lois were both doing well in their jobs, and could maybe afford to give Jamie a bit more. Lois said she'd be prepared to contribute, and so the evening ended in an edgy peace. It was not until Lois lay awake in bed, listening to Derek's snores, that she thought about the woman behind the curtains, and how she could get to speak to her. An idea came to her, and she smiled. That would do it. She was asleep in minutes.

Thirteen

ॐ

LOIS ARRIVED LATER THAN USUAL AT HERBERT'S house. It did not matter much when she arrived. Herbert would not be there to be annoyed by unpunctuality. She wondered if Cowgill had made any progress in finding him. She was no nearer, and determined to speed things up a little. After an hour or so cleaning, she took a key from the ring Reg Abthorpe had given her, went out to the garden shed, and unlocked it. Leaving the door ajar, she went back into the house and looked across the

road. Sure enough, she could just see a shape behind the
net curtains and set out to ask for help.

It was some time before the front door opened, and a
furious barking from somewhere at the back of the house
accompanied the wispy woman as she held the door
open. She did not remove the security chain. "Good
morning," said Lois, in her best professional manner. "So
sorry to bother you, but I wonder if you could help?"

"What d'you want?" the woman said in a scratchy
whisper. Lois smiled encouragingly. "It's just that I've
noticed the garden shed across the road is open. Door not
locked. The gardener must've forgot, and there's quite a
lot of valuable tools in there. I wondered if you maybe
had a key to the shed? Or could you tell me where the
gardener lives? Oh, and by the way, I'm Mrs. Meade, the
cleaner. My daughter keeps the village shop. Quite respectable, in case you were wondering!" She was glad to
see a faint smile crossing the woman's face, but it vanished in seconds.

"I don't have any keys to Mr. Everitt's house," she
said. Her voice was slightly stronger, and she added. "But
I've got that gardener's name and address somewhere.
We thought of using him ourselves. You'd better come in
a minute." She removed the chain, and held the door
open. Lois stepped in quickly, thanking her and apologiz-
ing again for wasting her time.

She followed the woman into the room with the net
curtains and waited while a desk was searched and a
small address book produced. "Ah, here we are," the
woman said. "Mr. Adams, that's him. He lives down
Church End. Number three. His wife'll be there, if he's
not." She returned the book to the desk, and just as Lois
was about to venture a conversation about Herbert
Everitt, a car drew up outside and a man rushed up the
path. Evidently he had a key, because there was no
knocking or ringing of the bell. Lois could hear the door
opening, and as she turned, was confronted by a familiar
face. It was Reg Abthorpe, and he did not look at all
pleased to see her.

Lois was the first to speak. She had every right to be there, doing her duty in keeping an eye on the Everitt house, and faced him with confidence. "Hello again, Mr. Abthorpe," she said. "I've been trying to get hold of you." She waited. He was obviously making a great effort to adjust his face, and made it with a mirthless smile.

"I've been away a lot," he said, and turned to the wispy woman. "Sorry for just walking in. I hope you don't mind. I saw the door was ajar, and I was desperate for some help." The woman appeared to be turned to stone. She stared at him, and said nothing.

"I wonder if you could tell me the way to Round Ringford," he said. "It's not marked on my map." He addressed himself to Lois, who replied that he could just follow the signpost on the corner by the pub.

"You can't miss it," she said. Still the woman said nothing, and Reg Abthorpe turned as if to leave. "By the way," Lois said quickly, "I wanted Mr. Everitt's address. Local people would like to visit him. That phone number you gave me belonged to someone else, and she'd never heard of you."

"Oh God, sorry. Must have given you the wrong number. I'll send you all the details. Uncle's address, telephone numbers and everything. Can't stop now, though. Late already. Thanks, missus," he added, turning to the woman. "Sorry again if I alarmed you, bursting in like that. Cheers."

He was gone before Lois could reply, and the door banged behind him. She watched him drive off at speed, and then turned back. "Are you all right?" she said.

The woman was pale, and her hands were trembling. She nodded slowly, as if waking up, and said in her whispery voice, "Yeah. I'm all right. Who was he? Never seen him before."

It was like an automaton speaking words that had been programmed in, and Lois knew without doubt that she was lying. She was absolutely certain that the front door had been closed, and only a key could have opened it from outside.

"Can I make you a cup of tea? You look shocked. Was it him coming in like that?"

"No thanks. And yes, I am a bit scared of burglars," she said lamely.

"Is that why you have the dogs?" Lois said, leading her on. She nodded again, and Lois said, "Funny they didn't bark at him, isn't it?" At this, the woman burst into tears, and Lois helped her to a chair and decided not to brave the kitchen and the two killer terriers. "Sit quietly for a bit," she said, patting the woman on her heaving shoulders. "I'll be off now, but you can always get me on this number." She produced a New Brooms card from her pocket and put it on the coffee table. "Oh, and perhaps I should have your name. I'll look in tomorrow to make sure you're all right."

The woman scrubbed at her face with a tissue, and said quickly, "Oh no, thanks, that won't be necessary. You're very kind. I'll be all right now. Can you let yourself out? I'm feeling a bit wobbly, but I'll be OK in a minute or two. Oh, and I'm Mrs. Wallis. Frances. Bye."

Lois went back to Herbert's garden shed and locked up. Thinking time needed. She looked up at the cloudless sky. She'd take Jeems for a walk. This morning had been very peculiar, and the more she pictured Reg Abthorpe's face when he saw her, the more she was convinced he had something very dodgy to hide.

Fourteen

Inspector Cowgill was thinking about Lois. Since his wife died, he had felt numbed. Nature's way, his daughter had said. Protects you from unbearable grief. Now feeling was beginning to return, and it was like freezing cold hands beginning to thaw. His brain throbbed, confusion reigned, and he wondered again if he should retire. He had a few years to go, but his pension would be adequate, and he'd put a bit by for a rainy day. His wife had insisted on that, but now she'd not get the benefit. He sighed deeply. How many times had he wished he was a single man? His wife had not been easy to live with, but they'd been married for so long, he had no real picture of life without her.

Now he was thinking about Lois, and the old surge returned. She had been nice to him that day in the café, and when he remembered her sympathetic smile he realized it was the sharp-tongued Lois that attracted him. Masochism? He thought not. Although she could be brusque to the point of rudeness, there was always warmth behind it, and it was warmth that had vanished from his marriage. He decided to go over to Long Farnden and hope to see her. The whereabouts of Herbert Everitt was still a mystery, although his boys had been working hard on it. Nor had he had any luck tracing the man who employed Lois, Reg Abthorpe. Cowgill was aware that he had not treated the case with any urgency. In the first place, he could see no hard evidence for disbelieving the retirement-home story, and second, he had not been functioning as he should. But all the usual avenues had been explored, and so far nothing had turned up. Still, sooner or later Abthorpe would be flushed out, and the old man found. Meanwhile, he would try to see Lois. She might have made some progress. He hoped she had forgotten about pitying the bereaved.

IN THE VILLAGE SHOP, FLOSS PICKERING WAITED PATIENTLY to be served. It was lunchtime and a number of customers had rushed in to buy sandwiches and filled rolls. She was last in the queue, and Josie smiled at her. "Hi, Floss," she said. "Hope you don't mind me using your nickname. I know you work for Mum. Enjoying it?"

"Floss is fine," the girl said. "Anything's better than Florence. My grandmother was Florence, and so I have to suffer! And yes, I love working for New Brooms."

"What can I get you?" A couple of stamps, I expect, Josie thought. But she was wrong.

"I want a present for someone. I know you have those expensive Belgian chocolates, and he's got a very sweet tooth."

"*He's* a very sweet lad," laughed Josie, "if your some-one is Ben Cullen from Blackberry Close. Yep, I've got a new lot in. Here we are."

"How did you know about me and Ben?" Floss looked alarmed. If Dad knew she'd been up in the woods with a boy and had seen something mysterious, he'd be apoplectic.

"Shopkeepers know everything," Josie replied. "It's like a clearing house for gossip in here. Nothing escapes my notice, but I'm the soul of discretion. So you needn't worry. Anyway, you're old enough to have a boyfriend, surely?"

"Course I am," Floss said quickly. "It's just that my dad's . . ."

". . . a bit old-fashioned," finished Josie. "Well, now, which box d' you want? This one's got a gold heart on it. A selection of milk and dark chocs. Cor, makes my mouth water just looking at them!"

Floss paid for the chocolates, and smuggled them back into her bedroom. She was meeting Ben that evening—his birthday—and looked forward to sharing her present. Not much money left for her savings, but so what? No one need know.

IN HER OFFICE, LOIS SAT IN FRONT OF THE COMPUTER, surfing the web. She was more than competent now with the new technology which Derek had said she'd never master. Now she was searching for sites on badger-baiting, and was surprised at the long list which came up. She read carefully, and after an hour or so, knew a great deal about the whole sordid business. Now she had come across records of cases up in court. Names were named, and addresses, and the sentences the guilty men received. They were all ages, and were from all over the country. A thought struck her and she checked for Abthorpes on this site. None. There was a Reginald Tompkins, with a London address, but Lois passed over it. Reg was a common enough name. And Tompkins was nothing like Abthorpe.

She looked at her watch. It was time to get going. She had promised to look in on Frances Wallis, and could do it before setting off to the Tresham office.

Cowgill met her as she emerged from her house. She had driven her car on to the road and was shutting the garden gates. He lowered his window and waved, pulling up by the kerb. She hesitated, then, remembering his bereavement, walked up to his car. "Is this a good idea?" she said, and added quickly, "Oh, and how are you now?"

He nodded firmly. "Fine, thanks. This is an official call. Have you turned up anything interesting on Everitt?"

"Look," said Lois, "my mother and husband both suspect I'm what they call ferretin' again. If they see me talking to you . . ."

"Surely you can spare a minute or two without being rushed inside by Gran playing bodyguard?"

Lois's sympathy vanished. "Oh, very clever," she said. "I'll give you a ring. Now bugger off." His smile was broad, and he chuckled as he drove off. That was more like it!

FRANCES WALLIS DID NOT ANSWER THE DOOR. THE TERRI-ers were behind the side gate, frantic and deadly. Lois rang the bell again, and peered in the window. But the net curtains were a match for prying eyes. There was not even a shadowy movement inside the room. Ah well, she must have gone out, thought Lois. And I'm certainly not opening that gate! If she's out, she's feeling better, like as not. She turned away, and was suddenly aware that the terriers had stopped barking. She whipped round, but too late. No dogs, no woman, nothing. But somebody had taken them in.

FIFTEEN

ॐ

"WHERE ARE YOU GOING, FLOSSIE?"
"Out."

Floss's father sighed. "You're too old for that sort of cheek," he said. "We only want to know so that—"

"So that if I get kidnapped and never seen again, you'll at least know where I was going?" Floss had flushed, and wished she didn't have to deceive her parents. But really, Dad was too much.

"It happens, Floss," her mother said gently. "Is it the usual get-together with your friend?" And then, knowing exactly where Floss was going, she added to her husband, "I'm sure she'll be fine and safe with her, dear." She kissed the top of his head, winked at Floss, and went out to the kitchen to make a soothing cup of coffee.

Ben was waiting for Floss at the edge of the village, and they walked quickly away, up the hill towards the woods. "Don't worry, babe," he said. "Maybe I should come to your house more often, and your dad could get to know me. Find out that I'm not a serial rapist or worse."

Floss shrugged. "Doesn't matter, anyhow. Mum knows about us, and she can keep Dad at bay. But I don't like to lie to him. He's been a good dad . . . on the whole." Then she laughed and Ben hugged her, and she yelled, "Careful!" As he stepped back in alarm, she reached inside her fleece jacket and presented him with a parcel, birthday-wrapped.

"Happy birthday, Ben," she said shyly.

He took the parcel, placed it on a handy milestone, and held her face in his hands. Then he kissed her sweetly, and said, "Thank you, darling Floss. It's the nicest present I've had today."

Floss swallowed. "Um, well, how do you know, if you haven't opened it?"

Together they sat down on the milestone, and Ben unwrapped the chocolates. "I was right," he said. "Much the nicest present. Shall we indulge?"

They opened the box and indulged. Eventually, Floss closed the lid and stood up. "We'd better leave a few for tomorrow. Come on, let's walk up the hill and see if anything's going on in the woods." She was not eager to discover more scary lights, but was sure they would be more safe from the eyes of prying passers-by. They wouldn't have to go far into the woods for a bit of a cuddle . . .

They wandered slowly up the hill, and at the first turning into the woods silently climbed the stile and, closely entwined, found a path that led away from the road. It was well-marked, and Ben said, "People do come this way, Floss. See the footprints? Big 'uns."

"So you were a Boy Sprout! Got your tracking badge, did you?" She laughed and tickled him. " 'You'll never go to heaven, with a fat Girl Guide,' " she sang, " ' 'cos the pearly gates, ain't quite that wide. . . .' "

Ben put his finger to his lips. "Shush!"he whispered. "Could be some others in the woods, like the other night. An' I don't like the look of those footprints." His face was serious, and Floss sobered up immediately. Now they walked quietly and silently, until Ben stopped. "Come here," he said. "I want to give you a thank-you kiss." He gently moved her until her back was against the broad trunk of a tree. The silence was broken only by a nightingale, trilling a lovely song right on cue.

*   *   *

In another part of the wood, Reg Abthorpe frowned. "Listen!" he said.

One of his companions said, "Listen to what?"

"Thought I heard voices. Over there." He pointed to the far side of the wood, back along the path they had used an hour or so ago.

"It's that bloody bird. Nuthin' else." The man turned back to the business in hand.

"Shut up!" Reg said. "Lie low until I get back. I'm goin' to check. Can't take any risks, y' fool. All of you, find some cover and keep shtum." He watched them until they were hidden in the underbrush, and then set off back along the path.

Not far from the stile, Reg stopped. He could see a dark shape against a tree that had not been there before. He moved forward, and his foot caught in a snaking bramble, throwing him forward on to his face. He was on his feet in seconds, standing motionless for a fraction of time, and then running like a demon back along the path. But not before Ben and Floss had seen him. He could hear footsteps behind him, and knew they were following. Just as well I know these woods like the back of me hand, he said to himself calmly, and dived off into what looked like impenetrable thicket.

"Lost him!" said Ben, pulling up in front of Floss. Both were panting and scarlet with effort.

"Who was he?" Floss gasped.

"Not sure," Ben said, "but I think I've seen him in our Gardens. Visiting Mr. Everitt. Not lately, but I'm sure it was him."

"Was he a—oh, what d' you call them—voy . . . ?"

"Voyeur? Peeping Tom? Shouldn't think so. How would he have known we were coming? No, he was up to something else, though God knows what."

"D'you think he knew who we were?" Floss was beginning to tremble, and Ben took her hand.

"Course not," he said, but he was pretty sure the man had recognized them both. He had stood and stared before taking off, no doubt committing their faces to memory.

"Come on, love, let's go back. Quite a birthday adventure!" He made a big effort, and by the time they reached the road, Floss had stopped trembling and was smiling at Ben's attempts to cheer her up.

As they parted at the edge of the village, Floss said, "Ben, can I ask you to do something?"

"Anything," said Ben.

"Can you keep quiet about tonight? Not tell anyone at all? If my parents got to hear of it, they'd chain me to my bed."

"Trust me," he said. "Not a word to anybody."

"Promise?"

"Cross my heart and hope to die," Ben replied.

"Night then, Troop Leader," said Floss, and walked away.

EARLY NEXT MORNING, WHEN FLOSS'S DAD WENT OUT to put the wheelie-bin on the pavement, his eye was caught by something hanging from their gate post. He closed his eyes in disbelief, then retched. God, he must get rid of it! With his hand over his mouth, he approached and unhooked the limp body of Floss's ginger tomcat, and with a glance at her curtained bedroom window, crept round to the back of the house. Armed with a spade, he went to the bottom of the garden, dug a hole, and dropped the corpse into it. Poor old Sandy, he was nearly thirteen, and weighed very little. When the hole was filled in, and leaves scraped across it, Pickering replaced the spade, took a deep breath, and went back into the house.

Sixteen

❧

Philip Pickering decided to take a day off
work. He said to Floss for the umpteenth time that he
hadn't seen Sandy, but was sure he would turn up. Off
hunting somewhere, he was sure. It was the best way, he
had concluded. Floss wouldn't forget him, but she would
get used to his disappearance, and they could get her another kitten. Perhaps a black one. They were supposed to
be lucky, weren't they? Pickering felt as if he had a lump
of ice in his chest. It was anger, and it would not go away.
If the cat had belonged to anyone else but Floss, he would
have shrugged his shoulders and blamed it on those itin-
erant yobs who regularly stole a car in Tresham and took
joy rides around the villages at night. They probably
bashed into poor old Sandy as he crossed the road, and
thought it would be fun to string him up. This time, because it was Floss, he was determined to find them.

After breakfast, he went to the front gate to check
there were no traces of the execution, and as he turned to
go back into the house, he saw an empty cigarette packet
under the hedge. Litter louts, too! he swore to himself. As
he picked it up he saw something scribbled on the blank
side. He could just make it out, and the message was
nasty: "Keep out of the woods, else your father will be
told." Woods? Floss wouldn't be in the woods. Perhaps it
was meant for someone else.

He met Floss coming down the path on her way to
work. With difficulty, he smiled at her and wished her a
nice day. "Don't forget to keep an eye out for Sandy!" she

said, her eyes full of tears. "He's never missed breakfast before. I'm sure something's happened to him." Her father assured her he would have a good hunt, and encouraged her to concentrate on her work. Then she was gone, and he went into the house to think.

Mrs. Pickering was also on her way out. "Just going to the shop," she said. "Shan't be long."

Pickering knew this meant he had at least twenty minutes to take some action, and he had a plan ready. He put down the cigarette packet, noticing that a blob of chewing-gum had fixed it—probably to the gate post— and had failed as the disgusting grey stuff had dried out. He checked the telephone book and dialled a number.

"Good morning. New Brooms." Lois was feeling cheerful and efficient this morning, and looked forward to a productive day. When Mr. Pickering asked if she could spare him a few minutes, straight away, a small cloud crossed her blue sky, but she agreed. "It can't be more than half an hour, I'm afraid," she said.

"Fine, that'll be fine," he replied.

What on earth does he want? Lois hoped he wasn't planning to take Floss away. She was proving to be an asset, and the others were fond of her, helping her out and giving her tips on how to deal with pernickety housewives. Lois knew Philip Pickering was not too happy with his precious daughter being a skivvy—as he saw it—and both her parents hoped she would decide on a proper job or training soon.

Gran opened the door, as always. "Mr. Pickering?" she said politely.

"I have an appointment to see Mrs. Meade," he said.

"She didn't tell *me*," said Gran, holding her ground.

At this point, Lois emerged from her office, and smoothed things over. "Now, Mr. Pickering," she said, "do sit down, and tell me how I can help you." Lois could be professionally charming when she chose, and a disgruntled Gran returned to her kitchen.

"Right," he began. "First of all it is nothing to do with Floss." Lois smiled and said that was a relief, as his daughter was shaping up very well. "Well," he continued, "in a way it is to do with Floss," and then he told Lois about the hanging cat and the cigarette packet, fumbling in his pocket to show it to her.

Lois read it, and stared at him. "What on earth is this about?" she said. "Have you any idea?"

"Yobs, probably," he answered. "But I mean to find out exactly, and I wondered if I could ask for your help. I'll come straight to the point, as I know you haven't much time. I have heard that you often work with the police in clearing up crimes in this area. I reckon this constitutes a crime, don't you? So, as you employ Floss, I thought I'd rather ask you than go to the police. They'd probably be very sympathetic and do nothing."

"But what made you think I could . . . ?" Lois looked innocently at him. He shook his head, and she saw that he was near to tears. Oh, sod it! she thought.

"Well . . ." His voice tailed off, and he started to get to his feet.

"No, no, sit down," Lois said. "There may be something in what you say. And I'd like to help you for Floss's sake. Does she know the cat's dead?" Lois had a mental picture of another hanging, and shivered.

"No, I buried it before she got up. And I haven't told my wife, either. I thought it best if they both think he has just gone missing. Cats do sometimes. Then I can find another kitten for Floss in a while."

Lois sighed, and was silent for a few seconds. "All right, then," she said, "I'll see what I can do. But try to think why they should threaten Floss. It seems as if the message was meant for her. Ask her gently if she ever goes up to the woods. And don't sound angry or suspicious, else she won't tell you anything! I've got a daughter, and I know what they're like at that age. Now, I must be going, so I'll be in touch. And if you have anything to tell me that might help, however small, ring my mobile." She gave him the number, and saw him to the door.

"I'm off now, Mum!" she shouted, and without waiting for an answer she set off for Blackberry Close.

Frances Wallis could not hide from her for ever, and now Lois had an added incentive for finding out just what those terriers did for a living.

IN AN IMMACULATE BACK BEDROOM IN THE CRUMBLING farmhouse, William Cox shook the shoulder of an old man fast asleep in a comfortable armchair. "Bert!" he said. "Herbert! Wake up. Time to go for a little outing before lunch. A nice walk in the woods with kind Mr. Abthorpe. Come on, shake a leg!"

The old man opened his eyes, and for a minute looked around him in drugged confusion. "Where is this . . . ?"

"Never you mind," William Cox said, and sighed. "A luxury hotel, that's what it is, and you've got salmon for your lunch. I've asked the chef to cook it just as you like it."

Herbert Everitt shook his head, as if clearing the mist from his eyes. "Don't I know you from somewhere?" he said.

"Should do," Cox replied. "I've been assigned to look after you for a while now. We like to take care of our guests, so if there's anything you want, you only have to ask. I'll leave you to wake up properly, and then come down with your coat on, ready for your walk."

Cox frowned as he went down the narrow stairs. He was not enjoying this pretence, and greeted Reg Abthorpe with a scowl. "Nearly ready," he said.

"Does he suspect anything?" the grim-faced man asked.

Cox shook his head. "Nothing. He's seriously confused, poor old bugger. Don't worry. He knows nothing."

SEVENTEEN

❧

"COME IN, DEAR, DO." OLD ELLEN HOBBLED IN front of Lois and pointed to her usual chair. "Sit yerself down, and I'll bring in the tea."

"But I can do that!" Lois protested.

Ellen shook her head. "While I can still put one foot in front of the other, I like to be mistress in my own house," she said firmly. Lois sat down.

"It's a nice gingerbread today, for a change," Ellen said. "Hope you like gingerbread?"

"My favourite, along with chocolate," said Lois diplomatically. In fact, she loved anything with ginger flavour. Her own grandmother used to make a wonderful dark, sticky gingerbread, and she had never forgotten the taste. "Mmm!" she said with her mouth full. "Best I've tasted since my granny's. Was your sister Martha a good cook like you?" Lois had got around to the loaded question sooner than she'd hoped.

"Not bad," Ellen said. "Mind you, she had to learn a lot of fancy recipes. What was good enough for me and them up at the Hall, weren't good enough for the Cox family. And the Standings at the Hall are real gentry. Them Coxes were a jumped up lot. Poor old Martha. I reckon they broke her spirit. She was a lively girl, pretty, too. I watched it gradually fade, until she looked like one of them dreary sheep she had to help look after. Just a drudge, she was. Lost interest in how she looked, and everything. Made me feel bad. She lost the will to live, I reckon."

"Poor girl," said Lois sympathetically. "Did you have much to do with them? What was William Cox like? He must have loved her to marry her, when his family disapproved."

"He was a good-looker," Ellen said grudgingly. "Wouldn't think so now, would you!" Ellen cackled. "Still, as Martha found out, good looks aren't worth much in the end. He used to boast in the pub that he'd tupped every girl in the village before he married. An' I don't reckon he changed his ways all that much after the weddin'."

Ellen looked sad, and Lois tried to cheer her up. "Water under the bridge now, Ellen. What d' you think of him now, now he's fallen on hard times? Does he ever come to see you?"

"Does he hell!" Ellen said. "And don't believe all you see. I'm told he's let everything go. Farm, woods, himself. All he cares about is that dog. Well, I reckon he's got a pile hidden under the mattress, so to speak. There was money in that family, an' they're all gone now. If you ask me, he's got it, crafty devil. Still, let's talk about something more interesting," she added, pouring out second cups. "How's Josie getting on in the shop? Not easy taking over from somebody else, I know."

Lois abandoned efforts to bring the conversation back to the subject of William Cox. She'd heard quite a lot to be going on with, and told Ellen the latest gossip from Long Farnden. As she said goodbye, Ellen said, "And if you're thinkin' of calling on Cox again, just you be careful. Nasty friends, he's got. Always did have. Cheerio, then, dear! See you next week." She shut her door and Lois drove off thoughtfully.

She decided to go home via Cox's house, and coasted to a halt at the first entrance to the woods. She looked at her watch, and reckoned she could spare half an hour. The woods were silent at first. There was almost no wind stirring the trees, and Lois, still at heart a town girl, was not listening for the rustles and whistles in the undergrowth, as small creatures scurried to safety. She followed what she assumed was a footpath, though thought it narrow for tramping feet. Not far in, where the trees were still at some distance from each other, she noticed an earthy mound, peppered with three or four holes, and thought confidently of rabbits. But the holes were huge, much bigger than a rabbit would need. Here and there were small hollows, filled with what looked like turds. Ugh! It was like a miniature camp site, with tunnels instead of tents, and small latrines neatly dug by a tidy-minded camp leader.

Badgers! Derek would have known straight away. She knew they came out to feed at night, and wondered if this was where Floss saw the lights. She doubted it. It was really quite close to the road, and easy for a cruising policeman to spot. Still, the badgers were probably spread out all over the woods. She glanced at her watch again. Not time now to go further, but as she turned back, she heard a voice, a man's voice, faintly in the distance. Now there were two voices. She certainly did not want to face them by herself, and retreated rapidly. Back on the road, she looked around, but there were no cars parked. Everywhere was quiet and still. Those voices could have carried a long way. But as she got into her car, she heard a shout of anger, much closer, and drove off at speed. She was almost certain the angry voice was that of William Cox.

"I THOUGHT I TOLD YOU TO KEEP AWAY FROM THOSE woods!" Derek was shouting, and Lois assured him she could still see the road from where she found the sett. "Of course it was badgers," he said. "Those are the lucky ones. Too near people passing by to be tormented by them killers. But the voices could easily have been men keeping a lookout."

"But it was broad daylight," Lois protested.

"Don't make any difference, me duck." Derek was calming down. "They bring terriers and send them down the tunnels to pick a fight. Then they dig 'em out and kill 'em when they've had enough sport. Sport! If I got my hands on 'em . . ."

"There weren't no cars parked. They'd have to have cars to get there."

"Probably hidden. There's plenty of places to hide a car. Old Cox's yard, for a start."

"He doesn't like the badger diggers. They wouldn't have hung a dead badger on his gate if he was one of them." Lois wished she hadn't told Derek about the voices. She hadn't expected him to be so furious, but now he was, and that confirmed the warnings she had had already.

"Just forget all about it, Lois," Gran said anxiously. She knew from long experience that her daughter seldom took notice of advice that didn't suit her. Even when she was a little girl, the way to get her not to do something, was to tell her to be sure and do it. Contrary Mary, her dad used to call her.

"That Mr. Pickering phoned," said Gran, changing the subject. "I said you'd ring him back. Wouldn't tell me what he wanted. Probably found a proper job for Floss to do."

Derek held his breath, waiting for Lois to explode. But she frowned and seemed not hear, "Right, I'll ring him after tea. I've just got one or two things to do in the office now."

After she'd left the kitchen, Derek looked at Gran and whistled. "Wow," he said, "that was dangerous ground you were on. She don't usually take remarks like that so calmly!"

Gran shook her head. "No. It's a bad sign, isn't it, Derek. She's still up to something. And what's Floss's dad got to do with it?"

"All will no doubt be revealed," shrugged Derek. "All in good time, when our Lois is ready, or needs some urgent help. Not too urgent, I hope," he added, and stumped off out to the garden.

EIGHTEEN

꩜

"Hello? Is Mr. Pickering there, please? I'm returning his call." Lois rubbed her eyes. She was tired and worried. Derek was seldom angry with her, and this, more than any warning from Cowgill or Ellen Biggs, had made her realize that the whole business of Herbert Everitt's disappearance and the badgers in Cox's Wood could turn very nasty indeed.

"Thank you for ringing back," Philip Pickering said. "It's just that I've had a friendly conversation with Floss—" I bet it was friendly, thought Lois—"and she said one or two things about herself and her friend Ben. I admit I was not pleased to know that the two of them had been up in those woods in the dark, but, as my wife says, young people will be young people."

"Yep, I'm sure," said Lois, sighing. "But what did Floss say?"

"She said they were spotted by someone coming along from deeper in the wood. A man. He tripped over a bramble, she said, and then he saw them and turned round and ran back into the wood. They followed him, but he vanished. So they came home. I think she was still frightened, and that's why she told me, but I said perhaps that would teach her not to?"

"That's really your business," said Lois quickly. "But did they get a look at him? Notice anything about him?"

"Only that Ben said he thought he had seen him before, in Blackberry Gardens. And they both reckoned he must have known the woods well, as he disappeared completely into the middle of a thicket. But it was very dark in amongst those trees. Frankly, Mrs. Meade, I can scarcely bear to think about it!" His voice had risen now, and Lois attempted to calm him down.

"Well, no harm done," she said. "I'm glad she told you all this. It will be very useful. Leave it to me, Mr. Pickering, and don't be too hard on Floss. Daughters will be daughters, you know. Bye."

Lois sat quietly at her desk, digesting this new information. So Ben thought he had seen the man in Blackberry Gardens before. It was certainly not the missing Herbert, nor William Cox, as the man had been athletic and presumably young or youngish. Probably not Mrs. Wimp Wallis's husband, either, as he was a big bull of a man, according to Jean Slater, and would have been immediately familiar to Ben. That left the one who repeatedly turned up and then disappeared again, and who should not have had any business being anywhere near Long Farnden. Reg Abthorpe.

But could he have killed and strung up a pet cat? He had been such a mild man when she first met him. Then she remembered his chilly smile, and his strange behaviour in Frances Wallis's house. She doubted whether he would have done the deed himself. Probably had friends—or associates—who would think nothing of bashing an old cat. After all, a much bigger animal had been done to death and tied to old Cox's gatepost.

A whimpering outside the office door demanded Lois's attention. She opened up and admitted a shivering Jeems. Lois hadn't noticed the rumbling thunder but now lightning was flashing across the village and heavy drops of rain tapped against her window. She picked up the little dog and spoke soothing words. She knew dogs disliked thunderstorms and fireworks, and Jemima was no exception. But as Lois hugged the warm puppy, she reflected that if she were as small and defenceless as Jeems, she too would be terrified.

And then, as the rumbles became fainter, a thought struck her with force. Suppose those men in the woods whose voices she'd heard had found out that she was interested in them? And to frighten her off, decided to kidnap Jeems! Or . . . She could not bear to think of a small white body tied to the . . . Oh, no, no! She would have to keep her with her wherever she went. It would be so easy for anyone to nip into the garden, pick up the puppy and scarper to a waiting car.

For the first time since years ago, when her son James had been in danger, partly because of her ferretin', she wished she had said no to Cowgill. After all, Herbert Everitt was nothing to her. Let the police get on with it. Maybe if she told Cowgill she was pulling out, he would galvanize his boys into getting a result.

Then she thought of Enid Abraham, her loyal, brave cleaner. She was genuinely upset at Herbert's disappearance, and would expect Lois to do everything she could to find him. Lois squeezed Jeems, and showed her the sun coming out over the village. "No, sorry, Jeems, I can't give up now," she said. "But we'll all have to be very careful, and not let you out of our sight."

THE PICKERING HOUSEHOLD WAS VERY QUIET. As Lois had guessed, the father and daughter conversation had been far from friendly. Father shouted and blustered, and Floss ended up weeping bitterly. She regretted having told him anything, but was secretly still alarmed at what had happened. She had hoped for fatherly reassurance. Ben had been very comforting, but ever since that evening, Floss had looked anxiously at every man she met to see if he was the one who had stared at them.

Philip Pickering had been almost driven to telling her about her cat, but fortunately had managed to control himself. It would have made things worse between them. Floss would have castigated him for keeping it from her, and it was too late now.

"Lunch is ready!" called Mrs. Pickering, and her husband made his way slowly to the kitchen.

*   *   *

In Blackberry Gardens, Ben sat with his elbows
on the table, watching his mother decorating a fruit tart
she was making for the WI Bring and Buy sale. "Why
don't *we* get fancy edges and pastry flowers all over the
top?" he said. "A few crisped up cornflakes is the family's lot."

"And very nice too," said his father, coming in from
the garden. "What would be the good of your mother
spending hours decorating a tart for us, when it'd all be
gone in a few mouthfuls?"

Ben did not answer, but grinned at his mother and disappeared to his room overlooking the road. He wished
they lived in the High Street, where there was some action most of the day to demand his attention. He was applying for jobs, but many of them did not even have the
courtesy to reply to his application, and others wrote but
regretted he was not what they were looking for. It was
depressing, and he was beginning to wish he'd appren-
ticed himself to a plumber instead of wrestling with IT.
Computer studies graduates were ten a penny these days,
and after the bubble burst there were not enough jobs
around.

If they had a house in the High Street, there'd be kids
coming out of school, young mums taking toddlers to the
playgroup, people going to work, most in cars but some
on bikes, and, always good for a few words, Josie from
the shop delivering the post. In this cul-de-sac development, where, as far as he knew, no blackberries had ever
been seen, it was dead. First thing in the morning, perhaps, there was a trace of life, when commuters set off
with a roar of engines. After that, nothing. Once a week
a neighbouring housewife would go off in the car to the
supermarket, and two or three others to keep fit at
Tresham Leisure Centre.

Here was one of them coming back, no doubt. Ben
went closer to the window and watched the car move
slowly, until it stopped outside Herbert Everitt's house.
Who was that then? He stiffened as a man got out,
opened his boot, and struggled up Mr. Everitt's garden

path with a huge parcel. Ben knew who it was! Last seen leaping into a bramble patch in Cox's Wood. He stepped back behind the curtain, and watched. The parcel was causing the man some trouble, and he finally put it down whilst he fumbled for a key. Then he opened the door, lifted up the parcel, and, staggering under its weight, vanished into the house. The door shut behind him.

Ben shivered. What the hell was going on? He knew that Floss's boss, Mrs. Meade, came once a week to dust around in there, because all Mum's friends said they couldn't think what she found to do for a couple of hours. Money for old rope, they said. But nobody else came. None of Herbert's friends or relations. Mind you, he always said he had no family, so that figured. Then who was this man? And what was in that package? It looked like an orange crate well-wrapped, or it could be a miniature coffin for old Herbert's dog. What had happened to that yapping menace, anyway? Ben's thoughts were buzzing, and he needed to talk to someone. No good worrying Floss, and his parents would just laugh and tell him to think about something useful, like bringing some money into the house. There was always Josie at the shop. Ben counted the change in his pocket. Just enough for the local paper. There was an extra sports section today, and a friend of Ben's was in the news for making it to the Tresham Tigers. With luck, he'd have the shop to himself and could bring up the subject of Mr. Everitt naturally.

"Morning, Ben." Josie was about to tidy the stockroom, but turned with a smile. Ben was a nice lad, always so polite and pleasant, and she didn't mind when she saw his only purchase was to be the local paper. Always a chance he might be tempted by something else.

"Hello, Josie," he said. "What's in this rag today? I expect you've given it the once-over to make sure it's suitable for tender customers like me."

"Come off it!" Josie took his money, and leaned on the counter. "Today, I'm afraid, no murders, no robbery with violence, no spectacular car crashes. Very boring today."

"Not even a mysterious disappearance?" Ben watched her closely.

She shook her head. "Not even news of our old friend Herbert Everitt," she said obligingly. "I miss him and his little dog, y' know. We always had an interesting chat. Still, I don't suppose he'll be back again now. Probably institutionalized in an old people's detention centre."

Ben laughed. "I don't think they're that bad these days. But he did seem so chipper just before he was taken off. I saw someone at his house this morning, and wondered if he was ready to return. Could've been a social worker, preparing for him to come home?"

Josie shook her head. "You mean that man with the crappy old car? No, he's a distant relation, I think. Keeping an eye on the place. Mum goes in, dusting and getting rid of spiders and mice. She doesn't like it much, says it's creepy." Josie could see that Ben had more to say, and knew that her mother would want to know what it was.

"This man was carrying an enormous great package— I thought maybe it would be a portable loo or something like that. An aid to independent living, as the catalogues say."

Josie shrugged. "Might be. I hope he is coming back. We could all give him a hand. Keep an eye on him. Meals-on-wheels, that kind of thing. Now, I've got work to do, so if that's all?"

IN MR. EVERITT'S CLEAN BUT CHILLY HOUSE, REG Abthorpe put down his burden and felt in his pocket. A small key unlocked the large chest freezer in front of him, and he shivered as the blast of cold air hit him. He moved aside some frosted packages, and with some difficulty pushed the latest into the space. The lid would not shut, and he swore. He wanted to be out of here as soon as possible. More shoving and pushing finally enabled him to close the freezer and lock it firmly.

As he scurried down the path, his collar turned up, he

glanced over to the Wallis house. No signs of movement, thank goodness. He could see the terriers looking expectantly at him through the window, and ducked into his car. It started at the third attempt, and he drove off quickly. As he turned into the High Street, he saw a tall youth walking towards him. Ah, yes, young Romeo, but without his Juliet. Reg was reminded that he had unfinished business to attend to there, and looked the other way as he passed.

NINETEEN

"ARE YOU COMING TO THE BRING AND BUY, LOIS?" Gran had made two loaves of bread, one wholemeal and the other a fruit loaf, so tempting that she had shut it in a tin so that Derek could not see it.

"I'm not a member," said Lois, without looking up from the local paper.

"You can come as my guest," Gran said. "It'd be nice for me, if you'd come just this once. Lots of others are taking guests . . ."

"Oh, blimey, not the emotional blackmail, Mum! Of course I'll come if you want me to. There's usually good bargains to be had. Are you off now?" Gran nodded, and as she went to get her jacket, she smiled a small, smug smile. She was glad she could win sometimes, though Lois was a tricky one.

The village hall was full of people, mostly women, milling about from stall to stall, and Gran greeted many of them. Lois, too, knew almost everybody, and joined in the fray, buying useless things she did not need, in the general fever to grab something before somebody else got it. She came upon Enid, sitting quietly behind a stall set out neatly with small, framed watercolours, landscapes of the villages and fields around.

"Enid! Did you paint these yourself?"

Enid nodded modestly. "It's just a hobby, Mrs. M."

"But they're lovely! Let me have a look and see which one I like best."

"Oh, you just choose one, and have it as a present," Enid said quickly. "I'd really like you to have it."

"Don't be daft, Enid," Lois said. "That's not the way to run a business. Here, this one of Dallyn Hall is beautiful, with the park and the trees. And it'd remind me of keeping the place clean! How much?"

Enid silently pointed to a card which priced the paintings at twenty-five pounds each. "But you have it for ten, Mrs. M. Please."

Lois said nothing, but found two tens and a five in her purse and handed them over. "It's worth much more to me," she said. "And this'll pay for more paints. I'll go and find Mum. She'd love one for her room, I know."

"Just before you go, Mrs. M, have you heard anything more about Herbert Everitt? I think about him a lot, and would really like to get in touch. Sorry to pester . . ."

Lois shook her head. "No, I'm the one who's sorry. Reg Abthorpe promised to send me his address and telephone number, but so far nothing. My cleaning money keeps coming, and I don't have a real reason for trying to find Reg. Various people claim to have seen him in the village, but somehow I only ever see the tail end of his car disappearing down the road. The only time I met him again, he was in a tearing hurry and cleared off quickly."

"Never mind, then." Enid's face had dropped, and Lois wondered if she had been more fond of the old man than she admitted. Perhaps a little romance had been blossoming? Oh dear, if that was so, she'd have to try even harder to turn up some information. She pushed her way through the throng and found Gran.

"Go and have a look at Enid's paintings," she said.

"I've seen them," Gran replied. "She kindly gave me

one as a present. It's the High Street, with the shop and Josie standing at the door. Wasn't that kind of her?"

"Huh!" Lois was lost for words for a moment. She sighed. "Well, I must be off now. I've spent out, and there's paper work to do at home. Thanks for bringing me, Mum. I've enjoyed it."

She reached the door with difficulty and found it blocked by a large figure coming in. It was a bulky, bald-headed man with a bull-dog face, and behind him crept Frances Wallis. "Not much left to buy," Lois said cheerfully.

Frances smiled nervously. "Um, Victor," she whispered, "this is Mrs. Meade, who cleans Mr. Everitt's house."

The man looked down at her. Lois was tall, but he still towered over her and she retreated a few steps. "How do," he said brusquely. "Don't know how you've got the nerve to take the money. Nobody to make any mess. Not even the dog. Still, Reg always was a fool. Come on, Frances, let's show our faces and then get out quickly."

Lois opened her mouth to take up the challenge, but he'd gone, Frances following close behind. Lois's face was scarlet, and she started back into the hall to ask him what the hell he meant. But Gran was there, smiling at her and saying she was ready to go herself now.

"You all right, Lois?" she said. Lois muttered something about it being very hot in the hall, and went out with her mother into the cool night air.

So he was Victor Wallis, and he knew Reg Abthorpe. And he wasn't too keen on Lois Meade. She was annoyed to feel herself shaking. It was a fact, then, that whoever they were and whatever they were up to, there was a gang of them with something to hide, and they would go to nasty lengths to keep their secret.

"Must be badger-baiting," Derek said, when she gave him an edited version of what had happened. "But that's maybe not all," Lois said. "OK, so they're tormenting wild animals in Cox's Wood, but that wouldn't explain why Reg is so interested in his Uncle Herbert's house, nor why he is keeping his whereabouts a closely guarded secret."

"If Herbert *was* his uncle," Gran said. Lois looked at her. "Well, he was pretty convincing that first time he came," she said. "You seemed to be all over him."

Gran bristled. "A person can be mistaken," she said. "And anyway," she added, "why are we all talking about Herbert in the past tense. D' you know something you're not tellin', Lois?"

"Of course she does," said Derek flatly. "Though no doubt a full report will go to that copper," he added. "Why don't you put the kettle on, Gran, and let's have a cup of that revolting Sleepytime muck you bought. It did put me out like a light, I will say that for it."

"It'll take more than that to send me off tonight," said Lois. "That bald bugger will haunt my dreams, anyway. If you don't mind, Derek, I'll go and sort out some papers in my office. Shan't be long. You go on up. Night, Mum," she added. "It was a nice evening until them Wallises came along. Thanks for taking me."

She sat in her office without moving. Everything was neat and orderly, and there was nothing for her to do. Reg Abthorpe, William Cox, Victor Wallis, and others. An unsavoury bunch. Perhaps she should pay another visit to Cox, who was, outwardly at least, on her side. No doubt he would try to get something from her, but she was pretty good at not answering difficult questions. He seemed to be at the hub of whatever was going on, even though he was a frail and dozy old man. Perhaps he wasn't frail at all, but had deceived her for a purpose? She looked at the telephone. Should she call Cowgill, tell him the latest, and see if he had any ideas, or anything to add to their sketchy sum of knowledge?

No, it was too late, and he would be alone. Not a good idea. Lois stood up and stretched. She went into the kitchen, and found Derek gone, but Gran still tidying up. "Where's Jeems?" Lois said.

"I thought she was with you," Gran answered, looking under the table, Jeems's favourite sleeping place.

Panic sent Lois around the house and into the garden, calling the puppy's name loudly. There was no response. Derek came down in his pyjamas and joined the hunt.

"Oh my God," Lois said finally, bursting into tears. "They've got her. Those rotten sods have taken her."

Before Derek could stop her, she leapt into her van, grated the gears, and backed down the drive.

"Hey! Lois, wait! The gates are shut!" Lois screeched to a halt, and sat with her head in her hands over the steering wheel. Derek opened the passenger door and sat beside her. "She'll turn up, me duck," he said. "Don't fret. We'll comb the country tomorrow." He put his arms around her, and she sobbed into his shoulder.

"Lois! Lois!" It was Gran, calling from the back door. "Look! I've found her! She was shut in the larder!"

Derek and Lois were very still for a few minutes, and then he said, "Now do you see what I mean? No good can come of this ferretin'. Give it up, me duck. We all need a bit o' peace and quiet."

"If Jeems can be found, so can Herbert Everitt," she said slowly. "Though I doubt he's in the larder." As she said this, she remembered being told about a man seen struggling up Herbert Everitt's path with a large package. There was no larder in that modern house, but there was a very large freezer, and it was firmly locked.

TWENTY

꒱

NEXT MORNING, LOIS SET OUT FOR BLACKBERRY Gardens earlier than usual. Nothing stirred in the Gardens, except for the terriers, barking excitedly at her approach. She hoped that Victor Wallis was still there. No lorry outside, but perhaps he had parked it elsewhere. She couldn't imagine the good folk of the Gardens would put up with a huge articulated vehicle being parked in their trim, well-ordered little estate.

She knocked, and was not in the least put off by the minutes passing and no one coming to the door. She knocked again, harder and more insistently. Then she peered through the windows, but couldn't see much because of the net curtains. Back to the knocker. She banged it as hard as she could, and then shouted through the letterbox, "Open this door, and soon. It's the police." She knew this would not fool them, but it was worth a try. It worked. A chain and bolts were withdrawn, and the door opened a crack.

"What the hell do you want! An' it's a crime to claim to be police if you're not!" Victor was wearing boxer shorts and a vest, and his face was not pleasant.

"A joke, Mr. Wallis," said Lois calmly. "I want a word with you. And in case you were thinking of inviting me in, I'd rather stay here on the doorstep. So, what d' you mean by accusing me of taking money for nothing?"

"You're not comin' in here. Not on your nelly! An' what I said was what I meant. I always mean what I say. An' now, if you're not off my property in ten seconds, I'll call the police and have you done for trespass."

Lois laughed loudly. "It's my guess you'll go nowhere near the police. So listen to this. If I hear that you or your poor wife have said anything more about New Brooms in general or me in particular, I'll see my lawyer and have your guts for garters. Right?"

Victor Wallis watched her walk out of his garden and across the road to Herbert Everitt's house. "Wow!" he said admiringly, turning to his wife, who was sheltering behind him. "She's a goer! Pity you can't be more like that, Frances," he added, and pushed her aside as he retreated upstairs.

Inside Herbert's house, Lois went straight to the freezer and stared at it, as if staring long enough would spring the lock. She needed help, and either the police or an experienced safe-breaker would do the trick. But she wasn't sure she could persuade Cowgill to do it, without a lot more evidence of something criminal going on. And unlike all those fictional detectives, she didn't have a criminal acquaintance who could use a bent pin and have it open in seconds.

Perhaps Derek would have a key that would fit. But how would she persuade Derek to take any part in it? He would no more break into someone else's locked freezer than burgle a jewel box. But supposing there was a power cut, and the electricity was off for hours? Whatever was in it—she shuddered—would deteriorate, without doubt. It could be a health hazard.

She plugged in the vacuum cleaner and began work. The house was stuffy and the air outside was quite balmy, so she decided to open all the doors and windows and shake out rugs and cushions, pillows and duvets, then drape them all over bushes in the garden to catch the sun. That would give Victor Wallis something to think about.

The windows were dusty and rain-streaked. A bird had splattered its purple-stained droppings on several of the panes, and Lois decided on a general cleaning and polishing job, including outside. This would give her ample opportunity to keep an eye on the terriers and their master, as well as demonstrate how she more than earned her fee.

The front windows finished, she took duster and spray, and the step-ladder, round to the back of the house. She was on the last window, when she heard hoarse shouting and a woman's cry of pain, then a door slam. She waited a few minutes, but there were no more shouts or screams. She walked quietly round to the front and stared across the road. Nothing. A net-curtained façade looked back at her blankly. She went in through Herbert's open front door, and saw a torn-out page of a magazine on the mat. Her pulse quickened, and she bent to pick it up. When she saw the photograph, she gasped and threw it on to the hall table. Feeling sick, she swallowed hard and closed her eyes. Then she slowly picked up the page again, and forced herself to look at it.

The photograph was from a country magazine, and illustrated an advertisement for an animal rescue organization. On a surgery examination table lay a small white terrier. It was horribly damaged, and very dead. "SOME PEOPLE WILL STOP AT NOTHING!" the accompanying text shouted, and continued, "PLEASE HELP US IN OUR WORK."

Lois got the message. Reg and Victor and unknown others would stop at nothing.

THE FIRST THING SHE LOOKED FOR AS SHE CAME INTO the kitchen back home, was, of course, Jeems. The little dog rushed to greet her, as always, and she picked her up and gave her a hug.

"Well, I thought I'd never see it," said Gran.

"What?"

"You being soft about an animal. Softer than you ever were with your own children." Gran sweetened the criticism with a smile. "Mind you," she added, "I reckon they couldn't have turned out better, bless 'em."

"In spite of me being so brutal?" Lois said sharply. She had had enough for one morning, and retired to her office, taking Jeems with her. She had replaced the sickening advertisement exactly where she found it. Maybe next time one of those villains went in to the house—she believed that at least Reg and Victor went in frequently—it would puzzle them. They would expect her to have torn it up and got rid of it. Well, if they wanted a battle of dirty tricks, they could have it.

She listened to her messages. No complaints, but a short request from Mrs. Cullen, Ben's mother. She needed help in the house, she said, now that she was starting a new job. An interesting place at the hospital in Tresham had come up, and she'd been offered it. She intended to accept. Would Lois ring her back?

Lois looked at her watch. Nearly lunchtime, so Mrs. Cullen would probably be at home. She dialled the number. "Ah, thanks for calling." Lois remembered that Gran had liked Mrs. Cullen at the WI. Always willing to do jobs nobody else wanted, she said. Lois arranged to see her on the way to Ringford, where she intended to visit Ellen Biggs. She needed to ask Ellen a few more questions about William Cox.

Twenty-One

BEN CULLEN WAS DISMAYED TO HEAR OF HIS mother's new job. He was used to having all his needs catered for, and the prospect of getting his own lunch, not to mention doing his own laundry, had shaken him up. If the house was going to be empty all day, he might just as well find any old job to do until a real opportunity came up. Or, to put it more realistically, until someone decided to give him a job in computers.

"I might even ask you to do a bit of housework," said his mother cruelly. "No reason why you shouldn't wield a duster and hoover around the place." His face fell, and she relented. "Well, as a matter of fact, I've been in touch with Mrs. Meade at New Brooms, and she's coming to see me. At least I'll know it will be done properly."

"You'll probably get Floss," he said gloomily. "I don't want her doing my room, nosing into all my ghastly secrets."

"By which you mean smelly socks and sweaty T-shirts, I suppose? Well, there's one remedy. You know where the washing machine is, and I'll show you how to use it."

Ben groaned. "I can't take any more," he said, and announced his intention to go for a walk and ponder on his future.

*   *   *

AT THE EDGE OF COX'S WOOD, BEN HESITATED. He couldn't decide whether to go straight on and take the footpath across the fields, or plunge into the woods and find a shady place to sit down and think. He had to admit to himself that he wasn't too keen on the woods option. That night when the mysterious man watched Floss and him having a smooch, was still fresh in his mind. It was the way the man had disappeared instantly, like a ghost into the thicket. Still, who's afraid of the big bad wolf? He braced his shoulders and climbed the stile. Come to think of it, it'd be nice to have a big dog, perhaps a Doberman or an Alsatian, padding along beside him. He decided not to go too far, just far enough to find a mossy stump suitable for contemplation of his future.

Several hundred yards along the well-trodden path, he heard whistling coming closer. He stopped and looked around for a hiding place. It would be quite useful to know who this one was, and in any case, there was no time to go back undetected. The broad trunk of an oak, twenty yards or so from the path, looked likely. He dodged through the wild garlic, and with the heady scent in his nostrils, he concealed himself behind the tree. The whistling was very close now. It was no recognizable tune, but a monotonous wandering across three or four notes. Then the whistler came in sight. Ben peered cautiously round the tree trunk, and was not happy to see the mysterious man, the man who was a ghost, with the clapped-out car and was a suspicious lurker in Blackberry Gardens.

Suddenly the whistling stopped and there was silence except for the usual sounds of the woods. Ben had heard crunching footsteps as the man approached, and now they too had stopped. He held his breath. A low muttering came from the path, and to his horror the footsteps began again, coming precisely in his direction. He took one peek around the tree and saw the man staring at him. Best to stand his ground. He had no chance against this character who knew his way around the woods so well.

"What d' you think you're doing?" The man frowned threateningly.

"Come to that," said Ben, "I could ask you the same question." He was shaking, but determined.

"I've been looking for foxes," said the man, and Ben saw he had a gun in his hand. "All quite legal. No need to concern yourself about that. Now you answer my question."

Tell the truth, Ben said to himself. "I came for a walk in the woods. I have left college, have no job, and wanted to think out my next move. All quite legal."

A chilly smile crossed the man's face, and he said, "I'll leave you to think, then. But I advise you not to go too far in these woods. You can get lost for hours. I've known people who went for a walk in here and were never seen again . . ." He turned and went on his way, resuming the whistle, and as he disappeared through the trees, Ben noticed that though he moved quickly he had a slight limp.

IN ANOTHER PART OF THE WOOD, TWO MEN SAT ON A fallen tree trunk and stared into the dark interior, where no sunlight penetrated and the underbrush was thick.

"He told us to cover the tracks," the thin one said. "Make sure there's no trace."

"Easier said than done," said the other. "How do we cover up footprints and bloody great holes in the ground?"

"Fill 'em in, I suppose. The holes, not the footprints. I don't see what we can do about those."

"Except rake every single one until it's gone."

"And then cover it with dead leaves? Sounds like bloody Hansel and Gretel. Perhaps he'd like us to lay trails of rice to lead the fuzz away from here? The man's bloody mad."

"And dangerous," said the bald, tubby man, getting to his feet. "We know exactly how dangerous the bugger can be, don't we. That poor old man, never knew what hit him. Come on, we'd better get busy. Sooner we start, sooner we can get away from here. I hate these bloody woods."

"I hate *him* even more," said the other, and picking up his spade, he brought it down viciously, halving an innocent worm making its way out of the turned earth.

"That's what I'd like to do to him," he said, and they both began work.

Mrs. Cullen saw Lois coming down the road, and opened the door. "Here we are!" she called in a welcoming voice. "Come on in. Would you like a cup of tea?"

Lois shook her head. "It's very kind of you, but no thanks," she said. "Just had what Gran calls a light lunch. Goodness knows what she'd produce for a heavy one!"

"She's a good cook. I know that from the goodies she brings to WI." Mrs. Cullen indicated a chair in the comfortable sitting room, and began to explain again why she needed help in the house. "I thought just once a week, to give the whole place a good clean-up, if that's OK with you?"

"Fine," said Lois. "And if you've got people coming to stay, or some special date, we can always give you some extra hours. Now, I've done some thinking, and have decided the best one of my team for you would be Floss Pickering. I know she's Ben's girlfriend at the moment, and if that bothers you, I can certainly think about sending someone else. But she's shaping up very well, reliable and trustworthy. I expect you've met her?"

"Well, no, actually we haven't. Not formally, that is. I've seen her around the village of course, but Ben says she doesn't want her father to know and so they meet secretly."

"Nothing's secret in this village," laughed Lois. "You can be sure the gossips' network has been busy. Mind you, if Mrs. Pickering knows, she's probably kept it from hubby. Though why Floss should worry about her dad, I don't know."

"Seems he welcomes boyfriends with open arms, and, according to Floss, overdoes the whole thing so stupidly that the boys get frightened off. Ben says he's proof against that, but so far he's not been invited up there."

Lois remembered her own rules about gossip, and said, "Yes, well, the private lives of my staff are their own affair, and should have nothing to do with the job. I'll send Floss along next week, and if you have any concerns about her work, let me know at once."

She had not been entirely honest about her reason for sending Floss. It had quickly occurred to her that having Ben and Floss legitimately in the same house for a while might produce some more information about the encounter in the woods. Floss was a chatty soul, and if Lois contrived to see her on her own occasionally, useful details might emerge. She had denied many times that she used her staff to snoop, but believed that if interesting information turned up in the course of natural conversations, this was fine.

"Well, thanks for coming, Mrs. Meade." Mrs. Cullen ushered her out to her car, saying, "Off on your duties? I expect you have a lot to do keeping everyone in order."

Lois nodded. "But I'm off to see an old lady in Ringford. I've known her for years, and she's fairly immobile now. She likes visitors, and to hear what's going on. Bye, then. I'll be in touch soon to see how Floss is getting on."

By the time Lois reached Ringford, it had begun to rain, and Ellen appeared at her door with a cautious look at the sky. "I knew it'd rain," she said. "Red sky in the mornin', shepherd's warnin'."

"You're right," Lois said. "Are you going to keep me on the step getting soaking wet, or can I come in?"

Old Ellen cackled. "Course you can, ducky. Mind you, I wasn't expecting you. Have I got me days mixed up?"

Lois assured her that her memory had not deceived

her. "I was passing by," she lied, "and thought I'd drop in and make sure you're OK."

She sat down in the dark sitting room, and gave up protesting that she did not need a cup of tea. "I'll not be accused of forgetting me 'ospitality," Ellen said, hobbling into the tiny kitchen.

Settled with a cup of good strong brew, Lois steered the conversation round to William Cox. "I'm going to see him later," she said. "Shall I give him your regards?" It was meant as a joke, and she was unnerved to see how it misfired.

"Don't you dare!" Ellen said vehemently. "And if you don't mind, we'll talk no more about William Cox. He's bin enough trouble to me, without goin' over it with you. Now, did I tell you what our Ivy said about the gyppos' settin' up camp in the bottom field?"

Lois was puzzled. Ellen had had no qualms about discussing her brother-in-law on other occasions. There was no point in arguing with her, Lois knew that from bitter experience. But why was she clamming up now? Reluctantly, she listened to Ellen's tale of Ivy Beasley and the gypsies. "They were up there in the woods, Ivy said, trappin' rabbits an' that. I reckon they'll cop it if they're not careful. Dangerous place, them woods. Still, serve 'em right, I say. I expect we'll get one of them funny-lookin' women round, selling lace they claim is hand-made. Straight from a factory in Birmingham! I know hand-made when I see it, and it ain't what them gypsies got!"

Lois's ears pricked when Ellen mentioned the woods again, but knew she couldn't ask what she meant. For some reason, Ellen had closed the subject, and that was that. After offering help with washing-up, and being refused, Lois left, promising to come on her regular day, and licking her lips at the prospect of a dough cake spread thickly with butter.

As she turned her car in the direction of Cox's Wood, Lois felt uneasy. Had Ellen been told to keep quiet? Had her despised brother-in-law paid her a visit at last? At this thought, Lois was angry. If that nice old lady had been threatened, then William Cox would get the rough side of Lois's tongue. And then, heaven help him.

TWENTY-TWO

ᔫ

HAZEL THORNBULL WAS LATE FOR WORK AT THE OF-fice of New Brooms in Tresham. Her small daughter, Elizabeth, had produced a high temperature in the middle of the night, and it was still high when she woke up this morning. Hazel's mother, Bridie, had said on the telephone that children must come first, and Hazel should take her in to the surgery at once. Hazel needed no persuading, and after she had argued with the doctor's receptionist who had offered her an appointment in three days' time, she went in to Tresham. "Just one of those little bugs children pick up," the doctor had said. "Keep her warm and give her this to keep the temperature down. She'll be as right as a trivet in a couple of days. Is your mother looking after her? Fine. Nobody better." And she pressed her button for the next patient.

Hazel took Elizabeth back to Bridie, and was late for work in Sebastopol Street. Her mind was still on little Lizzie as she parked her car fifty yards away from the shop. As she walked towards it, she saw a small crowd of people outside. Oh no, not a queue! She quickened her step, and as she drew up to them, saw the reason why they stood there. Not a queue, but a crowd of shocked observers. The big plate-glass window, always sparkling and clear, was shattered, and glass had spread everywhere. "Oh my God!" gasped Hazel, and pushed her way through to the door.

"We've sent for the police, me duck," said a fatherly man, taking her arm. "You got the key? Right, let's open up, but we mustn't touch anything for the moment."

"When did it happen?" Hazel said. She was not in need of the man's support, and began to shake with anger. She glared hard at all the bystanders, who, unwilling to be implicated in any way, began to melt away.

"Not sure," said the fatherly man. "But the man in the video shop over the road said he heard something in the small hours. Lives over the shop, since it changed hands."

"Right," Hazel said. "I'd better ring the boss now. Thanks a lot for your help."

"Sure you'll be all right, me duck? I'll stay until the police come, if you like."

"No, I'll be fine, thanks." She dialled Lois's mobile, and filled her in with the details. "No need for you to come beetling over," she assured her. "I can handle the police and organize replacing the window. I'll keep you informed. Have you got a busy day?"

"Yeah, as always," Lois said. "Just off to the Hall, to check Mrs. T-J is happy. But give me a ring any time if you want help. I expect the cops will want to see me anyway. I'll leave it to you for the moment."

She had pulled over on the hill up to Cox's Farm to answer the call, and now sat motionless for a few minutes, considering who had smashed the window, and why. So they were after her, she decided. A campaign to warn her off. Strange that they should risk alerting the police, but maybe the job was done by a known gang, roving young villains who plagued the lives of people in Tresham. Probably breaking windows was run-of-the-mill for them. Still, enquiries would be made, interviews carried out. It was risky, even though they had covered their tracks.

She set off again towards Cox's Wood and the farmhouse. As she got out of the car, she at once missed the barking assault of Rosie, the sheepdog. Perhaps William was out with her, checking his land. Unlikely! She opened the collapsing gate and walked in. Nobody around, and no one answered the door when she knocked. Then she peered through the windows and was startled to see a completely empty house. Not a stick of furniture, no curtains, everything gone.

Lois glanced around quickly, feeling eyes upon her. But there was nobody in sight. A couple of chickens wandered up and looked at her hopefully. Had they been fed? They certainly looked hungry, and Lois thought maybe she should find something to give them. In a small barn across the yard, she found a bin of corn, and threw the anxious birds several handfuls. They ate furiously, and Lois reckoned they had not been fed for some while.

Then she heard a sound in the barn behind her. It was a whining sound, a dog's whine. She whipped round and went forward nervously. In the far corner, behind sacks piled up, Lois found Rosie, shivering and whining, and clearly unable to stand. Frantically pulling away the sacks, she found the dog lying on straw, wagging a feeble tail. When Rosie struggled to get up, Lois saw her legs buckling under her, and the dog screamed in pain. No! Not a defenceless dog, too! Lois picked her up with difficulty, and got her into the back seat of her car. Next stop, the vet.

As she went round to the driver's door, a flashy car drew up and the window slid down. "Excuse me, is this Cox's Farm?" The young man grinned winningly at her.

"Yes, it is," Lois said. "But there's nobody here. Except an injured dog, and I'm taking it to the vet before it snuffs it. You'll not find anyone at home."

"I know," said the man, his grin fading as he peered into Lois's car. "I'm from the estate agents, and have to put up a For Sale board." Like a parody of a property salesman, he added, "Can I interest you in an historic old farmhouse with great potential for restoration?"

Lois glared at him, and drove off rapidly, sending a shower of grit and gravel over the young man as he got out of his car.

*   *   *

As luck would have it, Lois found Bill on duty, helping out at the vets. He was now part-qualified so that he was trusted to do preliminary examinations, and Lois was very glad to see him. "I was hoping it would be you," she said. "Here, can you help me with a dog in the back of the car."

"Not Jeems!" said Bill, knowing Lois's feelings for the terrier.

Lois shook her head. "Nope, a sheepdog. I'll explain in a minute. Let's get her looked at first."

As Bill lifted her, Rosie once more yelped in pain. "Never mind, old girl," he said as he put her on the examination table. "I'm just having a little look." He took each leg in turn and very gently moved it. His face was dark when he looked up at Lois. "This dog," he said quietly, "has four broken legs. And she's emaciated and dehydrated. Almost no pulse. For God's sake, Mrs. M, what's been going on?"

Lois explained as clearly as she could, and her voice shook. "Bill," she said finally, "is it possible somebody could've broken an old dog's legs deliberately?"

"Or she could have been run over. But there's no crushing or other injuries you would expect." Bill was silent for a moment. "Would you like to stroke her, Lois? Calm her down? I'm afraid there's really only one thing to do. I'll get Mr. Wright to come in and confirm. It'll be the kindest. We'll give her some peace."

Rosie looked up pleadingly at Lois, who held her head gently, stroking her and speaking consolingly. Mr. Wright came in, and quite soon the light went slowly from the dog's brown eyes and she was still.

TWENTY-THREE

ॐ

"Lois! What on earth has happened to you?"
Gran was dressed in her best, and about to set out
for the village hall, where the annual Flower Show was in
full swing.

"It's not what happened to *me*," said Lois, slumping
down on a chair.

"Who, then? For God's sake, Lois, not one of the
children . . . or Derek?"

Lois looked up at her, and her eyes were full of tears.
"No, just an old dog. Left to die in agony up at Cox's
Farm. Four broken legs and no food or water. Oh Lord,
Mum . . ." And she got up quickly and rushed to the
cloakroom, from where Gran could hear the unmistake-
able sounds of Lois being sick. When she came back,
Gran had the kettle on.

"Sit down there," she ordered, and continued, "now
you just tell me what you were doing at Cox's Farm. As
far as I know, he hasn't required the services of New
Brooms?"

Lois shook her head. "No, he hasn't. And now he certainly won't. The house is empty, everything gone, and a
man was about to put up a For Sale notice. I heard Rosie
whimpering when I was scouting round to see what was
happening. There were chickens needing food, and I
found some in a barn. And I found Rosie. The vet's put
her to sleep."

Gran patted her shoulder. "I'm sorry, duckie. You did
the right thing. But it really is none of our business, is

it. No doubt the vet will tell the police, if he thinks there's been cruelty. Well, all this explains why Mrs. T-J phoned to ask where you were. Worried me, I can tell you. Anyway, you'd better give her a ring. You know what she is."

Lois groaned. "Yep, all right. I'll do it now. Stand by with the brandy." She went off to her office, and Gran heard a contrite Lois explaining with an excuse that had nothing to do with an injured dog. "I'd better be off," she said, coming back into the kitchen. "The old bag is livid. It was only my routine check, but apparently Floss didn't turn up, either."

"I know," said Gran. "She rang after you'd gone, saying she had a migraine and was throwing up. She was sure she'd be fine by tomorrow. I explained that to Mrs. T-J, but I don't think she was listening."

"Not my day," said Lois, taking her car keys off the hook. "See you later."

"What about food?"

"No thanks. Not hungry at the moment. Bye."

WHEN LOIS ARRIVED AT THE HALL, THE HOUSE-keeper answered the door. "I'm afraid Mrs. T-J has gone to the Flower Show," she said. "She's a judge."

"I bet she is," muttered Lois. "I had an appointment," she said, and the woman flushed.

"So sorry," she replied. "Mrs. T-J mentioned it, and said I was to ask you to wait. I think you were supposed to be here earlier? She was quite cross . . . In fact," she added, "she was furious. Not used to being kept waiting, I'm afraid."

"Nor am I," Lois said. "I have work to do, and I'll give her a ring to fix a convenient time for me to come back. It was only a routine check on the cleaner."

"She didn't turn up either," said the housekeeper nervously. "That made it a lot worse."

"Well, I'm sorry for *you*," said Lois. "But Floss's absence was explained. Perhaps you would tell Mrs.

Tollervey-Jones I shall be sending a replacement tomorrow. If that's not convenient, let me know. Goodbye."

She drove off at speed, down the tree-lined drive and out into blinding sun at the gates. Just in time, she saw a dark shape crossing the road and stood on the brakes. She leapt out of the car and looked along the grassy bank. It was a badger, and it hardly moved when she approached. From her research, she knew badgers were nocturnal animals, and if seen out in daylight, were likely to be diseased. As she stood wondering what to do, it shambled off, disappearing into the thick grass and undergrowth. Maybe it wasn't sick. Perhaps it had woken up too early and was confused. Lois turned back to her car. More likely to be sick, maybe with tuberculosis, and a danger to cattle. Quite legal to shoot it, then. She thought of the law, and realized it would be good to talk to Hunter Cowgill. It was treacherous ground she was treading. She needed help, and reached for her mobile.

"Hello? Is that you?"

"Who else?" Cowgill smiled. His Lois. His day brightened instantly.

"Well, listen." she said. "I need to talk to you, and it would be best face-to-face. There's quite a lot to say, and I'd like some advice."

"Well, my dear Lois, I never thought to hear you say that!" He fancied he could hear her draw in her breath ready for a blast, and added quickly, "Of course we can meet. Usual place? Eleven o'clock tomorrow morning soon enough?"

"Yep. Oh, and by the ways how's everything?"

"Improving," said Cowgill. "See you tomorrow."

BEFORE TURNING INTO HER DRIVE, LOIS REMEMBERED again the For Sale board and the pushy young man. She had been able to think only of poor Rosie, but now she decided to drive on and call in at the estate agents in the next village. It was only five or six miles, and she was quickly there. The street was deserted, and she pulled up outside the offices. First she looked at every property advertised for sale in the window, and Cox's Farm was not among them. Probably not this agent, but one in Tresham. It was worth asking, and she went in. New Brooms cleaned these offices, and she was welcomed warmly by the blonde receptionist.

"Morning, Mrs. Meade, how are you?"

They got the small talk out of the way, and Lois said she was pleased Bill was still satisfactory. Then she said casually, "Did I hear Cox's Farm is for sale?"

The blonde shook her head. "Not with us, Mrs. Meade. I must say it's a surprise to me. Isn't that where old William Cox lives? Has he gone into a home, or, well, passed on . . . ?"

"I have no idea," said Lois. "It was just that I heard through the grapevine. Well, I must be on my way. I'm glad everything is going well. Bye."

The afternoon was nearly gone, and Lois felt she had achieved nothing. Might as well go home and do some paperwork, she decided. Then she remembered Floss being ill, and thought she would call in and commiserate. The quickest way back home was through narrow roads and past Cox's Wood, but she felt a stab of nausea again at the thought. By the time she reached Long Farnden, Mr. Pickering's car was in his drive, and she hesitated. He was bound to want to know if she'd discovered anything more. No, she'd give them a ring and enquire after Floss. She accelerated and drove past.

"So, are we telling Derek about your finding that dog?" Gran had been thinking, and had decided to take a firm line.

Lois stared at her. "Of course," she said. "Why not?" This took the wind somewhat out of Gran's sails, and she replied that she was well aware that Lois kept a number of things to herself and she didn't want to put her foot in it.

"Lovely flowers," Lois said, with an obvious change of subject. "Where did you get them?"

"Flower Show, of course," Gran said. "They had a stall selling them. I think these came from the Hall."

"Should be the best, then," said Derek, coming into the kitchen with a cheerful smile. "How's everybody?" He looked at Lois, and added, "No, don't tell me. Not until I've had a cup of tea."

When he'd washed and changed, and they were sitting down to tea, he said to Lois, "All right then, let's have it."

"It's just a little hiccup," said Gran desperately.

"Don't be daft," Lois said. Then she gave Derek an account of her day, and he raised his eyebrows.

"Poor old love," he said. "I hope they catch the buggers who done it. Old William was fond of that dog, even if he did yell at it a lot. And what's this about the farm being for sale? I've just come by, and saw the sign. No sign of old Cox. Nothin' going on there at all, except for a couple of chickens wandering in the road. Nearly squashed 'em."

"There was something else," said Lois, and she told him about the badger.

"Don't worry, gel," he said. "I'll ring old Fred Watts. He'll go out there with his gun and put it out of its misery. He does a good job."

Lois suddenly felt very tired. She smiled at Derek with difficulty. "Thanks," she said. "I'll go and put the telly on, shall I, and we'll catch the news." She would try to push the whole dismal day from her mind until she saw Cowgill tomorrow.

Gran looked at them both. "Telly news is always bad," she said. "Why don't we wash up and then have a nice game of Scrabble? Forget the telly for once?"

They stared at her. "Are you mad?" they chorused, and Lois went to switch on the television.

TWENTY-FOUR

～

T HE SUPERMARKET WAS CROWDED, AND LOIS WAS glad. She acknowledged that the meeting place was a clever one, and once in the little room at the back of the bakery section, she felt quite safe from prying eyes. But getting there was different. She always met someone she knew, and had to make sure they weren't watching her. This time she was lucky. The supermarket seemed full of complete strangers, and she went straight to the bread counter.

"Four iced buns, please," she said. "And a wholemeal loaf." As she took her purchases, she made her usual request. "Um, I need to go to the loo urgently," she whispered to the assistant. "Bladder trouble . . . you know . . ."

The girl nodded sympathetically. "Through there," she whispered in return. "Second on the right, end of the passage."

At the first door on the left, Lois knocked. Cowgill opened it, and she walked in.

"Morning, Lois," he said, his eyes shining. "How are you and yours?"

"Fine," she said. "I'm just supposed to be having a pee, so it'll have to be quick."

"Fire away," he said, and she gave him a succinct account of most of the developments, leaving out her visits to Ellen Biggs in Ringford. She was not having blundering policemen upsetting the old thing. Nor did she mention Pickering's concern about his daughter, as he'd specifically said he didn't want the police involved.

When she had finished, he nodded gravely and said, "I knew you'd be in touch. We had a call from the vet yesterday. Dreadful business. It'll have to be investigated. And this apparent disappearance of William Cox—well, maybe the old man has gone to a relative, or an old folks' home. Until somebody gives us evidence for real concern, there's not a lot we can do."

"Same as Herbert Everitt?" Lois snapped. "How much concern do you need? That old man's got no relatives, except a dodgy bloke who says he's his nephew. *I'm* concerned, and so's my mother. And so is Enid Abraham. Have you contacted Reg Abthorpe yet?"

"Lois," Cowgill said patiently, "I'm not making excuses, but . . ."

"But Herbert Everitt is low on your list of priorities? An old man apparently taken into a nice comfy home by his loving nephew. No real complaints? Just a general feeling that something's not quite as it should be? Right at the bottom of the queue." Lois was scarlet with rage, and turned towards the door.

"Lois," replied Cowgill, smiling desperately at her, "I was going to say that we're almost sure his name is not Reg Abthorpe. We have several leads, and are on his trail."

"In other words, you've got nowhere. Any more thoughts about retiring?" she added, and immediately wished it unsaid.

His smile vanished, and he was every inch the policeman. "All right, that's probably enough for today," he said. "Do you need my help at all?"

"Yes," she said. "I need to know what to do next."

"Just carry on in the way you know best," he said. "I wouldn't dream of giving you any instructions. But I will say this, Lois. Be very careful. It begins to look like something more dangerous than a few locals carrying on a traditional village pastime. We'll be getting round to that. You're right, I've not given it enough thought. For reasons which I don't have to spell out. Leave it with me, and I'll be in touch. Thanks for coming."

Lois walked away through the supermarket, cursing herself for being so unthinking. Poor old sod had not long lost his wife, and she had attacked him mercilessly.

"Hey! Penny for 'em!" She looked up and saw Bill, basket over his arm.

"Oh, hello," she said. "Sorry, I was miles away."

Bill looked at her and wondered exactly how many miles away. "Just doing a spot of shopping for our nice old thing at Hall Cottages. She's very grateful for our help, and finds it difficult to get out."

"Well done," said Lois, making an effort. "But next time, it's in your contract that you use Farnden village shop whenever possible . . ." She managed a smile, to show it was a joke, and they parted.

LATER THAT DAY, FLOSS RECEIVED A CALL ON HER MObile. "Hi, Ben here. Are you better? Doing anything tonight?"

"Yes, I am better. It was a migraine, as usual. And yes, I'm going out with Prince William," she replied.

Ben was indignant. "Why, when *I'm* around? Anyway, ditch him and meet me at the end of the village as usual. Six o'clock? Or you can bring His Princeship with you, if you like. Seems like a decent sort. Bye, beautiful. See you soon."

At ten to six, Floss walked up the village street and met nobody. The only activity was round the pub, and that was in the opposite direction. Even so, she was aware of eyes behind lace curtains watching her as she passed. God, I wish I lived in a big town, she thought. Then I could live my own life without the watchers. She didn't really mind being watched, if it brightened their pathetic lives, but objected strongly to having her every move misinterpreted and relayed by devious routes to her parents.

Ben was waiting for her, and they walked away from the village arm-in-arm.

"Well," said Ben, "where's Himself?"

"I dumped him," said Floss. "Said I had better fish to fry. Satisfied?"

Ben laughed and kissed her. "Sensible girl," he said patronizingly, and she thumped him on the upper arm where it hurt. In this fashion they walked on, and when they came to the lane that led to the woods, Ben steered her into it.

"No, Ben!" she objected. "Not up there. Let's go straight on and across the fields."

"Boring," said Ben. "And anyway, there's something I want to check up there. Come on, Flossie, you've got me to defend you. *Courage, ma petite!*"

"Blimey, I don't know what I see in you," she said, but walked obediently beside him up the hill. It was a dull evening. Rain had been threatening all day, and now a huge bank of black cloud approached over the woods. "I wish I'd brought an anorak," Floss said.

"Any more complaints?" Ben said, and this time he sounded genuinely irritated.

Floss pulled herself together, and said she'd be perfectly all right. There were plenty of trees for shelter, and anyway, she was sure he'd lend her his jacket. In this rather less than harmonious atmosphere, they came to the woods and Ben stopped.

"We're going in. It'll be quite safe. Men were in here this afternoon, so they wouldn't come back so soon. I'd like to see what they were up to."

"What makes you so sure they won't come back?" Floss stepped reluctantly over the stile, and followed Ben closely along the path. "What were you doing up here this afternoon, anyway, when I was slaving away on my hands and knees with a scrubbing brush?" She paused, but Ben did not reply. "Hey!" she continued. "I've had an idea! Would you like me to suggest you join the New Brooms team? Just until you get a proper job? You could be a sort of spare—"

"Sssshhh!" Ben stopped in front of her, and she cannoned into him. As they listened, Floss could hear quite clearly a liquid whistling tune not far away.

"Blackbird," she whispered. "They often sing at twilight. Isn't it great?"

Ben exhaled loudly, and resumed walking. "I was thinking," he said. "Sitting on a log and thinking for a long time. Then I went exploring further into the wood, and found something which I'm going to show you. Very interesting."

"Is it nasty?" she said nervously.

"Not exactly," he replied, and said no more. Best not to mention talking to the mysterious man, he thought.

After ten minutes or so, they came to a clearing and Floss gasped. "What's been going on?" she said, still in a whisper. "Looks like someone's been making a garden." The sandy soil in the cleared patch had been newly dug and smoothed over, as if with a rake. They crunched on a thick layer of leaves to the edge of the patch, and Floss grabbed Ben's arm. "Look!" she said, pointing to a roughly-made flag on a knobbly stick pushed into the fresh earth. The flag was made of white material, a piece of old sheet, with a black skull and crossbones crudely drawn on it. Floss turned to run, but Ben held her back. She was astonished to see that he was chuckling. "For God's sake!" she hissed. "What's funny?"

"It's kids," he spluttered. "Kids playing pirates. Couldn't be further from the sea, but still . . . And I thought it was something sinister going on!"

He turned with Floss and began to walk away. "Sorry, love, to drag you in here to see the remains of kids' games," he said.

"Not kids," said a voice from the shadows. "You're trespassin' 'ere. Bugger off, the pair of ya. We got work to do. Go on, clear off, and don't come back. Else you'll be dealt with . . . An' no blabbin'! We always know when there's bin blabbin'. Now sod off!"

Floss did not need telling twice, turned and ran.

Reluctantly Ben followed her. As he went, he heard raucous laughter. Two men laughing, he was sure.

TWENTY-FIVE

ॐ

Lois and Derek were both asleep in their armchairs, and Gran's eyelids were half-closing. Her knitting slipped to the floor, and then she too was asleep. The television flickered on, but nobody watched. After a while, Derek began to snore.

"What the hell!" All were rudely awakened by a frantic hammering at the front door, and Gran was first out of her chair. Lois rubbed her eyes and stood up, and Derek swore under his breath and hunted for his slippers.

"Mr. Pickering!" Gran said at the door. "What on earth's the matter?"

"Floss," he blurted out. "Floss is the matter. She went out to see her girlfriend, and she's not come home. Her friend hasn't seen her—we phoned—and has no idea where she is. My wife can't stop crying, and I need to see Mrs. Meade. At once, please."

Lois appeared, tactfully thanked Gran, and led Mr. Pickering into her office. She suggested Gran might make some coffee, asked her to explain to Derek, and shut the door. "Right," she said. "Sit down, and begin at the beginning." He had barely begun his story, when there was another knock at the door. This time it was a very irritated Derek who went to open it. His irritation melted away when he saw a white-faced Floss holding tight to young Ben Cullen.

"Good God, come in," he said. "Go in there"—he indicated the sitting room—"and I'll tell Lois you're here."

He had meant to give Lois time to think what to do next, but before he could stop him, Philip Pickering had burst out of the office and was confronting his trembling daughter.

"Just a minute, Mr. Pickering," Lois ordered, wide awake now. "This is my house, and I'll thank you to behave decently. Sit down, and I'll ask the questions. If you don't want that, then you can all go home and leave us in peace. At this time of night!" she added for good measure.

"Now, Floss," she began. "Introduce Ben to your father, please. The rest of us have met him."

Under Lois's furious gaze, Floss stuttered out a brief introduction. "We've . . . well, we've been . . . um . . . friends for quite a while now," she said. "This is Ben. Ben Cullen."

"Hello, sir," Ben said quietly. "I'd like to explain . . ."

"I'll say you'll explain!" Pickering's colour was high, and he stood up again, advancing threateningly towards Ben.

"Sit down, Pickering!" Derek had gone out to the kitchen with Gran, but returned just in time. He took Floss's father by the arm, pulling him back none too gently to the sofa.

Lois continued. "Perhaps we can go on, then?" she said. "Tell us, Floss, what happened. Ben can help you out, but I'm sure your father would like to hear it in your own words. Take your time." Derek raised his eyebrows and looked at his watch, but he said nothing.

"Thanks, Mrs. M," Floss said. "Well, it was like this. We—Ben and me—went for a walk, and as it was a nice evening we decided to go up the hill and see if we could hear a nightingale in the woods. I've always wanted to hear a nightingale . . ."

You'll have to do better than that, thought Lois, but she nodded encouragingly.

"Anyway, when we got up there, all we could hear was

a kind of scream coming from the woods. So I persuaded Ben"—Lois saw her squeeze Ben's hand hard—"that we should go in and see if it was an animal in a trap. Then we could . . . um . . . set it free."

Too pat, much too pat, thought Lois. She waited for Floss to continue. "Then it was awful," Floss said in a very small voice. "We walked towards the screaming, but it soon stopped, and it was getting dark. We wandered about for hours and hours, completely lost, and I was getting frightened. But Ben was very good and cheered me up, and eventually we found ourselves at the edge of the wood, but in a completely strange field, and then it took us even longer to walk round until we found the way back to the right road." She took a deep breath, and looked her father straight in the eye. "So that's why I'm so late, and I'm very, *very* sorry if I've worried you and Mum. She told us to come straight up here to see you. But I'm glad you've met Ben now, and we don't have to keep secrets any more."

Silence. Tears began to run down Floss's cheeks, and Ben put his arm around her. Then Mr. Pickering stood up. "Right," he said, and now he was calm and dignified. "I think it's time we let these good people go to their beds. And us too. I'll see you in the morning, young . . . er . . . Ben. Come along, Floss. We must go and see that your mother is all right now."

When they had gone, Lois sat on in her chair, saying nothing, until Derek took her hand and pulled her up. "Come on, me duck," he said. "Don't you remember when we were young, and your dad was waiting on the doorstep when we got back at five in the morning? It'll blow over, you'll see. Floss'll be back to work tomorrow, right as rain, as if nothing's happened. Wish I was young again," he added nostalgically, and led the way to bed.

But Lois lay awake for a long time, becoming more and more convinced that Floss had been lying. What had really happened up in the woods? Her last thought before finally falling asleep was that her first job tomorrow would be to find out the truth.

*   *   *

Ben Cullen let himself into his quiet house and went straight upstairs to his room. No anxious parents awaited him, and he thanked God his father was nothing like Pickering. Poor Floss. He had been very unwilling to concoct a story instead of telling the truth, but she had been so desperate and terrified, he had had to agree. When that man had given them such a fright, Floss had been hysterical and it had taken him ages to calm her down. Then she wouldn't go home. Her father would find out, she'd said. He was good at knowing when she was hiding something. So he'd taken her to Blackberry Gardens. His parents were out, and he made her coffee and they just sat and worked out a story to tell the Pickerings. Ben had said it didn't sound very convincing, but Floss was insistent. She knew what her father would swallow, she'd said. Then they'd watched some television and lost count of time. When they arrived back at Floss's house, and found her weeping mother, it had suddenly become much more serious. They'd obediently gone up to find her father at the Meades. Floss had been very good. She'd done well, but Ben was quite sure that even if Pickering had swallowed it, Lois Meade certainly hadn't.

He sighed, and got into bed. This was not the end of it, by any means. He had a nasty feeling they had stumbled into something he didn't understand, and he had a strong urge to get on a train in the morning and disappear. But then he thought of Floss, dear little Floss, and he knew he'd stay and deal with it as best he could.

TWENTY-SIX

୬

LOIS KNEW SHE HAD TO GET TO BEN CULLEN BEFORE
Pickering. The lad would get such a pasting from an
angry father that he would clam up completely in the face
of more questioning. But when she had swallowed a
quick breakfast and set off for Blackberry Gardens, she
was dismayed to see Pickering's car outside the Cullen
house. She stood for a moment, undecided what to do
next. No Wallises were around, but the terriers were barking at the gate as usual, warning off any callers. Lois had
no wish to call there, anyway. Then she remembered the
Everitt keys were in her pocket, and decided to go in and
do some cleaning while keeping a sharp eye on
Pickering's car. As soon as it had gone, she would walk
over and enquire politely how Ben was after the night's
adventure. She also had a couple of things to tell Mrs.
Cullen about New Brooms, so had every reason to be
there.

After half an hour or so, she heard a car engine start
up, and went to the window. Yes, he had gone. She locked
up and walked across the road, about to knock at the
door, but Ben had also been looking out of the window,
and saw her coming. He was halfway down the path before she got there. Damn! Lois guessed he would invent
an excuse to get away from her, but she was surprised
when he stopped, greeted her cheerfully, and said if she
was going home, he'd like to walk along with her.

"So how're you feeling this morning?" she said, as
they set off.

"Fine," Ben said. "I was expecting a roasting from old Pickering, but he was nice. Too nice, really. Said I must go up and have supper with them, and we'd all get to know one another. Actually thanked me for looking after Floss in the woods!"

"Mmm," Lois said. "I've heard he overdoes it with Floss's boyfriends and frightens them off. Be a shame if it happened to you. She really cares for you."

"Me and Prince William," answered Ben, "but anyway, it's nice of you to warn me."

"Um, I was wondering," began Lois, as they drew closer to the shop, "whether you told him the true version this morning?"

Ben stopped dead. "What d'you mean?" he said, staring at her. He was thinking quickly. He'd been right that Mrs. M would not swallow the stuff about getting lost in the woods.

"I mean what I said," Lois said gently. "I am certain Floss was not telling the truth last night, and I was sorry for her. She's not an untruthful girl, and it must have been something pretty serious she wanted to conceal. And not just going up to the woods with a boyfriend. Long Farnden girls have been doing that for generations. Fortunately they don't end up with a bun in the oven so often nowadays. No, what really happened, Ben?"

He hesitated. He had promised Floss he would tell nobody, but it would be a huge weight off his mind if he could confide in Mrs. M. "You're sort of right," he said finally, "but I'm sworn to secrecy and couldn't betray poor Floss."

"OK," said Lois, "I can wait. When you or Floss are ready to tell me, you know where I am. Now, I must call in and see Josie," she added and began to walk on.

"Hey! Wait a minute!" It was Ben, pursuing her. "I guess I can give you a clue," he said quickly. "We weren't alone in there," he blurted out, and was gone.

"Hi Mum," Josie said, as Lois walked into the shop. "What's up?"

"Nothing's up," Lois said shortly. "I need some apples. Two pounds, please."

"Fine, don't tell me then." Josie weighed out apples huffily.

"Oh, sorry, love." Lois smiled and began again. "Hi Josie, how are you? How's business?"

Josie laughed. "I'm fine, thanks. Business is not bad. Next rush will be when the kids come out of school. Am I allowed to ask if anything's up?"

Lois nodded. "It's still this business with old Everitt disappearing. It looks like being nastier than at first thought. Have you seen Mr. Cox lately? The farmer from up by the woods? Looks like he's done a bunk, or been persuaded to . . ."

Josie shook her head. "No, not for a week or two," she said. "Mind you, he didn't come in very often. I think somebody did his shopping for him, and it wasn't from me. Supermarket, probably. But Mum," she continued, "surely you don't think there's a gang kidnapping old men? For God's sake, what for?"

"Money?" said Lois. "Herbert Everitt must have had a bit stashed away, with no children and no close relatives. And William Cox was rumoured to have bags of the stuff under the mattress. Both old men living on their own and vulnerable."

"I suppose so, and no relations left. Somebody told me that old lady you visit was his sister-in-law."

"She was, or is," Lois answered, "and she was not at all fond of William. Seems he was not a good husband and the family treated her sister like dirt. Ellen Biggs was very outspoken on the subject!" But then Lois remembered that the last time she called on Ellen, she had been different, unwilling to talk about William or anything to do with him. Why the change? Perhaps another visit would be more productive. An idea struck her. "Do you fancy a ride over to see Ellen tomorrow, Josie? It's my day for the cake. She'd love to see a new face, and you'd have lots of Farnden gossip to tell her."

"In the evening?"

"No, afternoon would be best. I'm sure Gran would hold the fort. She loves it . . . mops up all the local stories."

"Yeah, well. I know she likes doing it, but between you and me her arithmetic's not too good. Nobody's complained, but balancing the books is always a bit tricky after Gran's been in charge."

"Well, up to you. You decide." Lois wondered whether to persuade her, but that had never worked when she was small, so probably wouldn't now.

Then Josie nodded, and said, "I'll come. It'd be nice to get out for a bit. This can be more than a full-time job. Will you pick me up—three o'clock?"

It was so seldom that Lois and her daughter went out together that Lois found herself ridiculously pleased at the idea. She hoped Ellen would be in a better mood, and that somehow the subject would get around to William Cox.

WILLIAM COX'S EARS WERE NOT BURNING. BUT THEN he was unlikely to worry if people *were* talking about him. He was finding it difficult to think at all. His head felt muzzy and he found himself drifting off to sleep almost as soon as he woke up. He had no idea whether it was night or day, and his watch had been removed from his wrist. Food, delicious food, arrived at regular intervals, but he could never get a good enough look at who was bringing it to him. The door was always locked behind the stranger, and when William asked why, he was told it was for his own safety. Sick patients are vulnerable, he was told. But why should he be? He'd done a few foolish things in his time, but not to merit confinement. And who had decided he was sick, and brought him here? It wasn't Reg Abthorpe, though he half-wished it had been. At least he would know who was responsible. He had never trusted Reg, ever since . . . He'd carried on doing a few jobs for him here and there, just to keep him happy. And for others, of course. All those others, who were either clients of Reg, or worked for him because he had something on them and could get their labour cheap.

It was dark in the small room, and only a dim light bulb enabled William to see roughly were he was. The walls were painted clinical white, and he could see his narrow bed and a white-painted table and chair. A more comfortable chair, like those in day rooms in hospital, stood by the wall. The uneven floor was covered with rugs, and high up was a small window with bars. Although it was clean, very little light came in through it. One corner of the room was curtained off, and behind it an old-fashioned bowl and jug were filled each morning with hot water for washing. No razor, of course. He was too vulnerable. His beard had begun to itch. A portable toilet was emptied and cleaned scrupulously every day, and a row of hooks served as a clothes cupboard. He hadn't much in the way of clothes, and his washing was collected and returned neatly laundered every few days. As far as he could remember, no doctor or nurse had visited him.

I should be trying to get out of here, he told himself, but even as the thought went through his mind, his eyelids closed and he slumped on to his bed and began to snore. He dreamed, and the dream developed into a nightmare. He was in the woods, woods he'd known since a child, but he was lost and couldn't find his way out. Men were chasing him, brandishing sticks, and he and his old dog were slowing up. Finally they stopped and were caught. He was forced to watch as they began to beat Rosie until she collapsed on the ground. Then they advanced on him, and he awoke screaming. He was sweating, although the room was chilly. The door opened a crack, and a man's voice said, "Did you call, Mr. Cox?" The door shut again, and everywhere was silent. He was just drifting back to sleep when he heard a distinct tap on the wall next to his ear. He was awake instantly. The tap came again, and this time it was followed by two more taps. William, suddenly awake, succeeded in a wobbly attempt to get up, and was able to pick up a metal mug from the table. He held it carefully and tapped sharply on the wall. Then twice more.

If he could have seen Herbert Everitt's joyful expression, he would have wept with relief. All that time in the village Scout troop, learning tracking and Morse code, wouldn't be wasted after all. So Herbert had been a Boy Sprout too. Maybe they had other things in common, like wondering what the hell all this was about.

TWENTY-SEVEN

꒱

IT WAS A BEAUTIFUL MORNING, HIGH WHITE CLOUDS scudding along in a clear blue sky. Child's picture-book morning, thought Floss, as she sat next to Lois driving to Dallyn Hall. She smiled, thinking she was nearer to childhood than the rest of New Brooms' cleaners. But she loved the work, the variety of it, and the satisfaction of leaving a client's home clean and fresh for them. Most were friendly and grateful, but Dallyn Hall was different. It was more professional. They were hired as a team, and apart from the sniffy manageress, who ridiculously gave herself the title of Director of Hotel Services, there was unlikely to be an opportunity to get to know anyone else. The hotel staff kept themselves to themselves, and Mrs. M was not keen on getting too close to them anyway. "We're here to do a job," she'd explained to Floss, "and we do it and then leave."

Floss's father had begun to drop hints about "proper jobs" again, but the longer she worked for Mrs. M, the less she thought about looking for other careers. And the idea of going anywhere too far away from Ben was too painful to contemplate. Now that he was accepted by the family—which meant by her father—she had relaxed, and their relationship had blossomed.

As they drew into the staff car park, Lois suddenly braked hard, put the van into reverse and backed dangerously out on to the narrow road that led across the park to the Hall. She got quickly out of the car and shielded her eyes from the sun with her hand. "Are you looking for something?" Floss said, coming to stand beside her.

"Did you see that car pull out as we came in?" Lois sounded breathless.

Floss shook her head. "Didn't really notice," she said. "Is it that one, just past the church? Looks like he's stopping." They could just see a figure setting off from the car and disappearing in the direction of the lake. "Taken short, I shouldn't wonder," said Floss, laughing. "Come on, Mrs. M, else we'll be late, and Her Majesty the Director of Hotel Services will give us the boot."

All morning, as they cleaned bathrooms, hoovered carpets, opened windows to let out the smell of cigarette smoke, and binned evidence of whoopee the previous night, Lois thought about the car. She was certain it was Reg Abthorpe's old banger, and wondered how she could find out what he was doing at Dallyn Hall, and why he always seemed to be disappearing every time she glimpsed him. As she gathered up cleaning materials and walked with Floss towards the car park, she felt certain now that he did not live miles away in Suffolk, but not all that far from Long Farnden itself.

"They've really extended this place, haven't they, Mrs. M?" Floss said chattily. "I suppose the conversions over there were stables once."

"And barns," Lois replied, and as she said this she looked more closely across the stable yard which was now the car park. "Some of those store rooms over there would have been for hay and straw, I expect," she said.

"Must have been lovely in the old days," Floss said.

"Lovely for some," Lois replied. "The nobs who lived in the Hall, anyway. Not so good for the servants at the mercy of their masters."

"Well," Floss said, "we could say the same about us and our Director of Hotel Services."

Lois laughed now, and they got into the van. She started up and was away quickly, but by the time they reached the path leading to the lake, there was no sign of the red car. Not surprising, really. Reg was unlikely to hang about all morning. Lois was silent, trying to work out what Reg could possibly have been doing at Dallyn Hall. It was a smart hotel, and the prices were high, relying on corporate hospitality and rich holiday-makers from all over the world. It was in all the lists of most luxurious hotels, and the cars in the guests' car park proved it.

"Never seen so many fancy cars," said Floss. "Where do they all come from?"

"God knows," said Lois, not concentrating. "And anyway, the one I'm interested in is an old banger, colour red. Belongs to the man handling old Mr. Everitt's affairs. This bloke in the red car claims to be his nephew, but it all looks a bit dodgy. Keep your ear to the ground, Floss, and let me know if you hear anything interesting on the subject."

"Thought we weren't meant to gossip?" Floss said. She was still too new to anticipate Lois's wrath.

"Don't you quote rules and regs to me, young lady!" Lois sat ramrod straight, and was silent for a moment. Then she turned and smiled. "OK, point taken," she said, "but what I ask is in the line of duty. New Brooms is cleaning the old man's house, and I like to know exactly what's going on with my clients. If there is something dodgy, the last thing I want is to have the business involved."

"Yeah, well, I'll let you know," Floss said, as Lois dropped her outside her house. Once out on the pavement, she leaned back through the window and said, "Oh, by the way, Mrs. M, any chance of taking Ben on as a cleaner in a temporary capacity? He's still applying for jobs in IT, but needs to earn some money. He's quite keen."

"Ah," said Lois. She wasn't too happy about temporary cleaners. They generally let her down, and departed for good without warning. "I'll think about it, Floss, and maybe get in touch with him. See you later, then." She drove off home, her thoughts momentarily deflected from Reg Abthorpe to the possibility of another male cleaner. She'd had two in the life of the business. First Gary, whom she'd liked, but who had left her under a cloud. Then Bill Stockbridge, still with her, and a tower of strength. But now that he was expecting a baby—or rather, Rebecca was—he might well decide to get a better paid full-time job. Some clients were happier with a male cleaner, and Lois was reluctant to send the girls to one or two of her clients.

"I've decided to give Ben Cullen a try as a temporary cleaner, " she said conversationally to Gran. It was a good idea to mention things to Gran, as she nearly always had something useful to contribute, mostly gleaned from her sessions as shop assistant.

"Goodness gracious!" Gran said. "He's only a boy. And anyway, does he *want* to be a cleaner?" Lois explained, and Gran said nothing for a while. Then she set down a plate of salad in front of Lois and said, "Well, he's a nice, clean, polite boy. And you could do a lot worse. But take my advice, which, of course, you won't, but don't send Ben and Floss together to the same job. Like to Mrs. T-J, for instance. I know you send in two now and then for big occasions. But you'll never know what's going on in them empty bedrooms and long corridors!"

Lois laughed. "For heavens sake, Mum! They'd know better than to waste New Brooms' time snogging, and if they don't know, I'll soon tell them. No, it's really whether I want a temporary chap or not."

"Give him a try," Gran said. "You can always say it's not working. What's more," she added darkly, "he does live opposite where poor Herbert lived, and might be a useful lookout for you and your copper. And don't deny that anything's afoot, because your husband and me know all the signs. Now, it's time for me to catch the bus. I'm going over to Ringford to visit Ivy Beasley. I met her at WI last month, and she invited me for a cup of tea."

"Better wear protective clothing, then," Lois said with a straight face. "She's known to be a right battling Bessie. She'll gobble you up if you upset her."

Gran drew herself up. "I don't intend to upset her," she said. "I'm taking her some shortbread I made yesterday. Now, I must be off."

"Cheers, Mum. Give the old bat my love—no, on second thoughts, give her my respectful greetings. That'll do. Bye."

Lois went into her office and looked at the diary. She was picking up Josie to visit Ellen Biggs, but before that she might give Ben a ring, and make a date to see him. She dialled his number, but got the answer phone, and so left a message asking him to call.

Twenty-Eight

Two stately homes in one day! Floss drove round the back of Farnden Hall and parked in front of the stable block. She went over to greet the black mare who snickered in return, nuzzling in Floss's palm for the usual Polo mint. What a nice friendly old girl, Floss thought. She hadn't ridden for a while, but had enjoyed it when she was still at pony-girl age.

"Ponies out, boys in," she muttered to herself, before turning and making for the back door of the house. It opened before she got there, and Mrs. Tollervey-Jones stood unsmiling on the doorstep.

"It is really not very convenient to have you here this

afternoon," she said. "Still, now you're here, you'd better get on with it. I hope this is not going to be a regular occurrence."

Floss did not say that she did exactly as she was told, and had no idea if mornings, afternoons or evenings were what Mrs. M had in mind. Instead, she said pleasantly, "What a nice old mare you've got there, Mrs. Tollervey-Jones." Why couldn't the woman be Mrs. Jones? It was such a mouthful every time. Still, at least her change of subject had produced a chilly smile.

"Ah, yes, the old queen, we call her. Her name's Victoria, and I've had her for years. Only horse left in the stables now. I'm too old to do much, and Queenie and I move at about the same pace."

"Nonsense!" said Floss daringly. "I've never seen anyone as active as you, Mrs. . . . um . . . Jones."

"Tollervey-Jones," was the sharp reply. "And now we must get on. I have a meeting in Tresham at three, so I have to trust you to let yourself out when you've finished. Make sure you lock up securely. Houseful of treasures here. It really is most inconvenient," she added, and strode away.

Still, a nice girl, that, Mrs. T-J considered, as she fetched her papers and handbag. Superior to the usual run of cleaners. Must find out a bit more about her. *And*, as far as she could tell, the girl was good at the job. I just hope she leaves the place secure, she said to herself as she drove off down the drive.

Meanwhile, Floss was singing softly to herself as she began work. Downstairs first, then up on the first floor. On the top floor, there were servants' bedrooms, dark and tiny under the eaves, but Mrs. T-J had told her not to bother with those every week. Once every couple of months was enough. They were never used now, except by spiders and mice.

Floss moved into the entrance hall. She loved it, with its large black and white tiles like a gigantic chess board, good as new after she'd dealt with them. She admired the long windows, with damask drapes, looking over the park, sparkling in the sun. The ceiling was covered in elaborate plasterwork, and Floss took advantage of being alone in the house to look up at the scrolls and cherubs and roses, until her neck ached. Fancy owning a house like this, she thought. Ah well, if I marry Ben, the best I'll do is a house in Blackberry Gardens, or similar. Still, I'd rather have Ben than any son of Mrs. T-J! Imagine her as my mother-in-law . . . Her gaze was interrupted by the line of trophies, dusty and moth-eaten, all down the side of one wall.

Today, Floss decided to be brave and have a good look at them. She usually gave them a quick glance and moved on. They were too high to reach, even with a cobweb brush. And so far, thank goodness, Mrs. T-J had not suggested a step-ladder. The first was a small, insignificant creature. Floss supposed it was one of those small deer she saw occasionally crossing the park. The next was more impressive, and there were several of these. Stags, still with a tinge of red in their coats, and great branching antlers that looked too heavy for the animals to carry on their heads. Floss imagined them standing proudly on the horizon, outlined against the sky and monarchs of all they surveyed on the moors of Scotland. She shook her head sadly, and looked at the last of the line. It was a different animal, its jaws fixed in a permanent snarl, showing vicious pointed teeth. Faint stripes remained on its bristly coat. A badger, she supposed. It certainly looked like something you wouldn't want to meet in the dark. She had seen a small one on the road this morning, on her way to work. Must have been knocked by a heavy vehicle into the side of the road. Heavy enough to kill it dead, poor thing. Suppose it was a mother and had cubs waiting for her to come home? She moved on to the display cabinet, and saw the elaborate ormolu clock on top. She realized time was passing, and climbed the curving staircase to the next floor.

*   *   *

IN THE HALF-LIGHT OF HIS BEDROOM THE OLD MAN sat up in bed, thinking. This was a strange place, and he couldn't remember how he got here. Not a hotel, that was for sure. And not any kind of nursing home, either. The room was like a cell, and the good food was a bit of a puzzle. And who was the nice young man who brought him his pill and cup of tea early in the morning, and was gone again almost straight away, saying he'd soon be back with breakfast? As Herbert put the pill on his tongue, he raised the tea to his mouth, and then stopped, spitting it out into his hand. What on earth was the pill *for*? He had obediently taken it every morning, and felt much too muzzy to ask questions. But now he considered. No doctor had seen him for a couple of years, and he was always given a clean bill of health. This morning the young man had been later than usual, and Herbert supposed yesterday's pill had more or less worn off. He looked again at the little white tablet in his hand. Well, we'll see which bit of me falls to pieces if I don't take it, he said, and slid it into his trouser pocket.

Time for a message to whoever is in the next room and knows the Morse code, he thought next, and realized his head was clearing. I suppose it's a bit of fun for whoever it is, perhaps just a passing travelling salesman on his way to Tresham and staying in this cheap billet for a couple of nights. Probably hopes I'm female, young and plump with long blonde hair, Herbert thought, and smiled. It was the first smile he could remember since . . . since when? The past was shut off from him. Then he had a sudden flash of memory. His dog! Where was his dog? Were they being kind to him? Was he having his three dog biscuits every afternoon after his walk, each biscuit a different colour?

Maybe I've had a stroke, he thought next. Affected my brain. Perhaps I was in hospital and now they've moved me on to this weird place to convalesce. But *why* am I locked in? And why do I have to pee in a bucket?

He began to tap sharply on the wall, and listened hopefully for a reply.

William Cox was asleep. Very sound asleep, as the result of one of the ubiquitous white pills. He did not hear the tapping, but dreamed on. Nightmares again, and then, half-waking, he realized he was soaking with fear-induced sweat. As he succumbed again to the heavy drowsiness, he muttered, "I'll get that bugger." But nobody heard.

THERE WAS NO MESSAGE FROM BEN WHEN LOIS RE-turned to her office. Well, if he couldn't be bothered to return her call, he was unlikely to be of much use. Perhaps she would call in at Blackberry Gardens when she and Josie got back from seeing old Ellen.

Gran had returned limp and exhausted yesterday from her visit to Miss Ivy Beasley. She had met her match, and admitted it. "She never stopped, Lois! On and on and on, all about her father, who was such an important man, and her mother, who—and this crowned it all—after she died still spoke to Ivy and kept her company. Honest! I'm not making this up. Oh, and by the way, she asked me to make sure Bill was staying with New Brooms, even if he is to be a father."

"So when are you asking her back to tea?" Lois had enquired.

"Never! Not unless you stay to help me out. Honestly . . . well, you know me, Lois, I'm not usually backward in coming forward, but I only spoke about two sentences the whole time. The one good thing was the lemon sponge, and that was made by Doris Ashbourne."

Now Lois was on her way to make conversation with another feisty old lady, except that last time Ellen had been far from feisty. Monosyllabic would be a better word. Josie was waiting on the steps of the shop, and greeted Lois cheerily. "Hi, Mum. It's a real treat to have an afternoon off. Let's go."

"I wish it was something more exciting," Lois apologized.

"Oh no, this'll be fun. I've always liked old ladies. In

spite of Gran . . ." They both laughed, and chatted amiably until they reached Round Ringford and drew up outside The Lodge, a typical little house built in the period of Victorian Gothic decoration, with its carved wooden barge boards, twisted chimney and ecclesiastical windows. Even the window in the door was a pointed arch, with stained-glass lilies obscuring the light.

Lois knocked loudly as usual, knowing that Ellen was more than a little deaf. No reply. Lois knocked again, and peered past the lilies and into the dark hallway. No sign of Ellen, and no sound of movement. "Surely she can't have forgotten," Lois said. "This is my regular day. Has been for ages . . ."

"Perhaps her memory's going. She's probably asleep in her chair somewhere."

They walked round the house, looking in all the windows, but could see no sign of Ellen. "There's dirty dishes on the draining board," Lois said. "That's not like Ellen. If she was being taken out to the shops, she'd never leave the dishes like that."

"Oh, Mum, you're too suspicious. I bet she's gone round to see Ivy or Doris. Forgotten all about you coming. Let's leave it, and go into Tresham. I could do with some new shoes."

Lois followed reluctantly down the garden path, and out into the road. As they were getting in the car, a voice hailed them. "Is that you, Mrs. Meade?" Doris Ashbourne, neat and tidy, was walking swiftly towards them. "I'm afraid Ellen's not there," she said. "She had a couple of funny turns and they've taken her in for a few days."

"In where?" Lois said.

"Tresham General. She was in there once before. It's a bit of a mystery why she collapsed this time. Right as rain when I saw her the night before. I took her down a steak pie I'd baked, and she was her old self. Critical and grateful at the same time! I sometimes think what with Ivy and Ellen, I ain't got time to look after myself, but keeping busy keeps you young, they say, don't they?"

She smiled at Josie. "Shop going well, dear?" she added, and said she'd be seeing Ellen tomorrow and would give her good wishes from Lois.

On their way back to Farnden, Lois said, "Josie, would you mind if we didn't go to Tresham? I do need to talk to young Cullen, and now I've got some time it would be a good opportunity." She looked anxiously at Josie to see if she was disappointed, but was relieved to hear her say that she'd been meaning for a long time to pop over to Waltonby to see an old friend, so not to worry.

"I'll get out here," she said, as Lois turned into Blackberry Gardens, "and walk home."

Ben opened the door, and said, "Hi, come on in. I tried to ring you, but got the answer phone. Would you like a cup of tea?"

Lois refused, as always, and wasted no time in getting down to the subject of Ben as a cleaner. "I must tell you frankly, Ben, I don't see you in the job," she began.

His face fell. "But I can wear a frilly apron with the rest," he said.

"Exactly," said Lois. "That's my point. If you think you're doin' it for a laugh, that's no good to me. I know Floss is very fond of you, but my team think of cleaning as a profession. It's skilled and reasonably well paid. With your degree an' that, you'll be looking for something different. I'm not saying better, but different. So I'll be going now, and wish you luck in the job hunt."

"Hey, hang on, Mrs. Meade, can't we talk about it a bit? It was a silly joke about the frilly apron. I really would like to be a New Brooms cleaner." Liar, he said to himself. But he'd promised Floss he would take it seriously and the money would certainly be handy just now. "I know your Bill Stockbridge," he said, "and everybody respects him, thinks he's a good bloke. No, it'd be really great, Floss says. Every day different, meeting new people, and taking pride in the work."

"Yes, well, that's Floss speaking, not you." Lois thought for a moment, and then said, "I tell you what I'll do, Ben. You can have a couple of weeks' trial, and if it turns out well, I'll think some more. Come along to the meeting on Monday, twelve sharp at my house, and you can meet the rest. Now I must go. Oh, and don't forget, if you want to tell me more about that night in the woods, I'm a good listener."

After she'd gone, Ben looked at himself in the hall mirror. "Hi there, skivvy," he said. "Here's the scrubbing brush. Now get on with it."

LOIS MADE HERSELF A QUICK CUP OF TEA AND LOOKED out of the window. It was still a lovely day, and she was aware of Jeems's pleading face looking up at her. "You win," Lois said, locked the house and set off with a delighted dog trotting by her side.

"Which way shall we go?" Walks were easier now. The training classes in Tresham were paying off. And just as well, thought Lois, considering how much they cost her! Down by the edge of the woods and out to the footpath beyond would be best, she decided. Jeems could have a run and chase rabbits. Derek had said the For Sale notice was still up at Cox's Farm, so she could check that. It wouldn't be a very quick sale, she reckoned. So much work to do there.

The woods were quiet, except for the usual sounds of creatures and birds. No distant voices, no howls of pain or gunshot reverberating through the trees. No clues as to who had kept Ben and Floss company that night. Lois was away from the familiar section of the woodland path, but it was still quite clearly visible through the trees, and she walked on, disappointed and at the same time relieved that nothing sinister seemed to be happening. The farmhouse, too, was silent and empty. Doors all locked, and outbuildings exactly the same as when she had last seen them.

Now she was into the field, and a cool breeze lifted her hair. In her pocket she found an elastic band to anchor it into a ponytail. Getting a bit old for a ponytail! Lois walked smartly, with Jeems trotting behind her, departing from the path every now and then to chase a rabbit. So far, she had never caught one, and Lois hoped it stayed that way. They were soon on the road that led back into the village, and passed by the entrance to Blackberry Gardens. On an impulse she decided to go in and see if Jeems would like a barking confrontation with the Wallis killer terriers behind the gate. If Frances Wallis came out, she could easily say she was going to check the Everitt house. It was a silly idea, she knew, but Derek always made the detour with an old retriever he walked for a neighbour. Trained it to be a good guard dog, he said.

She would pass the Cullens again, but knew nobody was at home. Ben had been going out as soon as she left, to see a mate in Tresham for the rest of the day, and his parents would not yet be back from work. As she approached their wrought iron gates, standard for the estate, she stopped dead. Something was hanging there. A brace of . . . a brace of what? Lois moved closer, and Jeems began to bark fiercely. Oh my God! It was not a brace of pheasant, but two large black crows, heads askew, anchored by their necks with a length of orange binder-twine, and bleeding dark red drops on to the pale gravelled drive. An ancient warning.

TWENTY-NINE

꒰

A S SOON AS SHE GOT HOME, LOIS WENT INTO HER office to make a call to Cowgill. Surely he would think there was enough evidence now to take some action? The pattern was quite clear. Anyone wandering in certain parts of the woods got a warning. Floss had had the hanging cat, Ben the crows, and William Cox the mutilated badger. She had been given the "stop at nothing" warning. Now both Cox and Herbert Everitt—Herbert had been known to walk in the woods with his dog—had disappeared. What had they in store for her? But then, she had only visited William Cox in a professional capacity, and her walks in the woods had been confined to daytime. She had never actually seen anything sinister herself. Then she remembered Rosie, and her broken legs. But that had been aimed at Cox, not at herself. They— whoever "they" were—could not have anticipated that she would find the animal. But they might know she had tried to rescue her.

Cox was the real mystery. It was hard to believe that he did not sanction the badger-baiting in the woods. He'd been a farmer with beasts, after all. If he'd been against it, he could easily have shopped them to the police. Badger-baiters were caught every day and hauled before the courts. In fact, the fines were not large enough to prevent them setting up somewhere else, Lois considered. But if he had been a part of it all, even if reluctantly, why would they threaten him with the dead badger? And why had it been necessary to remove him? Lois was convinced he had been removed in the same way as Herbert Everitt, although she had no proof. And the removal must have been permanent, or how else would the house be on the market?

Two things to do, then. One, visit old Ellen and try to get her to talk some more. She would have to tread gently. The last thing she wanted was to worry or frighten the old thing. And two, call in at the estate agent handling Cox's Farm. Easy enough to pretend she was interested in buying.

She sat down at her desk, and saw that she had a telephone message. Checking it, she heard Cowgill's voice. "Call me as soon as you are home." That was all. No name, no please or thank you. So, Cowgill in policeman mode. She dialled his number and waited.

"Ah, there you are, Lois." His voice was brisk, efficient. "We need to talk. Usual place, tomorrow morning, ten thirty. Can you make it?"

"As it happens," Lois said, "no, I can't. Afternoon is OK. Two o'clock?" Thinking quickly, she decided to visit Ellen in hospital after her meeting with Cowgill. If she missed lunch, she could also call in at the estate agents before having to lie about her weak bladder at the supermarket.

"Very well," said Cowgill. "There's been a development that I'd like to discuss with you. Don't be late. I am extremely busy."

"Sod you! You're paid for snooping! And have I ever been late, huh? In case you've forgotten," Lois added, "I have a business to run!"

Hunter Cowgill, at the other end of the line, heard the click and smiled. He loved her when she was angry . . .

LATER THAT EVENING, THEY WERE ALL SITTING watching television, and Gran said suddenly, "Hey, Lois, I forgot to tell you. When I was in the shop this afternoon, that little wimbly-wambly woman from Blackberry Gardens came in. She looks frightened of her own shadow. Anyway, you know I like to put people at ease with a bit of a chat—" Lois and Derek exchanged a smile—"but try as I might, she just answered yes or no, and we got nowhere. *Until . . .*" Gran paused dramatically and looked at each in turn. They waited patiently. No good trying to hurry Gran. "Until . . ." she repeated, "I mentioned about living in Tresham before we came here."

"So what did she say?" Lois prompted.

Derek surreptitiously lowered the volume, and Gran continued, "Seems she's lived in Tresham herself. And knew the Churchill Estate well. Lived in those semis over on the other side. She's been in lots of places before coming here, apparently. They move around quite a bit. She seemed sad about that. Said she liked the Churchill. Plenty of people to talk to. Kids playing on the streets.

Always something happening. Then she started on Blackberry Gardens. Hates living there. Real snotty people, she said. All out at work all day, and then they spend weekends cutting the grass and cleanin' their cars."

"Did she mention her husband?" Lois held her breath, willing Gran to remember more.

"No, but I did." Gran laughed at herself, and continued, "You know me, Lois. I asked her where he worked. Said I'd seen the lorry parked outside, and supposed he was a driver. But I failed you there, duckie. She clammed up like an oyster, took her shopping and practically ran out of the shop. Still, there you are. Can't win 'em all."

"Did she say anything about those bloody terriers?" Derek said. "One of 'em took a bite out of a mate of mine who tried to go round the back to find somebody at home. Should be taken to court, them Wallises."

Gran frowned. "She did say something, but I'm blowed if I can remember what it was. I think it was to do with them not being really hers. Yep, that was it. Said she'd never choose to have terriers. They were no company, she said, and she'd always wanted a chocolate-brown Labrador. A nice big companion who wouldn't make such a lot of noise."

"She's got that already," said Lois glumly. "But then maybe not. Her foul husband is certainly big, though not so nice nor much of a companion. And I've heard him make a lot of noise, the bum."

"Lois! Language! But yes, she did say she was lonely a lot of the time, and I offered to have her up for a cup of tea some time. But she was quick to refuse. A very funny woman all round."

"Well, at least she had a nice chat with you," Lois said, wondering if any of it was particularly useful.

Then Gran said, "Oh, and when we were talking about neighbours, she said the only nice one was poor Herbert Everitt. Always talked to her when he was going walking with his dog. Then she went bright red, and changed the subject to the weather. Do you think she fancied him?

Now, that really is all, Lois. I'm off to bed. See you in the morning."

After she'd gone, there was silence for a minute or two. "Worth waiting for?" Derek said.

"Could be," Lois said, and reached for the television remote control. "I can't hear what they're saying. Where's the plot got to?"

"He's just strangled her," Derek said, and closed his eyes.

THIRTY

ᴢ

THE ESTATE AGENCY WAS NOT THE SMARTEST IN town. In a narrow lane off the High Street in Tresham, Lois found the dark, dusty office, which had once been a butcher's shop. She fancied she could detect an unpleasant, lingering smell of raw meat. A middle-aged woman, hunched up in a severe cream-coloured blouse that had seen better days, looked up. "Yes?" she said.

Ah well, Lois thought, makes a change from the dizzy blonde who smothers you with charm.

"I'd like to have some details of Cox's Farmhouse at Long Farnden," she said. No good trying to approach the subject by side alleys, not with this one. "Do you know the house I mean?"

"Of course I do, Mrs. er . . . ?" The woman got up and opened a drawer in the filing cabinet behind her chair.

"Meade," Lois said. "Lois Meade. I live in Farnden." The woman pulled a sheaf of papers from the file, and handed one to Lois.

"That's it," she muttered. Then, as if remembering instructions, she added, "If you're really interested and would like to look round, one of our agents would be pleased to show you. You'll have to make an appointment, as we're really busy."

Lois looked round. It didn't look exactly jumping. A pile of unopened post lay on a side table, and through a glass door she could see the outline of a man sitting with his feet up on a desk, reading a newspaper.

"Thanks," she said. "Can you tell me who's selling?"

"If you live in Farnden, you'll surely know," said the woman, "and anyway, I'm not allowed to release personal information."

Rat bag, thought Lois, but said, "I'll have a look at these particulars, and give you a ring. Bye."

The woman did not answer, nor did she watch her go out of the door and away down the street. She was too busy picking up the phone and dialling a number. "She's been in," she said cryptically, and put down the receiver.

THE SUPERMARKET WAS CROWDED. SCHOOL HOLIDAYS, and half the population of Tresham seemed to be doing their shopping. Tesco had sensibly set up a section of children's games and toys, and Lois fought her way past, heading for the bread counter. She had seriously thought about ducking out of this meeting with Cowgill. He had been so abrupt and cold, giving Lois the strong impression that he thought he could now take her help for granted. Well, he couldn't. She had never accepted any money for information, nor would in the future. If there was to be a future. She could easily carry on at her own pace, gathering evidence until she had something really concrete, and then go to the police station. There must be other detectives there who would listen politely and appreciate her efforts.

She stood at the counter, waiting in a small queue. A picture of Cowgill flashed into her mind, a grieving and defeated man, head down and nothing like the Cowgill of old. But that was a while ago, she told herself. No need to nurse him along for ever. Anyway, he sounded completely restored on the telephone.

"Yes, dear?" the assistant said.

"Large wholemeal and three doughnuts, please," Lois replied. She walked away with her bag full, but hesitated at the checkout. Cowgill was a policeman, an important policeman in Tresham. He was a professional, good at his job, so people said. What did she expect? She knew he fancied her, always had, but the law was a desperately serious business. It was not a game, and nor was her part in it. She turned back, and headed once more for the bread counter. Using her usual excuse, she walked through to the back.

"Morning, Lois," Cowgill said, indicating a chair. "Thanks for coming."

"No problem," said Lois. "I had to come into town anyway. I know you're busy, so you can come straight to the point."

A small placatory smile crossed his face. "I would really appreciate your thoughts on this. We have had a report that several people in Farnden have had frightening threats in the form of dead animals strung up on their premises. Mrs. Cullen, one of your clients, I believe, rang us in a lather this morning. Seems two freshly-shot crows were attached to her gate yesterday, and she knows exactly what that means."

"A warning," said Lois flatly. "I saw them myself."

Cowgill raised his eyebrows. "So why didn't you ring me?" he said.

"Because I knew what you would say," Lois replied. "That you were too occupied with really serious crime to waste time on a practical joke." Silence. "Is there more?" Lois said sharply.

"Yes." His voice was weary now. "I'm sorry, Lois. Maybe you're right. But this is not the first of these incidents in Farnden, is it? And now we need to look more closely. If it's a bunch of hooligans amusing themselves, they need to be stopped."

"It is just possible," Lois said in an icy voice, "that these warnings are connected with something much more serious. Like the disappearance of two well-off old men, and the true identity of Mr. Houdini in his old red banger. Did you know Cox's Farm is up for sale?"

"Yes, of course. We are keeping an eye on it, and I have not forgotten Reg Abthorpe, as he calls himself. Now, my dear," he added, being careful to keep an avuncular tone, "if you could focus on the dead animal warnings, perhaps ask Derek if he hears anything in the pub, I'd be most grateful."

Lois stood up. "And if you could kindly keep me informed with what dribs and drabs of useless information come your way, I shall carry on doing exactly what I think. I know by now when to call you. But then, I realize I am a very small frog in a whopping great puddle. But I can swim and jump. I'm off now in the hope of catching a few flies, so cheerio."

To her surprise, he roared with laughter, stood up and, before she could take evasive action, gave her a big hug. "Very good, Lois!" he spluttered. "What should I do without you?"

"Bugger all, I reckon," Lois said, extricating herself rapidly. "I'll be in touch," she added, and left.

It was a long walk to the General Hospital on the edge of town, but the car park was permanently full, and even if there was a space, it cost a fortune to leave a car there. It had always annoyed Lois that sick people, or their families visiting, had to pay for their misfortune. As she turned finally into the road leading to the hospital and all its treatment centres and consultants' chambers, research labs and mobile X-ray vans, she reflected on how lucky her family had been. Derek had only been in this hospital once, and that was when he'd been in a car accident of the deliberate hit-and-run variety. Gran was as tough as old boots, and the children, apart from the usual sniffs and sneezes picked up from school, had been remarkably healthy.

The receptionist here was pleasant and helpful. "Follow the yellow line on the floor, dear," she said, "and you'll come to Mrs. Biggs's ward. I'm sure she'll be delighted to see you." It was a formula, of course, spoken to all visitors, but Lois felt reassured. She bought a bunch of white marguerites from the flower stall, and walked along, following the yellow line, until she found the ward. She saw Ellen at once. The old lady was sitting up straight in an armchair, neatly dressed and with her hair cut and arranged in an attractive style.

"Hello, Lois!" she shouted, as she caught sight of her visitor. "You've come just the right day. Just had me 'air done. What d'yer think?" She turned her head from side to side, and Lois said all the right things. "Them for me?" Ellen said. "Did you get them from your garden?"

Lois thought of lying, but decided to own up. "At the flower stall," she admitted, "in reception."

Ellen cackled. "Thanks anyway," she said, and handed them to a hovering nurse. "Put these in water, there's a good girl," she ordered. She turned and said confidentially to Lois, "They look after you well in here. Better than a hotel."

Lois sat down in a chair beside Ellen, and was delighted to see her so strong and chirpy. It was not going to be so difficult after all.

Lois and Ellen exchanged inconsequential conversation until a nurse politely enquired if Lois would like a coffee, directing her to a machine out in the corridor. "What d' you think, Ellen?" Lois said. "Would you like me to stay, or are you too tired to talk?"

Ellen cackled loudly, causing heads to turn. "Good God no, dear!" she said. "You're a long time dead . . . Plenty of time to rest then." And she directed the nurse to fetch her friend a cup of coffee at once. "Black or white, Lois?" she said. The nurse winked at Lois and obeyed orders.

"Now then, Lois, let's get to what you really want to know," said Ellen, settling herself more comfortably in her chair. "It's about them Coxes, ain't it? Go on, then, ask me some questions."

THIRTY-ONE

~

I<small>T WAS JUST BAD LUCK, THOUGHT</small> L<small>OIS, DRIVING</small> home from the hospital. Bad luck that a nurse had appeared at just the wrong time and said she must take Ellen off to have an X-ray. Apparently her ankle was very swollen, and they wanted to have a good look at it. She was very sorry, but perhaps Mrs. Meade would be able to come back tomorrow? No, she wasn't sure how long the X-ray would take, as there was always a queue.

Of course I can go back tomorrow, Lois tried to reassure herself. It's a busy day, but I can make time. Not likely, though, that Ellen would be in such a loquacious mood, nor so openly willing to talk about her brother-in-law. Damn, damn, damn! Lois banged her hands on the steering wheel in frustration, forgetting that this would produce a raucous beep. The driver of a white van in front stuck out his hand and raised two fingers, and she could see in the wing mirror his face contorted with rage. Lois calmed down. She turned down a side road to take a different route back to the village, and avoid the van driver.

This way, she passed through Round Ringford, and decided on the spur of the moment to call on Ivy Beasley. If she was in a good mood, perhaps she would have some memories of Ellen's sister, Martha, and her unfortunate marriage. Just at this moment, Lois had a strong feeling that if she could sort out the mystery of William Cox she would have a good chance of unravelling the tangled mess. Not for the first time, she reflected that it must be more than badgers.

For once, the main street of Ringford was busy. A small gathering of people stood at the bus stop. A Jack Russell terrier wandered down the middle of the road, seemingly belonging to nobody. The vicar pinned a piece of paper to the notice board by the shop, and a woman sat on the top step, blinking at the sun and chatting to an old lady. Lois pulled up outside Miss Beasley's house, and switched off the engine. Then the old lady turned around, and Lois saw it was Ivy herself. That was that, then. Nothing would persuade Ivy Beasley back into her house if she had decided to take the air. Lois noticed that she did not have a stick with her, and as she took a couple of steps towards Lois, she was walking well. Caught you, Ivy B! Ah, well, not my day, thought Lois, and turned on the engine once more.

"Wait!" It was an imperious voice, and Miss Beasley raised a hand to emphasize the command. Now she was hobbling, and as she approached Lois's car, grimaced with pain. "What's the hurry, Mrs. Meade?" she said, breathing heavily. "Have you come to see me?" Lois nodded. "In that case, you can help me up the steps and make me a cup of tea. I think I've over reached myself." Lois obeyed, and as she glanced back to look at the shop-keeper, saw that she was smiling broadly.

Settled in her chair with a cup of tea, Miss Beasley said sharply, "Right, what have you come to see me about? Bill's not leaving, is he? If so, I shall blame you for not making enough effort to keep him."

Lois gritted her teeth and took a deep breath. "No, no," she said. "It's not about Bill. I was just passing. I've been to see Ellen, and she was much more like her old self. She sent her love," she added, though this was not strictly true.

"Huh! Love's not much use to me now! What I need is plenty of help. Still, I'm glad to hear the foolish old woman is getting better. Stubborn and stupid, I always tell her, and it doesn't do, Mrs. Meade. It doesn't do at all."

"You've been friends for a long time, haven't you?" Lois said.

"Longer than I like to remember," said Ivy, draining her cup. "Any more in the pot?"

Lois refilled her cup, and said, "I expect you remember her sister. Martha, was it?"

"Of course I remember Martha. Different as chalk and cheese, those two. Ellen was always the leader, and Martha trailed behind. But she was the pretty one, and William Cox fell for her, not Ellen . . . who, I might tell you, was keen on him herself! But looks count when you're young." Ivy was silent, remembering her own lack of attraction for the opposite sex. "I fancy a biscuit. Over there, in the cupboard. Green tin with cats on it. Bring it here." Lois once more did as she was bid, and handed the tin to Ivy, who opened it and peered in. "Mm," she said. "Now I remember what I went to the shop for. Only three left."

"I won't have one," said Lois. "Haven't offered you one," snapped Ivy. "But you might go next door and buy a packet for me on your way out. Was there anything else, besides bringing me daft messages from Ellen Biggs?"

"I was interested to hear what you say about the Biggs sisters. Must have been quite a do when Martha and William got married? Was it here in Ringford?"

"Yes, though how that William Cox had the nerve to enter a church, I do not know. Considering . . ."

"Considering what?"

"Why do you want to know?" Ivy frowned, looking suspiciously at Lois. "Is this something to do with him gone into a home, and the farm being up for sale? Are you working with social services?"

Lois shook her head, and decided to jump in at the deep end. "Just nosey, that's all." She smiled. "It sounds like a sad tale, with the Cox family disapproving of Martha, and him not being a very good husband."

"Good! He was downright bad! Always was bad. Spoilt by his family, and no sense of responsibility. Roving eye, too! He had all the willin' ones, and some of those that weren't willing, so I heard. There was scandal up at the Hall, when Joyce the garden girl produced a baby in amongst the runner beans, and swore it was William Cox who forced her into it. Looked just like Cox, some said, poor little soul."

"What a louse," said Lois feelingly. "What on earth made Martha marry him? Was she pregnant too?"

"Dunno," Ivy said. "Ellen won't talk about it much. But she was very upset when her sister started lying about bruises. Said she'd banged into a door, tripped over the dog, missed her footing on the stairs. All that kind of nonsense."

In the silence that followed, Lois wondered if she dare ask one more question. Well, why not? She was a match for Ivy Beasley, wasn't she? She opened her mouth to speak, but Ivy got in first.

"Time you were going. I'm tired, and I need a sleep before Doris Ashbourne comes down here with her latest gossip. Good day, Mrs. Meade. Remember what I said about Bill," she added. She leaned her head against a cushion and closed her eyes. Lois took the hint, and as she prepared to lock the front door behind her, heard Ivy shout, "Don't bother to lock the door. Doris will be down in a minute."

Lois walked down the garden path, and at the gate met Doris. "Hello, Mrs. Meade," she said pleasantly. "Been to see Ivy? How is she today?"

"Fine, I would say. But still Miss Beasley!" Lois held open the gate, and Doris walked past her. "By the way," added Lois, "do you remember Martha Biggs, Ellen's sister?"

"The one that married a Cox?" Doris's smile faded. "Couldn't forget her, could we. Poor woman. Still, money talks, and no more was said after she died. I can't look at that William Cox without a shiver. Oh, I can hear Ivy shouting," she added, and smiled again. "Mustn't keep the boss waiting! Bye, Mrs. Meade. Nice to see you."

Lois drove off with mounting excitement. What had

Doris meant by "money talks" and "no more was said'? Had old Cox had a hand in her death? And yet, she reminded herself, that time he had given her a cup of tea he had seemed nice enough. She had warmed to him. But then, even old devils know how to turn on the charm.

It was not until she was halfway home that she remembered Ivy's biscuits. Trouble! But she had been too taken up with the strange news that Ellen had been keen on old Cox too.

A CONVERSATION IN DOTS AND DASHES—OR, MORE exactly, in short knocks and long scrapes—is a laborious business, and William Cox was tired. He was always tired, and had trouble keeping awake long enough to reply to the message. He knew now that it was old Herbert Everitt from Blackberry Gardens next door. He had tried to concentrate on why both of them should be in this place . . . this place . . . where were they? He listened hard to the knocks coming through the wall and heard: "S . . . T . . . O . . P. T. . . . A . . K . . . I . . N . . . G. T . . . H . . E . . P . I . . L . . L."

What pill? Cox shook his head in a vain attempt to clear it. The pill . . . ? Ah! The pill that came with his morning cup of tea! But hadn't someone said it was necessary? The doctor had prescribed it. He could not clearly remember. Was it when he'd woken up from a long sleep and discovered himself in this . . . hotel? Hospital? His lids were heavy, and he struggled to stay awake to sort things out. His last thought before succumbing to sleep was that he must stop taking the pill.

THIRTY-TWO

‿

WHEN LOIS RETURNED TO THE HOSPITAL NEXT day, she was greeted at the ward door by the ward Sister. "Ah, Mrs. Meade, have you come to see Ellen?" Lois nodded, trying to look past the bulky figure to catch sight of Ellen. "Well, perhaps you could come with me to my office for just a minute or two? Thank you."

Lois followed obediently. "Please sit down," said Sister, pointing to a chair. "Now, I know you popped in to see her yesterday . . ."

"Yes, and I found her very well, and quite her old self," Lois said. "Has something happened?"

"Well, yes. During the night, the nurse checked on Ellen and saw that something was wrong. It seems she had a slight stroke. Nothing that she won't recover from, but she is an old lady and it will take a while. For the moment, we are keeping her calm and quiet, and so if you could perhaps come back in a few days' time, I am sure you will be able to have a few minutes with her." Lois nodded acceptance, and Sister resumed, "After you had gone yesterday, the nurse reported that Ellen was very excited and a little disturbed. Perhaps something was said that agitated her?" Lois said nothing. "Well, she's in good hands, and will, I am sure, be very pleased to see you again soon. Now, I have to leave you, but you know the way out? Good morning, Mrs. Meade."

Dismissed, thought Lois. She had felt sick with guilt when the Sister implied she had contributed to Ellen's stroke. But Ellen had seemed so well and cheerful! It was as if she was about to unload something which had been on her mind for a long time, and Lois had been delighted that Ellen had come to the decision herself, without any prompting, or being led to the subject of William Cox. Maybe their conversation had nothing to do with the stroke. After all, Ellen was a good old age. Oh, please God, Lois said to herself, don't let her lose her marbles. Lois acknowledged that it was a rotten thought, and self-ish and despicable, but she still had hopes of getting vital information from Ellen Biggs.

LOIS WAS BACK IN FARNDEN JUST IN TIME FOR THE weekly meeting of New Brooms. She felt frustrated and irritable. When she walked into her office and found all but Ben Cullen there already, she felt even more irritable. No time, now, for useful chat and pleasant togetherness. "Morning all," she said shortly, and there were answering murmurs. "All here already, I see. I hope you haven't skimped on this morning's clients." She could have bitten her tongue out, looking at the shocked faces in front of her.

Bill was the first to speak. "Oh, well, Mrs. M," he said in a steely voice, "we've all had a few drinks in the pub before coming on here. Excuse us if we're not too quick on the uptake."

There was a silence, and the ghost of a smile crossed Enid Abraham's face. Lois stared at Bill, and then slumped at her desk. "Oh Bill," she said, "and every-one . . . please take no notice of me. I've had a bad morn-ing so far, but that don't excuse it. Please forget I said that bloody awful thing."

There was an audible release of breath, and everybody spoke at once. Was there anything they could do to help? They'd thought she looked a bit pale when she came in. And everybody slipped up some time. She was not to think any more about it. And, from Bill, "As long as it doesn't happen again." Lois felt duly reproved.

At this point, a knock at the door was answered by

Gran, and she ushered Ben Cullen into the office. Lois introduced him to the team, and they smiled a welcome.

"He's on approval," Lois said. "Two weeks, to see how he gets on. Then either way, if it isn't working, he's free to leave or I'm free to let him go."

"I love that phrase," Bill said. " 'Let him go.' Puts all the blame on him, one way or another."

"I don't think so, Bill," said Lois, wondering what on earth was wrong with him this morning. She hoped it was nothing to do with Rebecca and the baby.

Ben beamed. "I know exactly what you mean, Mrs. M," he said, at once adopting the name the others gave her. "You can be sure I'll put my all into it. I'm really keen."

Floss choked to cover disbelief, but the others assured him he'd be fully hooked on the job after two weeks, and they all got down to the business of the meeting.

"You can go with Enid at first," she said to Ben. "You will learn a lot from her, so please take notice. You're at the vet's house this afternoon, aren't you, Enid? Right, then liaise together after the meeting." There were no other changes in the schedules, and Lois said, "Now, anything to report? Any complaints, or things you'd like us to talk about?" She looked around the team, and hoped the ensuing silence meant there was nothing.

But then Sheila spoke up. "There was one thing, Mrs. M. It's about that Mr. Everitt that you do the cleaning for."

"Go on," Lois said, keeping an even voice.

"Well, my Sam used to do a bit of woodin' for old Cox, and now the farm's for sale. I haven't heard where he's gone—probably into The Pines. That's where most of the old ones go when they need care. But anyway," she said, "about Mr. Everitt. Sam was in the pub and overheard a couple of blokes—strangers, he said—talking. They were speaking softly but my Sam's got very good hearing, you know. He's trained it up for when he's listening for foxes and badgers near the pheasant pens. He can hear everything and tell you what's goin' on in the woods!"

Can he, though? thought Lois, and willed Sheila to get to the point. She waited patiently, knowing Sheila was easily offended.

"Sam picked up the name Everitt, and listened carefully," Sheila continued. "They were saying they wished they could know a bit more about him. Specially his financial resources, they said. And they laughed. That was all, but I thought you'd like to know."

"Did Sam say what they looked like, these men?" Lois spoke sharply, and all turned to look at her. For them, this was no revelation, was it? Lots of people would like to know what had happened to Herbert Everitt.

"Yeah, he did. Now, let me see. One of 'em was tall and thin, with one of them nutcracker faces. And the other was bald and fat, Sam said. He's very observant, is my Sam," she added proudly.

"Thanks, Sheila. Sam certainly has a sharp eye and ear. No wonder his boss is so keen to keep him! I've heard he's trying to persuade Sam not to retire?"

"Quite right," said Sheila. "And I don't want him under my feet all day, so I'm backing his boss!"

They all laughed, and conversation became general. There were no more business matters, and the meeting closed. Lois went back to the kitchen and found Gran in deep conversation on the telephone. The smell of frying sausages was powerful, and Lois realized she'd had no coffee and nothing since an early breakfast.

"Who was that?" she said, as Gran came to the table.

"Mrs. Tollervey-Jones, ringing from Scotland. Seems she forgot to mention she'd be there on her annual holiday. Bit like the queen! Anyway, she wants Floss to go in as usual, but keep the work down to an hour, mean old bag. She'll be away for four or five weeks, unless something comes up and she's needed back here."

Lois nodded slowly. "How does she expect Floss to clean a dusty old mansion in an hour? Well, I suppose we'll think of something. Thanks, Mum. Now, I'm starving!"

AFTER LUNCH, SITTING ALONE IN THE KITCHEN AND mulling over the meeting, Lois thought again about Bill and his out-of-character behaviour this morning. Perhaps she would give him a ring, and have a chat. Maybe something he said would give her a clue. She got up and went into her office.

"Bill? How's it going?"

"Fine. I'm upstairs at Ivy's and she's out in the garden. Better make it snappy."

"Right. I just wanted to check that all was OK with you."

"Everything's fine, thank you. Oops, have to go now. She's on the move. Bye."

Lois put down the telephone and sat for a few minutes doing nothing except turning over in her mind what could have bothered Bill. She wasn't convinced that everything was fine. Not just her own gaffe, surely? He was always so sympathetic. Most likely something private, in which case it was no business of hers. She looked at her watch. Time to take Jeems for a walk and clear her head.

THIRTY-THREE

BLACKBERRY GARDENS HAD BEEN BUILT OVER AN EXisting footpath, and this had caused a great deal of controversy at the time. Petitions from the local ramblers were handed in to a hearing in Tresham Town Hall, objecting to the diversion, but in vain. The inspector hearing the case expressed his sympathy with local people, but said he could see there was a sensible alternative route for the footpath, and this would be easy to establish. It was only a matter of five hundred yards, and would be a reasonable solution. As this new route would pass close behind the proposed new houses, the developers then opposed the solution. Like a tedious game of tennis, the arguments went back and forth until at last the alternative route was approved by all.

Lois remembered all this, as she swung through the gate into the new footpath and began to walk along by the high fence concealing the back gardens of the Blackberry houses. Jeems stopped suddenly with an anxious look on her face and squatted down. Lois fumbled for the scoopbag she had in her pocket and waited. She looked at the fence and saw a knot hole at eye height. Peering through, she saw that it was the Wallis's garden and the terriers were stretched out in the sun on scrubby grass. Jeems finished the job and scratched a symbolic cover-up with her hind legs, giving a little yelp of success.

Pandemonium! The terriers were at the fence in an instant, barking ferociously, and now Jeems, safe from attack, stood her ground and joined in with enthusiasm. Lois kept her eye on the knot hole and watched the house. Jeems was pulling at the lead, ready to continue the walk, but Lois held her back. The terriers were still going strong. Surely someone would come and shut them up? But nobody appeared, and Lois was about to move on when she saw a figure appear at the downstairs window. It was a man, and he was familiar. Not big enough for Frances's husband. He moved away, and as he went Lois saw that it was Reg Abthorpe.

She turned, and dragged Jeems back the way they'd come. "Just a short call to make," she said to the little dog. "Then we'll go on with the walk."

No sign of life as she approached the Wallis's house, but that was nothing unusual. Lois knocked firmly at the door, and fancied she saw a curtain twitch. To her surprise, the door was opened straight away, and Frances stood there, smiling faintly.

"Hope you don't mind, Mrs. Wallis," Lois said casually. "I was on the footpath and thought I saw Mr. Abthorpe." She judged it best not to mention the knot hole. "If he's with you," she continued, "I wonder if I could have a word? It's just a small point about Mr. Everitt's house, and I still haven't got a phone number." Without it being too obvious, she stood to one side of the doormat, endeavouring to see behind Frances and into the house. But it was dark inside. Net curtains everywhere.

"Oh no, you must have been mistaken," Frances said, in an unusually firm voice. "I haven't seen that man since you were here and he burst in on us. Sorry, can't help," she added, and began to shut the door. Lois tried desperately to think of something to hold Frances in conversation. But Jeems suddenly began to bark again, this time in real fear. The terriers were at the side gate, and meant business.

Frances laughed, and Lois was amazed at the change in her. "Better get going, Mrs. Meade," she said. "They're killers, you know." The door closed, and Lois beat a hasty retreat.

Back to the footpath, and walking along with a now silent Jeems, Lois wondered if she could have been mistaken. Well, of course she could, but her first impression was very strong. The man had disappeared quickly, but there was something familiar about the way he carried his head, something weasel-like. She thought again of the change in Frances. She had had a boost of confidence from somewhere. Maybe the whiskey bottle, but it seemed unlikely. Perhaps her boorish husband had left her. And perhaps Reg Abthorpe had moved in? But there had been no old red banger outside.

She came out into a big field, where the path went straight across. It was muddy, and she had to concentrate to keep her footing. Here and there, dog excreta had been left, and she had to avoid that too. Once across the field, and into a grassy meadow, she relaxed and let

Jeems off the lead. Her thoughts returned to Frances Wallis. The woman had almost laughed at the idea of having Reg Abthorpe in the house. But, hey, wait a minute! What had she said? "I haven't seen that man since you were here." So she knew exactly who Lois had meant by Reg Abthorpe. But that proved nothing, except that Frances had been lying when she'd pretended not to have known him before. Lois had been more or less convinced of that anyway. But it was a small step forward, and Lois quickened her pace to keep up with the dog.

THE IRRITATING TUNE ON HER MOBILE STOPPED LOIS just as she was reaching a stile to climb into the next field. She could see bullocks quite near the path, and called Jeems back. "Hello? Lois Meade here," she said in a businesslike voice.

"Ah, yes, it's you, Lois."

Small statement of the obvious, she thought, but replied, "Who else? What do you want? Me and Jeems are just about to be attacked by young bullocks. Can you hear the stampede?"

Cowgill sighed. "That's not a very original put-down, Lois. Now . . . Oh, God yes! I can hear them! Run like hell, and ring me back."

Lois switched off her phone and grinned. She hadn't told him that she and her dog were on the safe side of the fence, and were stroking the steaming nostrils of the excited young bullocks.

"Calm down, " Lois said, patting one dark-brown animal on the shoulder. They were like the Chargers she remembered from school, bully-boys, all huff and puff, but easily faced. "Still, we'd better go round on the other path," she said. "Come on, Jeems. This way."

The path led her along by the side of the village's sewage works, and the wind was in the wrong direction. "Yuk!" she exploded. "Come on, dog, let's run." They scuttled round the corner of the works, and crashed straight into a young couple in a fond embrace.

"Floss! Ben! How could you? Right here by the stink! My God, I know love is supposed to conquer all, but this is ridiculous. Come back with us for a bit until we can breathe." She led the way, and the lovers followed laughing. They stopped in a small lane that had once been a single rail track, overhung with elder bushes and hawthorn. "Phew! That's better," Lois said.

"Did you want to speak to us specially?" said Floss, beginning to feel anxious. It was free time for them both, so surely Mrs. M couldn't object? They had been well out of sight until she arrived.

"No, just a thought. Might as well ask you now. Well, ask Ben, really. You're near the Wallis house, aren't you? I wondered if you'd seen a strange man around their garden recently. It's just that I still haven't been able to contact Mr. Everitt's nephew, but thought I saw him this afternoon in the Wallis's house." She was astonished at the reaction. An instant and furtive look passed between them, and Floss coloured.

Ben spoke quickly. "No, no, haven't noticed anybody. Haven't seen her awful husband lately, either. You know, the lorry driver who knocks her about. Sorry we can't help."

But you could if you wanted to, Lois almost said. The pair were frightened. Frightened of Reg Abthorpe? Instead, she said, "Knocks her about? Is it serious?"

Ben shrugged. "Who knows? Some women like it . . ." Floss glared at him.

"Yes, well," said Lois, "you should maybe report him to the police if it sounds serious."

"Perhaps he's left her," Ben replied. "Anyway, Mrs. M, we must get back. Both of us are on duty in half an hour. Floss is at the Hall, and I am going with Enid to those new people in Waltonby."

Lois nodded. "Fine, off you go, then. Bye." They almost ran away from her, and were out of sight in minutes. What was all that about? Time for a serious talk with those two, but not dangerously close to the sewage works. Lois looked at her watch, and walked on at speed.

*   *   *

As they approached home, Lois remembered that
her mother would be out. She had a front door key in her
pocket, and opened up. Jeems was growling, the hair
standing up on the back of her neck. "Just a minute, let
me get in!" Lois said and stepped over the rumbling dog.
She stepped on to something squashy, and jumped back
in alarm.

"What the hell?" Then she picked up Jeems and held
on tight.

On the mat, stretched out in *rigor mortis*, was a very
dead rat. A big rat, with a snarl on its vicious face.

"The cat must have brought it in," Derek said
later.

"We haven't got a cat." Gran spoke very quietly.

"Melvyn died," Lois said, staring into space.

"Oh, sod it," Derek said, taking her hand. "Lois, me
duck, what *have* you been up to?"

Thirty-Four

ॐ

Lois waited until next morning to telephone
Cowgill. She had been shocked, and for a short
while, frightened. So now she was a target, along with
Floss and Ben, and William Cox who had disappeared.
Another warning to keep our noses out of whatever was
going on, she thought. Well, bugger that! Her anger was
rising now, and as she waited for Cowgill to answer, her
resolve hardened. Nobody would tell her what to do! She
liked old Mr. Everitt, and had still to discover the truth

about Cox. No, if she watched her back she was sure all would be well.

"Ah, there you are. What took you so long?"

"Morning, Lois. And difficult as you may find it to believe, I do work pretty hard. Especially now we have a gang of serial rapists and potential abductors of young women on our hands. I expect you've seen the news?"

"Yep. Sorry. I take it all back. Under the circs, you probably don't want to know we've had another of them dead animal warnings. Me, this time. A dead rat on the doormat. And no, the cat didn't bring it in, because Melvyn snuffed it a few weeks ago."

"A warning to *you*?" Cowgill had snapped into official mode. "Have they got suspicious, whoever they are?"

"A reasonable deduction," said Lois acidly. "But that's not putting me off. Derek is not too pleased, and Gran is terrified, but tough. I've got a good idea now who is doing this dirty stuff, and a dead rat's not stopping me."

"Who is it, then?" Cowgill saw his hand was trembling at the thought of Lois in danger. You poor sap, he told himself.

"Not telling," said Lois. "I'll wait until I'm sure, otherwise you'll have your boys in hobnail boots blundering in and messing it all up."

"Lois! May I remind you we are the police, and upholders of the law? It is my duty to follow up any suspicious circumstances, so . . ."

"But you're not going to, are you? You trust me by now to choose the right time, surely. So I'll be in touch, soon, I hope."

"Lois! Before you slam down the phone, I must insist that you do not attempt anything dangerous, or even risky, but inform me immediately you have some useful evidence."

"Fine," said Lois, and put the telephone down as gently as she could.

*   *   *

WITH AN HOUR TO SPARE BEFORE SHE WAS DUE AT
Dallyn Hall, Lois decided to sit down at her computer
and surf websites concerning badgers. The reports of
badger-baiting cases up before the courts were the most
interesting. Young men, mostly, had worked in groups of
three or four and were often caught in the act as a result
of tip-offs. Lois looked at the fines. Only one of the cases
resulted in a prison sentence. The rest were fines ranging
from under a hundred pounds to over a thousand. The
maximum allowed, she discovered, was £5,000, but
found no fines even approaching this. Dogs were sometimes confiscated, and baiters forbidden to keep their
own terriers for two or maybe three years. In several
cases, the accused had East London addresses, but were
arrested in the Midlands.

Derek had come in softly and was standing behind
her, and she didn't have time to switch to some more innocent site. "Found anything?" he said. Lois was surprised. She expected him to blow his top and forbid her
to have anything more to do with badgers, dogs, policemen and walking in the woods. But no, he leaned over
her shoulder, kissed her cheek, and said, "Mind if I have
a butcher's?"

They sat together for nearly an hour, reading the
shocking evidence of cruelty and violence. Policemen
were threatened with spades by the baiters, terriers were
torn apart by badgers and badgers by terriers. Some dogs
got stuck down the badger holes, and were abandoned by
their owners, who took off into the night.

"Makes y' sick, dunnit," said Derek, sighing deeply.
"And it's a dangerous business to get mixed up in. You
can see that for yourself, Lois. Look at that one . . . revenge on a farmer who'd turned them off his land."

"Is there money in it? Or just a thirst for blood and the
fun of watching creatures suffer?"

Derek shook his head. "Don't know about money. The
other is probably right. But I heard an old bloke in the
pub say that they all did it in the old days. And once
you'd killed an animal, it was twice as easy the next time.

Makes you wonder if it makes it easy to kill, full stop.
Like in the war, I suppose."

Lois shivered. She thought of Herbert Everitt and
William Cox, two vulnerable old men disappeared from
sight. She wished she could find some hard evidence that
would get Cowgill going! "Better stop now," she said,
turning off her computer. "I'm due at Dallyn in twenty
minutes. Still, quite a lot to think about, isn't it."

Derek nodded, and put his arm around her. "You're
my most treasured possession, so remember what I said,"
he whispered in her ear.

She stared at him. "You've been reading too many of
Gran's romances! And I'm nobody's possession, so get
yourself back to work, you wally!"

Derek laughed. "That's my Lois," he said, and left her
office.

ON HIS WAY TO THE JOB HE WAS DOING THE OTHER
side of Waltonby, Derek considered badgers. He'd never
had much reason to give them a thought before. They
were just large striped animals, dead at the side of the
road, slowly rotting and eventually consumed by birds
and small mammals who scavenged and cleared up the
mess.

Now he thought about what he'd seen on Lois's computer. He knew farmers were able to catch and kill foxes,
but badgers were a protected species. He knew about TB
infections transmitted to cattle. He'd heard on farming
programmes reports of petitions to get government approval to gas the sick badgers, and petitions to stop the li-
censed cruelty, as it was seen by pro-badger lobbies. But
he was an electrician, a good one who knew his job.
Badgers were incidental to his life—or had been, until
Lois got herself involved.

He passed Cox's Wood and slowed down. On an impulse he stopped and got out of his van. Stepping into the
edge of the wood, he went a few yards and then stood still
and listened. Not a sound, except for rustling leaves and

birdsong. There must be quite a din when baiting was going on, what with dogs and fighting and encouragement from the tormentors. He turned back. Dark nights with no moon would be the most likely.

FLOSS WAITED FOR LOIS IN THE YARD BEHIND THE hotel. She was looking up at the huge trees surrounding the building, swaying in the brisk wind. "Must have been lovely in the old days," she said.

"Still on about that? Come on, you're a young girl with her whole life in front of her. Never mind about the old days," Lois said, remembering what the old man in the pub had said to Derek about the old days.

They went in through the servants' entrance and found the Director of Hotel Services waiting for them. There was no smile of welcome. In fact, she frowned and said she'd like a word in her office. Lois bit back a sharp retort, and followed the broad-hipped woman. Stately as a galleon, she thought. She put a reassuring hand on Floss's arm, and winked at her. The director walked into her office and glanced obviously at the ornate clock on the wall and said, "You're ten minutes late."

Lois thought of explaining she had been investigating the torture and massacre of an innocent wild animal, but decided against it. "Sorry about that," she said. "Unavoidable, I'm afraid, and we shall certainly be working ten minutes later to make up."

She turned to go, but the director snapped, "That's not all!" As she moved behind her desk, her high stiletto heels caught in a Chinese rug, and she stumbled, clutching a stack of CDs stored in a teetering tower. Before Lois could reach her, it had crashed to the floor, scattering the disks.

"Oh, bloody hell!" The director collected herself, and slumped into a chair.

"Don't worry," said Floss, clearly suppressing a giggle, "we'll collect them all up, won't we, Mrs. M."

Lois nodded. "Now, we must get on. What else was it you wanted to say?"

"Oh, nothing," the director replied peevishly. "Just leave me alone, and go and do some work. That's what you're paid for."

Lois took Floss's hand and drew her away out of the office, carefully shutting the door behind her. She put her finger to her lips, but it was too late. Floss exploded, spluttering and running as fast as she could to get away. In the safety of the Great Hall, full of fake designer lion heads and portraits by the yard, Floss whispered to Lois, "What d' you think she was going to say when so dramatically interrupted . . ." The thought set her off again, and Lois shook her head, pointing to a tin of polish and the long coffee table.

"Talk later," she said, and moved to the far end of the room.

As she continued on her way, cleaning every surface until it shone, and making sure no dropped cigarette ash had gone unnoticed, the same question occupied her thoughts. What was the director going to say? She could have no grounds for complaint about the work itself. Lois knew she inspected everywhere after they'd gone, but she and Floss made sure there were no faults to find. So what, then?

A thought struck her. Could she be in on the disappearances somehow? She didn't look like a potential badger-baiter, not in those heels. Lois smiled to herself. No, it would have to be something else. Spying? Spying on *her*? Lois shivered. It was not a pleasant thought, and the snarling rat flashed before her eyes. Well, it was possible, but very unlikely.

"Good afternoon, Mrs. Meade," said a sharp voice. Lois turned, and saw Mrs. Tollervey-Jones standing in front of her.

"What are you doing here?" Lois said, caught off balance. Not the politest thing to say to one of her snobbiest clients, but too late now.

"I fail to see what business it is of yours!" snapped

Mrs. T-J. "Unless I have upset your plans by returning without notice? I had trusted you to continue my routine, you know."

Lois answered immediately, "And so we have. No, I apologize if it sounded rude, but I was taken by surprise. I hope nothing serious has brought you back?"

"Only here for a couple of days. I have an appointment to see that manager woman, or whatever she calls herself. Give my regards to Floss . . . Oh, there you are, dear," she added in a softer voice. "Nice to see you. All going well at Farnden?" Not waiting for a reply, she stalked off towards the offices.

"Put your foot in it there, Mrs. M," said Floss. "Turning out to be quite an exciting afternoon. Is it tea-time yet?"

"It's after the usual time. Herself has probably forgotten. I'd give anything to be a fly on the wall when those two meet. A couple of Boadiceas there!"

"I'll go an' drop a hint in the servants' quarters," suggested Floss, and Lois nodded. She was thirsty, after cleaning out the dust and ashes where a real log fire had been lit in the great fireplace. A neat mound of ash must be left to be a base for the next blaze, and it was Lois's job to sculpt it once a week. She gazed at her handiwork, and Floss reappeared, saying, "Very architectural, Mrs. M—and the kitchen says she ordered there was to be no tea break for us this afternoon. They advise going on strike."

Lois stared at her. Then to Floss's surprise, she shrugged. They'd soon be finished and could go home for a cuppa. "In fact," said Lois, "I invite you to have tea with me and a piece of Gran's renowned chocolate cake. Come on, Floss. Let's get on with it and get out of here."

In Gran's warm kitchen, the two sat sipping hot tea and eating cake. "That's not fair, Lois," said her mother. "You've got a right to a tea break. I should tell that woman what you think of her."

"She's a valuable client, Mum. I know my place."

Gran sniffed. "It'll be the first time, then," she said. "Anyway, I'm off to the shop before it closes. Back shortly."

"She's wonderful," Floss said. "What would you do without her, Mrs. M?"

"God knows," said Lois. "But it doesn't do to let her know how wonderful she is."

"Well, I must be getting home," Floss said. "I'm meeting Ben early this evening. Big night! We're going to the movies." She finished her cake, and stood up to leave. "Oh, and by the way, I forgot to tell you what I overheard when I passed the office with those two battling away— I could hear every word."

"So what did you hear?" Lois said quickly.

"Well, Mrs. T-J was yelling that she had had no idea what was going on, and it must stop. Our director was yelling back that if Mrs. T-J didn't do as she was asked, she'd regret it."

"Was that it?"

"Yep. I didn't want to be caught lurking outside the door, so I moved on. A real shouting match it was, and I reckon our director was getting the best of it."

THIRTY-FIVE

❧

"IT'S FOR YOU, LOIS!" DEREK WAS SHOUTING FROM the hall telelphone. "House agents, they say they are." They had finished breakfast, and he was preparing for work.

Lois appeared at the top of the stairs. "What agents?"

"House," said Derek, and then Lois remembered. William Cox's house. She came down two steps at a time and took the telephone from Derek.

"Hello? Mrs. Meade here. New Brooms—can I help you?" This was for Derek's benefit. She wanted him to think it was a cleaning enquiry. It worked, and he walked away.

"It's the house you enquired about. I'll put you through to our Mr. Smith."

A man's voice, smooth and practised, said, "Ah, yes. How are you, Mrs. Meade?"

"Never mind that," said Lois. "What's this about?"

"The house you were interested in, Cox's Farmhouse. We wondered if you would like to take a look sometime? It does, of course, need a little work done, but basically it is a strongly constructed stone house. About three hundred and fifty years old, we think, if not older. Difficult to tell with these old farm houses. It has great potential, and we have had a number of enquiries. As you were one of the first, we'd love you to have the opportunity of seeing it."

"I've seen it," said Lois shortly. "Every day, more or less, as I go about my work."

"Ah, yes. Well, if you'd be interested in taking a look at the interior, we'd be only too pleased to show you round."

Lois considered rapidly. Would it be useful to take a look? Not just at the house, but at Mr. Smith, too? She made a quick decision. After all, she could always duck out of it. "I'm extremely busy," she said, "but should be free about six o'clock today. We're not considering it at all, really, but I'd like to take a quick look."

"Splendid," said Mr. Smith. "I'll meet you there. Six o'clock. Look forward to seeing you. Good morning, Mrs. Meade."

She went back upstairs, and Derek followed her. "Cleaning job?" he said.

"Sort of," Lois said. "They're trying to sell old Cox's house, and said it'd go quicker if we cleaned it up a bit. I'm going to have a look after work—sixish."

"Right-o. Better tell Gran you'll be late for tea."

Lois nodded, and gave him a hug. "You're my most treasured possession, Derek Meade," she said.

IN THE DARK, DUSTY OFFICE IN TRESHAM, MR. SMITH took his feet off his desk and looked through to the receptionist. "She'll be there," he said. "Six o'clock tonight. You know what to do."

The receptionist nodded. "Shall I tell the others now, or leave it 'til this afternoon?"

"Now," Mr. Smith snapped. "Use your loaf, Peggy. Sooner the better, in case they're off somewhere else. Then you-know-who will be at our throats. Get moving."

LOIS LOOKED AT HER DIARY. IT WAS GOING TO BE A long day. She'd planned to visit Ellen Biggs again, and also to catch Sheila's husband, Sam. He should be home at lunchtime, and might remember a bit more about the two blokes in the pub. Then she had to take Ben Cullen to introduce him to a new client at Waltonby.

First Ellen. She rang the hospital to make sure the old lady was still there, and they said yes, but she was coming on nicely and would soon be able to go home. Lois considered whether to wait until she was home, but decided to go today as planned. If there was any danger of a relapse, she wanted immediate medical help available. Not that she intended to upset Ellen. She would change the subject at any sign of reluctance to talk about her sister.

She could see Ellen at the end of the ward, sitting in a chair and looking out of the window. The view was of the car park, and Lois reckoned they'd told her she was coming. "Morning, Ellen," she said quietly. "How are you today?"

The old lady looked round quickly. "Ah, there you are, dear," she said. "I was expecting you. They'll bring you a drink shortly. Now, what were we talking about when I had to go off and have an X-ray?" Nothing wrong with her short-term memory, then.

"Not too sure," lied Lois. "Was it about the old days? You know I love to hear about early days in Ringford." This was not a lie. Lois loved to hear old people talk about their lives in the villages. She always turned first to the local paper's column written by a different senior citizen each week, a short memoir of something that had stuck in their minds. The last one had been an elderly man's memories of the High Street in Tresham in the Forties, and Lois had been fascinated.

"Now then," Ellen said. "It's coming back to me. You were asking about that old rogue, William Cox. And my poor sister. Mind you, if she'd had a bit more fight in 'er, it wouldn't't've turned out so badly."

Lois watched her closely for any signs of tension, but Ellen was completely relaxed and smiling. Whatever had caused her stroke, it wasn't talking about the Coxes. "Have you got a picture of her?" Lois said. "Did she look like you?" Ellen searched in her ancient black bag, and produced a scuffed leather wallet. She opened it, and handed it to Lois.

"There she is," she said. "Pretty girl. Not a bit like me!"

Lois stared at the lovely face of a girl, about eighteen years old, fair hair shining in the sun, her smile showing even white teeth. "Was this taken at the seaside?"

Ellen nodded. "We went to Brighton for an outing on a bus. Most of the day was on the bus! Them old things didn't 'ave much speed. Still, it was a nice day, and we 'ad our photos took on the front as we walked along."

"Who's that behind her?" Lois reckoned she knew, but waited.

"Well, it's 'im, ain't it? William Cox, o'course. They were walkin' out at that time, and I was playin' goose-berry." Ellen cackled at the memory. "'E tried to get rid of me, but I stuck like glue to the pair of 'em."

"He was quite handsome," Lois said. "'Andsome is as 'andsome does," Ellen replied briskly. "He was never no good, and she was a fool to marry 'im. He blamed her for not havin' kids. I think I've told you that before. He 'eld it against her."

"Still, I expect he was sorry when she died so young," Lois said.

"If he was, he didn't show it," Ellen replied. Her face fell for a moment. "Such a waste," she said.

"I suppose he grieved inside," Lois persisted.

Ellen shrugged. "'E was quick enough to get her buried and forgotten," she said, "and it was up to me to do the grievin'. Never any flowers on her grave, except what I put there. I never saw 'im in the graveyard, not once. In fact," she said portentously, "I did wonder . . ."

At this point, a middle-aged woman appeared with a trolley stacked with books. "Morning, Mrs. Biggs," she said brightly, "how are we today?"

"Who's *we*?" Ellen said.

The woman ignored that, and said, "Are you having a

new book this week? I've got two Barbara Cartlands you haven't read."

"I haven't read any of that silly woman's rubbish," retorted Ellen. "'Er an' 'er royal jelly. Wouldn't touch 'em with a bargepole. Anyway," she added, "I'm off home in a day or two, so shan't want any more books." She dismissed the woman by turning her back on her, and resumed her conversation with Lois. "Where was I, dear?" she said.

"Um, let me think," said Lois. "Was it something about Martha and William? Something you wondered about?" She held her breath.

Ellen frowned. "Yep, that was it. Now, what was I going to say?" She thought for a moment, then shook her head. "Nope," she said. "It's gone. Still, it'll come back to me. Next time you come to see me I'll be home, and we can talk again."

So my time's up, thought Lois, and stood up. "Well, I'll be on my way. Lovely to see you lookin' so well. Let me know which day you're going home, and I'll come over and check you're OK."

"Our Doris'll see to that. Don't you worry yerself about that. You got enough to do, with that cleanin' of yours. Thanks for comin', dear. Safe journey home."

WHAT HAD ELLEN WONDERED ABOUT? LOIS WAS driving away from the hospital and thinking back on the conversation. Ellen had been telling her about Martha's death, and being shocked at William's lack of piety over his poor wife's passing. In a village at that time, this would be a black mark for the widower. It was expected that every Sunday he would put fresh flowers on the grave, and maybe, if he was well off, donate a wooden seat in the churchyard in her memory. But William Cox had done none of this. Why? The way Ellen remembered it, he had wanted the whole thing forgotten as soon as possible. Why?

Lois turned into Waltonby and stopped outside the Stratfords' cottage. Sheila had seen her coming and was at the front door, smiling. "Something wrong, Mrs. M?" she said. "An emergency job for me?"

"No, nothing wrong," Lois said. "I just wanted to check with you next Thursday's jobs. I'm not sure I got it right on Monday. You having your lunch?"

Sheila shook her head. "We've finished," she said. "Sam's having a cup of coffee. You come on in, and have one with him."

Lois settled herself on a chair opposite Sam, and they talked farming for a few minutes. Lois was getting good at bluffing. She knew very little about farming, but had listened carefully enough over the years to talk reasonably intelligently. "It's non-stop hard work, isn't it, Sam," she said. "Thinking about retiring? But then," she added hastily, remembering that Sheila was anxious to keep him working, "what would you do with yourself? Old Ted Jones retired and just put on weight, with all his spare time spent in the pub!"

"He spends plenty enough time already in the pub," chipped in Sheila. "Mind you," she continued, "it's not the place it used to be. Full of strangers mostly. The old ones die off, and the houses change hands. We got commuters in Waltonby now! Back and forth to Birmingham every day."

"Strangers is right," agreed Sam. "Did Sheila tell you about them two I heard talking the other day? Nasty pieces of work, if you ask me. Didn't like the way they laughed."

"Yes, she did," Lois said. "You heard Mr. Everitt's name mentioned?"

Sam nodded. "Poor old lad. Nobody seems to know where he is."

"Were they local, these two? Did they talk like the rest of us?"

"No, no. They were from up London, I reckon. Real Cockney. What they were doing round here I don't know.

Selling something, you can bet. Anyway, I've never seen 'em again. Probably didn't have any luck in Waltonby. Maybe Mr. Everitt had bought from them before in Farnden, and they'd been to his house and couldn't find him in. Summat like that, I reckon."

"Could be," said Lois. "Well, perhaps I could just check your Thursday jobs, Sheila." She confirmed that they were fine, and thanked her for the coffee. "Better be getting back," she said.

"Have you had anything to eat?" Sheila asked, frowning. "I can make you a sandwich."

"No thanks. Gran will have prepared something, so I must run. Bye, Sam. See you, Sheila." Lois was on her way back to Farnden, and passed the woods. There was the For Sale sign outside the farmhouse. "Six o'clock, and I'll be back," she muttered, and felt a stab of apprehension.

THIRTY-SIX

HERBERT EVERITT FELT PROPERLY AWAKE FOR THE first time for what seemed like months. He had had difficulty in finding a place to hide his daily pill safely. If he'd had a flush lavatory, it would have been easy. But he didn't, and they'd be bound to notice it when they emptied his portaloo. He'd considered hiding them in his shoe, but after a while this had been too uncomfortable. Finally he hit upon the answer.

"I've got plenty of time, if nothing else," he muttered, and put the small white oval on a sheet of toilet paper. Then, with the heel of his shoe, he ground it into a fine powder. This he tipped into a couple of inches of the morning's pee and swilled it round. It was absorbed in seconds. Great! He waited anxiously until they brought the bucket, emptied and clean the next day, but nothing was said. Next he wondered how William was getting rid of his pill. Now he had plenty of energy to tap and scrape out a message, instructing him what to do. Footsteps outside, in what he imagined was a clinical corridor, were perfectly audible, and gave him adequate warning of an approach. Quite soon the reply came: "GOOD . . . IDEA." A broad smile crossed Herbert's face. His neighbour must have understood and stopped taking the bloody things.

Now Herbert looked at himself. There was no mirror, but it was enough to look down at his feet. He couldn't see them. The excellent food and lack of exercise, plus hours of unnecessary sleep, had increased his weight dramatically. To carry out the plan he was formulating in his mind, he would have to be fit. But how to get rid of the extra kilos? If he started leaving food on his plate, they would get suspicious. So it would have to be exercise. That would be difficult, in this confined space. Still, it was all there was, so he began to walk round and round, holding himself well and making sure all his muscles were in use. If only he had his dog! But they'd said they couldn't risk an infection because of his illness, and so he would have to wait until he was better. Illness! He felt as fit as a flea—if a little heavy! Round and round he walked. The only thing to do was to imagine a route he was taking with his terrier.

Now, out of his front door and down the path. Turn right at the bottom of the Gardens, into the footpath behind the houses. No, you can't stop here, doggie. Wait until we get into the field. Through the gate and into the sunlit meadow. Cows grazing over on the other side, and not in the least worried. They're used to seeing him, of course. The grass is cool and springy. Approaching the stile, and . . . there, over it safely, and walking quickly along by the sewage works. Not too bad today. Wind in the right direction. Ah, here's that nice young son of the Cullens. Morning, Ben!

Herbert's stockinged feet made no noise on the floor, and the entire conversation with Ben was in his head. On and on he walked, until he heard an unmistakeable knocking on the wall. He stopped and listened carefully. "I . . . HAVE . . . A PLAN."

"SO . . . DO . . . I."

The rest of the evening was spent in laborious conversation, but at the end of it, both men felt considerably more cheerful. "SLEEP . . . WELL." Herbert nodded and smiled. But he felt much too excited to sleep.

AT HALF PAST FIVE, LOIS DROVE SLOWLY UP THE HILL to Cox's farmhouse. She was deliberately early, and was relieved to see that the agent's car was not yet there. Since making the appointment this morning, she had thought a lot about his call. Why should he be so keen, when she had done her best to show lack of interest? Well, estate agents are pushy and thick-skinned. But Lois suspected some other reason. A trap? She had decided on an alternative plan, and driving past the entrance, she found the narrow opening half a mile up the road and managed to edge the car into it, more or less hidden in the tall grasses and hogweed. She locked up and walked along inside the edge of the wood towards the farmhouse. Seating herself out of sight behind the broad trunk of an old oak, she waited, listening for the sound of an engine.

At about a quarter to six, she heard a car approaching, slowing down, and then the engine cut out. He had arrived. She did not move, except to creep round the tree until she had a good view of the farmyard but was still concealed. She saw the agent go towards the house, looking around as he went. He opened the front door and walked in. There was silence for a while, and nothing happened. Lois had cramp in her foot and carefully changed her position. Another car! She heard it first, then saw it turn into the farmyard and drive across to the other side of the yard, where it disappeared behind a barn. Again, nothing happened. She looked at her watch. Exactly six o'clock. The agent reappeared and stood in the centre of the yard, frowning and looking from side to side. Then he walked out into the road and peered in the direction of Long Farnden. Back into the yard, he suddenly put his hand to his mouth and whistled. Blimey, thought Lois, where did a smoothie like him learn to do that?

Now, as she was half expecting, two figures emerged from behind the barn. One short and rotund, and the other tall and thin. Not quite Laurel and Hardy, but close. Lois's pulse was racing now. How long should she stay here? It was dangerous to move while they were in the yard, and she was certainly not going out to meet them, pretending she was house-hunting. A snatch of their conversation reached her.

"Well, where the bloody hell is she?"

"Been held up?" The tall one seemed to be spokesman for the pair. "Y' know what wimmin are," he added.

Ten past six. Time to go, thought Lois. But now another car, battered and dark red, turned into the yard. Oh God, not him! But it was Reg Abthorpe, and he strode over to the others. Now there were several raised voices, and Lois judged it a good time to leave.

"Look! Look, over there! There she is!" yelled the fat man suddenly. They all turned to look, and Lois ran. As one, they all followed, Reg Abthorpe galvanized into a surprising turn of speed. Then Lois tripped over a snaking bramble. They were gaining on her fast, and as she struggled to her feet, she felt a hand grasp hers and pull her up. Her feet hardly touched the ground as she was dragged along towards her van.

"Get in! I'll drive," said Derek, and they were back on the road and speeding towards Farnden in seconds.

"I expect you two would like to be left alone for a few minutes," said Gran, taking one look at their faces. "I'll turn the oven down, and then Lois can have her tea after."

Lois and Derek sat silently gazing at the carpet. Finally Derek got up and went over to sit beside her on the sofa. He put an arm around her shoulders, and she buried her face in his comforting warmth for a minute or two. Then she said in a muffled voice, "How did you know I was there?"

"I didn't," Derek said. "I was just walking along the road and saw you running. I'd seen the rest when I passed the farm. They were so busy shouting at each other, they didn't see me. I saw it all. And got you out."

Lois sat up straight, and looked at him. "Thanks," she said, "and sorry. But what were you doing walking up there on your own?"

"I suggest," Derek said slowly, "that we forget it happened. But I want a promise from you that you won't have no more to do with whatever's goin' on! Go on, promise!"

Lois sighed. "I can't," she said. "It's best I say now that I can't, and not have to break a promise. It's just that they know me now, and I'll have to watch out. Not up to me any more. But I *will* promise to be very careful, if that'll do."

After another silence, Derek said, "I suppose it'll have to do," and when Lois repeated her question about what he was doing up there by the woods, he said quietly, "It's dark early tonight," and turned on the television.

FOUR MEN WERE RUBBING THEIR SCRATCHED LEGS, and the short, fat one complained of a sprained ankle. "For God's sake, what's it all about?" he appealed to Reg Abthorpe.

The agent exchanged a quick glance with Abthorpe, and shook his head. "Enough for you to know we have to be very careful of this Mrs. Meade. Her cleaning business is a cover for snooping. Probably a snout for the cops.

Mind you, she's not that bright, if she comes snooping in a van with New Brooms all over it!"

Reg spoke now, and all turned towards him, as if he was the oracle at Delphi.

"Reg speaks," whispered the tall one to his mate.

"What was that!" Reg quelled them with a brutal look. "As I was about to say," he continued, "don't underestimate Lois Meade. She's crafty, and not in the least stupid. What's new is that her husband seems to have joined up with her. Never heard of him being involved before. So we have to be extra careful."

"How do you know all this about her, Reg?" The agent was respectful.

"I've got contacts," Reg replied.

They locked up the house, and moved towards their cars. "'Ere, Guv," said the short, fat man, limping back towards Reg, "What about them two old farts? We got to do somethin' about them soon, ain't we?"

"No questions," said Reg loftily. "Just do as you're told. As always."

THIRTY-SEVEN

ﭞ

HUNTER COWGILL WAS HAVING A BAD DAY. WHEN he awoke in his lonely bedroom, he looked at the rain lashing the window from a dead grey sky, and pulled the covers up around his ears, willing himself to go back to sleep. But what dreams would come? He had crawled wearily out of bed and gone through the morning routine. Shaved, showered and breakfasted—after a fashion— then he had driven through the rain to the police station, where the lost, misguided and downright criminal awaited him.

He stood at the window of his office, and, realizing it was market day, hoped he might see Lois's determined figure stalking through the rain. Instead, his internal phone announced that a Mr. Meade was in reception wanting to see him, at once if possible.

Cowgill sat down quickly. The last time Derek Meade had been in his office, he had accused the Inspector of having an affair with his wife. If only! Now what? "Send him up," he said, and waited.

Derek came in with a steely look on his face. "Sit down, please," Cowgill said. No good trying to be friendly, he realized. He would keep it strictly professional "How can I help you?"

"You know bloody well how you can help me—and the rest of my family," Derek said. "I'll come straight to the point. My Lois is involved with you again. Grassin', or whatever you call it. I want it stopped. Right away, as from this minute. Refuse to take her calls, and have no more contact with her. She's in danger already, from what I can gather, and I want it *stopped*!"

"Danger?" Cowgill said. "What danger?" What had Lois kept to herself? Perhaps this visit from Derek was opportune, if he divulged what Lois was keeping secret.

"Something to do with that farmhouse of old Cox's. She won't tell me anythin' about it, but what I seen was enough. And don't ask me any questions about it, else I shall be as bad as she is. So," he said, standing up, "I'm goin' now, and I expect my wishes to be acted on by you. I am," he continued, with the ghost of a smile, "still the head of our house, though you might not believe it."

Before Cowgill could remind him that he was in a police station, and that a Detective Inspector was entitled to ask him anything he liked, and expect to receive an answer, Derek was out of the door and on his way down the echoing stone stairs. Cowgill thought of asking reception to delay him, but decided against it. He knew Derek meant what he said, and he also knew that he should do exactly as asked, if only for Lois's sake. He knew she was headstrong, and however often she said she would be careful, in the excitement of the chase she could well do something foolish.

But then, she was an independent person. She had always refused money, and he knew he had no real influence over her. If he decided to have no more contact, she would just carry on by herself. It would be safer for her if he knew what she was up to, and could find out what she knew and hadn't told him. By coffee time, he had convinced himself that, in spite of Derek, he would carry on as before, but maybe make *more* effort to keep contact, not less. He would just have to be more discreet.

A new meeting place? Perhaps the supermarket had served its purpose. There must be a limit to how many times Lois could claim an urgent bladder call. It might already have been commented on, even though the manager knew all about it, and had been asked by Cowgill to say nothing. Where else could he think of? It had to be somewhere easy for Lois to get to, and where she would naturally be seen regularly. An establishment belonging to one of her clients would be ideal, he decided. The owner would have to know, of course, and be trustworthy enough to keep his mouth shut. Or *her* mouth shut. Cowgill had a sudden inspiration. Farnden Hall, and the eminently trustworthy Mrs. Tollervey-Jones. But would she agree, and would Lois agree to involve one of her best clients in this game of cops and robbers? No, of course she wouldn't. Nor would the ex-Chairman of the Bench.

He sighed. Perhaps if he forgot about it for a while, some other ideal location would come to him. Plenty of work to do, he thought, looking at the pile of papers on his desk. I'll get through these this morning, and this afternoon I'll prowl around, just like policemen are supposed to do.

*   *   *

LOIS KNEW NOTHING OF ALL THIS. SHE, TOO, HAD slept badly, but decided to concentrate on New Brooms' work today. It was time she called on selected clients again, just to check that they were satisfied. Although she knew that most would not hesitate to complain if they were not pleased, it was good public relations to call in periodically and be her most charming self. After she had checked messages and post, she fetched her raincoat from the hall and told Gran her plans. "Best if I skip lunch," she said, and then hastily added that she would make sure she picked up a sandwich somewhere.

"Huh!" Gran grunted.

A world of disapproval there, thought Lois, but continued out into the rain and drove off in her van.

"Good morning, Mrs. Pickering! Can I come in for a minute?" She was welcomed warmly and once more refused politely the offer of coffee. "I'm just looking in briefly," she said. "Now that you're a regular client, I'd like to check that you're pleased with Jean Slater's work. I know it must seem silly to you that Floss lives here and could do the job without going outside! But I do have a reason. If there was something wrong, you'd never complain about your own daughter, would you?"

Mrs. Pickering laughed. "You're right, of course," she said. "And yes, I am more than satisfied with Jean. Such a nice person, as well as doing her job thoroughly. I believe she had a very unhappy time recently?"

Lois never discussed the team's personal affairs, and said she believed it was quite a while ago. "Are you sure you won't have a coffee?" Mrs. Pickering was persistent, but Lois once more declined.

"Morning, Mrs. Meade!" Now Philip Pickering had joined them and was shaking her firmly by the hand. "Don't go before we've had a chat," he said. "Haven't seen you for ages, and so much has happened."

Lois at once agreed to sit down and have a chat. What could possibly have happened that Floss had not passed on? "Nothing bad, I hope, Mr. Pickering. Has Floss told you any more about that evening the two of them had been in the woods?" she said.

"No, no. And frankly, Mrs. Meade, I don't expect either of them to come clean about that. No, this is good news . . . sort of. Floss has finally found herself a suitable boyfriend. A charming fellow, young Ben. But if the relationship looks like developing into something more serious, we would want him to be thinking about . . . well . . . Oh dear, this is difficult. How can I put it?"

"Like this," said Lois bluntly. "You want to know when he's going to get a proper job. Cleaning is no job for a man, and, for that matter, not really one you'd want to see your daughter doing for ever." She smiled sweetly at him now, seeing his discomfort.

His wife rescued him. "That is exactly it, Mrs. Meade," she said. "Thank you for putting it so well. We knew you'd understand, didn't we, Philip?" He nodded, and was silent.

Lois looked at him. Surely there must be more to say? "I have to tell you," she said, giving him time, "I do not know Ben's plans, but I expect he'll be off soon. He is still applying for jobs, I know that. As for Floss, you'll know more than I do. She does enjoy the work, and has become a really good member of the team. Now, I must be going. Was there anything else?"

Philip Pickering put behind him thoughts of his beloved daughter being a skivvy for life, and said, "Well, yes. You remember that business with the cat? Nothing's been done about that, and then those horrible crows on Ben's gate."

"And the dead rat on my doormat," Lois added.

"What!" Mrs. Pickering's eyes widened. "Are they on to you now? What are the police doing about it?"

Lois laughed. "Oh, they have it in hand," she said. "Which means nothing much, I reckon. Still, it would do no harm to remind them. I'll give them a call when I get home. I suppose you haven't heard anything that might give us a clue?"

"Only something Floss's father heard in the pub.

Nothing he saw himself, but . . . well, why don't you tell Mrs. Meade yourself?"

She looked encouragingly at her husband, who said, "I don't know if it's relevant, but Sam Stratford was telling a couple of farming chaps that he was fed up with nasty-looking strangers invading *his* pub. You know what the locals are like. The pub belongs to them."

Lois remembered her father telling her how he'd once gone into a pub in the country, and everybody had stopped talking and stared at him. He'd had a quick half, and left as soon as possible. Frozen out, he'd said. Now she asked, "Did Sam say he'd recognized them at all?"

"No, complete strangers, he said. Mind you, I've seen a couple of unsavoury-looking characters up near the woods lately. Still, that's nothing to go on, is it. People can't help what they look like."

"Could be interesting," Lois said. "Would you give me a buzz if you see them again? Nothing like a bit of do-it-yourself policing. I can do without dead animals on my doormat, and poor old Gran nearly collapsed."

"Yes, of course," said Pickering quickly. "It's been nice talking to you. I must be off, dear," he added, turning to his wife. "Back at the usual time," he said, and left the room.

Lois was quick to follow. Next stop, Miss Beasley at Ringford. The old dear is getting more and more deaf, thought Lois, as she knocked and received no answer.

She rang the bell, and could hear Ivy Beasley shouting. "All right, all right! I heard you the first time! I'm coming." Lois stepped back from the door, and waited, knowing she'd be in for an instant raspberry. "Oh, it's you," said Ivy, opening the door a crack. "You of all people should know better. It takes time at my age to get to the door. What do you want, anyway? Not taking Bill away, are you?" She opened the door wider and glared at Lois.

"Certainly not," Lois said. "He'd be heartbroken. You're his favourite client." May God forgive me, she said to herself.

"Good. Then what is it you've come about?"

"Can I come in for a few minutes? Just one or two things I wanted to check with you." Ivy Beasley reluctantly stepped back and allowed Lois to enter. They sat in the kitchen, and Ivy's cat jumped on to Lois's lap. She stroked it absentmindedly, and it purred like a vacuum cleaner.

"Every few weeks I like to visit clients and check that they are satisfied," Lois continued. "There can be some small thing that people don't think is worth mentioning. So here I am, if there's anythin' at all."

Ivy narrowed her eyes. "You're not telling the truth, are you, Mrs. Meade," she said. "You know perfectly well I am very satisfied with Bill. I know what you come for. To pump me for what I remember about William Cox. Am I right?"

Lois sighed. "Yes, sorry, Miss Beasley. I'm owning up. You are quite right. The estate agents selling the house are trying to interest me in buying it. I went in to their office just to find out how much they want. Lots of people do it just to find out what their own house is worth. Now they phone me up, pestering like they do."

"So what can I tell you? Whether it's worth looking at? Or if the price is too high? I don't get out much and have no idea on such things. You'll have to ask someone else."

She made as if to get up from her chair, and Lois said quickly, "No, no. I wondered if you had any idea if the Cox family owned the farm, or were just tenants. There's several farms around here belong to Oxford and Cambridge colleges, and some of them stuck-up farmers just pay rent like any other tenant."

"Ah, let me think," Ivy said. She was quiet for a few minutes, then pointed with her stick to an old desk across the kitchen. "Look behind the clock," she said, "and you'll find a key. It unlocks the desk. Open it."

Lois obeyed, and inside the desk saw small piles of envelopes, yellow at the edges, and a clutch of photographs secured with an elastic band. "What am I looking for, Miss Beasley?"

"In that little drawer at the back, there's a few newspaper cuttings. Bring them to me," she ordered.

Ivy took them, and began to sift through. "Ah, here it is," she said, and handed a fragile cutting to Lois. "Read it out loud. I've forgotten exactly what it said."

"There's a picture, but it's difficult to see . . ."

"It's him, o' course. William Cox. Read it."

Lois began to read the fading print. "The headline says, 'Local Farmer Takes College to Court'. Then it goes on, 'Young son of the Cox family is accusing St Paul's College of putting up rent ex . . . or . . . bitantly, and intends to take the matter to court'. So it *is* a rented farm! That's worth knowing."

"Give it here, then. Now, you got your answer, so I'll thank you to put this back, lock the desk, and leave me in peace."

"Just one more thing, Miss Beasley," Lois said bravely. "Did the Coxes always give the impression the farm was theirs?"

"Oh yes. Old man Cox, William's father, said at the time that it was just a small piece of the farm they rented from the college, and the rest was their own. But I'm pretty sure that I remember my father saying otherwise. Now, good morning, Mrs. Meade. You can see yourself out."

As Lois got into her car, her mobile began to ring. "Hello? What do you want?"

"It's Cowgill here, Lois. Just keeping in touch. Are you working?"

"Of course."

"Fine. Keeping clear of those woods and Cox's Farm?"

"Why? What d' you know?"

"Oh, nothing. Just that although we've had no more reports of badger-baiting, that world attracts some very dodgy characters. Make sure you keep your eyes open. Anyway, anything to report?"

"Only that nothing seems to have been done about very dead animals frightening our residents. Not a sniff of a policeman anywhere."

"We are well into our investigations, Lois, and if you know anything else relevant to the matter, I'd like you to tell me. I rely on you, you know."

"Well, I can't rely on you, can I? Word gets round in villages, you know, and some of the older ones are dreading opening their front doors in the morning."

"We are almost sure there will be no more of this in Farnden. And I promise you we'll be there the minute another dead creature is used in a threatening manner."

"You sound like a policeman."

"I am a policeman. Goodbye, Lois."

THIRTY-EIGHT

FLOSS UNLOCKED THE BACK DOOR OF THE HALL AND looked around the kitchen. Everything looked exactly the same, except for a thin layer of dust, which was always there. Mrs. T-J had invested in a new Rayburn cooker, which heated water and radiators as well. Only the cooker was left on, turned down very low. In spite of it being oil fired, it seemed to create dust.

She began to work. As she dusted every surface in the kitchen, she came to an old polished oak table. If this place was hers, she thought, she'd chuck out everything in this kitchen and have it completely redesigned. Slate work-surfaces, those new Shaker-look units, painted a nice light-blue, a wood-block floor . . . Her thoughts were interrupted. She looked more closely at the oak table. O Lor, now what? There in the dusty surface was a handprint, a large handprint with long, thin fingers. Somebody had been in the kitchen since she was last here.

She told herself it could easily have been when Mrs. T-J returned for a day or two. But her hands were small and ladylike. Well, she could have had some man with her. Her bodyguard, maybe? Floss giggled, and dusted the print away, putting alarming thoughts from her mind.

The chequered floor in the Hall was unmarked. Floss was tempted to flick a dry mop over it and leave it at that. Who would know? Mrs. T-J would. And she would tell Mrs. M, and Floss would be in trouble. She fetched the mop and bucket full of soapy water, and began to clean the black and white tiles. As she approached the wide stairway leading to the upper floor, she looked more closely. So it wasn't completely clean, after all. On the white tile nearest the stairs, she saw a faint muddy mark, as if from a ridged shoe sole. So the bodyguard didn't wipe his shoes. Must be someone close to the old dame, who knew he could get away with it.

Floss began to hum a cheerful tune. She wasn't frightened, but she'd be glad to get through the job and out into the sunshine again. Upstairs in the bathroom, she decided to open a window. There was a musty smell in the house, and a fresh wind blowing through would do a power of good. But she must remember to shut it again. She leaned out and took a deep breath. Mm, that was better. Then she saw him. It was that man, the one from the woods. Her heart thumped so loudly she was sure he must hear her. She backed quickly away from the window, not daring to shut it and make a noise. She heard heavy footsteps on the cobbles outside in the yard, and doors opening and shutting. Then his unpleasant laugh. She shivered. More footsteps, and then silence. After a few minutes, she dared to take a quick look. Nothing there. The yard was empty, except for her own small car, and everything looked exactly the same as before.

She sat down on the bathroom stool and tried to relax. He was gone, so there was nothing more to worry about, was there? She took some deep breaths and began to feel better. Whatever he was up to, he had obviously decided not to come into the house, in spite of her car being very conspicuous. That meant he knew she was here, and his business was not with her.

The rest of the house was cleaned in double-quick time, and Floss locked up the house and got into her car. Then she looked up, and saw the bathroom window was still open. With great reluctance, she went back in and climbed the stairway. She shut the window, and began to make her way along the landing to the stairs. It was a gloomy corridor between bedrooms, and as she approached the head of the stairs, she drew in her breath sharply. A dark shadow had moved across the end of the passage, very swiftly, and almost instantly vanished. Floss had had enough. She rushed down the stairs, two at a time, and jumped the last four. Out in her car, she started the engine and was away down the drive in seconds. What the hell was going on? As she drove into the village, she passed Mrs. M's house. Maybe it was time she told her all. The night in the woods when she and Ben were threatened. That same man up at the Hall, and the shadow in the corridor.

She turned the car around, and parked outside the Meades' house. Gran answered the door, and said she was very sorry, but Lois was not at home. "She had a number of calls to make and won't be back until late. Is there a message?"

"No, it's OK, Mrs. Weedon. I'll catch her later. Thanks."

Gran went back into the kitchen, frowning. The child had not looked well. Very pale. She did hope she was not sickening for something. Lois was pleased with Floss's work, and already counted on her as a reliable member of the team. She shook her head. Probably too many late nights with that boyfriend of hers. Still, youngsters will be youngsters. She was one herself once, a very, very long time ago.

Thirty-Nine

❧

IT WAS QUITE DARK NOW, AND NO LIGHT CAME IN through the high, barred window in Herbert Everitt's room. He had feigned sleep when the man came in to settle him for the night. Now there was complete silence. This was broken as the distant church clock struck eleven sonorous strokes. Immediately a series of dots and scrapes came from William Cox. "ARE . . . YOU . . . READY."

Herbert's heart beat faster. With any luck, this would be the last message he would have to send. "YES."

He shouldered his makeshift bag—formerly a pillow-case—containing his few pathetic belongings, and went to the door. The lock had turned out to be an old one, and not difficult to pick. Thank God for those skills his old dad had taught him, before he had disappeared from sight for three years. "Guest of His Majesty" his mother used to say, and it had taken him a while to understand what she meant. It had been a terrible disgrace in the family, and he'd never discovered exactly what his father had done.

He tip-toed along to release Cox. This lock was more difficult, but after a few agonizing minutes he managed it.

"Christ!" said the old man, peering out. "It's outside! Where are we?"

"Never mind," whispered Herbert. "Close the door quietly, and follow me. Don't make a sound."

The darkness swallowed them, and silence settled once more.

FORTY

༄

LOIS SAT WITH GRAN AND DEREK, ALL OF THEM
dozing and waking and saying it was time they went
to bed, but nobody made a move. The telephone rang like
an alarm bell, and had them all on their feet. Lois got
there first, and heard Bill's voice, high and urgent. "Mrs.
M? Thank God. Can you come over? Rebecca's got
pains, and is in a panic. I've rung for the doctor, and he'll
be here shortly, they said. But we—Rebecca and me—
wondered if you could . . ."

"Give me ten minutes, and I'll be there," said Lois,
and after five minutes was on her way to Waltonby.

"Well, I don't know I'm sure," Gran said, tidying up
her knitting and turning off the television. "Lois is no
midwife—mind you, it's too early for that. We'd best go
to bed, Derek. She might be a long time, if that girl needs
to hold her hand."

It was a dark night, and Lois concentrated on her driving. At one point, she pulled up sharply, sure that in front
of her there was small dog on the side of the road, white
patches showing up in the car lights. But then there was
nothing there. Eyes playing tricks, she thought, and no
wonder, at this time of night.

Now she remembered that she'd meant to ask Bill why
he seemed so fed up. Perhaps Rebecca had had a scare
previously? It was just like Bill not to mention it. But this
time it sounded serious. Not much she could do, except
calm the girl down. Lois expected that the doctor would

be there before her, but when she pulled up, there was no car outside the cottage.

Bill must have been watching from the window, and stood at the open door as she came up the path. "Thanks so much, Mrs. M.," he said. "She's just drifted off to sleep, and the doctor is coming as soon as he can." He hesitated, and then said, "I know I ought to be used to all this, what with calving and lambing an' that, but . . . well, I'm scared, Mrs. M."

"Well, that's no help, is it?" said Lois briskly. "Now, when's it due?"

"Not for a few weeks yet."

"Right, well, has she lost any blood?"

Bill shook his head. "Just the contractions," he said. "But poor old Becky, she says they're strong."

"Mm," said Lois, trying to sound wise. It was such a long time since she had given birth, she had forgotten all the details. In any case, she reckoned crafty Mother Nature erased memories of most of it, especially the painful part, so women cheerfully got on with the next one. But now, looking at Bill's anxious face, she thought that the best she could do would be to prop him up until the doctor arrived.

"Contractions do come and go, as I'm sure you know," she said. "More of a practice for the real thing. Come on, let's put the kettle on and talk about something else until Rebecca wakes up."

Bill followed her obediently into the kitchen, and they talked in whispers, until suddenly a small voice called out, "Bill! Where are you?"

"Come on!" he said urgently, and ran up the narrow cottage stairs. Lois followed as calmly as she could, and was amazed to see Rebecca sitting on the bed, smiling at her.

"I thought I heard your voice, Mrs. M.," she said. "What are you doing here at this time of night? No, don't tell me, let me guess. This dear chap rang you?" Lois nodded, and Bill sat beside Rebecca and held her hand.

"It's fine now," she said reassuringly. "No more contractions."

Just then the doorbell rang, and Rebecca stared at Bill. "Who else?" she said.

"The doc, of course," he said, and went downstairs.

"WHERE THE HELL ARE WE?" WILLIAM COX LEANED against a tree trunk, panting. "Can we rest for a minute?"

"Better keep going if you can," Herbert said. His perambulations around the cell-like room had strengthened his muscles, and he was altogether in much better shape than William. "Here, give me your bag. You'll do better without it." He shouldered the two pillowcases and they both trudged on.

"Why can't we just go home?"

"Use your loaf, William." Herbert had the heady feeling of a liberated man. "They're not going to let us go home and tell all to the police. That was no hospital or clinic. We were imprisoned. A crafty job, admittedly, and they had me fooled. Until I stopped taking the pills. You too, don't forget. No, they'll be after us, and I hate to think what they'll do if they get us. We'll go into hiding for as long as possible, and hope the police are on to them already. After all, it's some time since we went missing. Come on, old lad, we're nearly there!"

They were not nearly there, but Herbert knew that it was vital to keep William on the move. With any luck, he and William would have until breakfast-time. His brain was whirling, trying to sort out what it all meant. And who were *they*? He had stepped straight out of his room into the pitch-black night. But things around him had seemed familiar, and if his guess was accurate, he was taking William to the only safe place he could think of. It was near enough to get there, and probably the last place they would look. In any case, it was all he could think of at the moment, and he plodded on, praying he would be able to get in when they found it.

*   *   *

"You're soon back," Derek said, as Lois came in and flopped down into a chair.

"False alarm," she said. "Poor old Bill. She's a bit of a silly girl. You'd think a schoolteacher would know better."

"Dunno," Derek said. "I do seem to remember a certain person who had me out three times taking her to the hospital before Douglas was born."

"That's because he was my first," protested Lois. "I was much calmer with the other two."

"Well, it's Rebecca's first, isn't it? Anyway, time for bed. Gran's gone up, so we might as well follow."

"Yeah," Lois said, not moving. "Come an' give us a cuddle first."

Derek looked at her properly, and saw her pale face and clenched hands. "Right," he said. "I see you need a thera-what's-it spot of lovin'. Come on, me duck, let's be having you."

Before she fell asleep, Lois stirred in Derek's arms and kissed his cheek. "Derek," she whispered.

He groaned. "In the morning, me duck," he said, half asleep.

"No, wake up a minute! I want to tell you something important."

Derek sighed. "Go on, then."

Lois said, "You remember Herbert Everitt's little dog?"

"Oh God, is that important? Of course I remember his dog."

"Well, I think I saw it tonight. It's a terrier, isn't it. And I used to think what a nice one it was. Longer legs than usual. I'm sure I recognized it. But when I got up to where it was, it had gone . . . Derek? Are you listening to me?" His answer was a light snore.

FORTY-ONE

ॐ

"NO MOON TONIGHT," DEREK SAID, HANDING A CUP
of tea to Lois.

She sat up in bed and said, "So? We're not planning on
a midnight picnic, are we?"

"Might be romantic for a walk in the woods y'know,
listening for nightingales an' that. Take Jeems if you
like."

Lois stared at him. "What's up with you, Derek? Are
you feelin' all right?"

He nodded, and smiled. "We could take Gran, if you'd
like a chaperone."

Lois slid out of bed. "No, not Gran, nor Jeems, nor
me. It's that quiz on the telly tonight, and I'm not missing the final. If you want to go for a walk in the pitch
dark, you can go by yourself."

"I might just do that," said Derek, and moved swiftly
into the bathroom before she could get there.

A SECRET INQUISITION HAD BEEN SET UP, AND IN THE
back room of William Cox's house, Nelson, Nelly for
short, and his mate Shorty—the tall, thin one—faced a
furious Reg Abthorpe. He had been told of the missing
men, and his angry face had suffused with blood, but now
it was an unhealthy grey and his eyes were chips
of ice.

He spoke quietly at first. "Shorty," he said, almost

whispering, "you are supposed to be the brains. Tell me exactly what you found."

"Hey, wait a minute . . ." protested Nelly.

Reg turned and froze him in mid-sentence. "*Shut up*!" he barked, and Nelly subsided, shaking.

"Go on," Reg whispered to Shorty, who was also trembling in fear. They knew Reg had a quick temper, but they'd never seen him like this before. "Well, we went to take them their early morning tea and pill, as usual, and found the birds had f-f-f-flown."

"Flown?" hissed Reg. "*F-f-f-flown*? What d' you think this is? A bloody Open University poetry course?" He got to his feet and stood over the pair of them, and now he had a gun in his hand. "You two will find those doddery old men within the next hour, or I shall be behind you with this." He waved the gun at them, causing them to duck down, accidentally banging their heads together. Reg laughed, a mirthless laugh which was gone in seconds.

"W-w-w-where shall we look, boss?" Shorty rubbed his head and shrank away from the waving gun.

"How the hell should I know? You'll have to use whatever limited intelligence you can muster between you. But be back here within the hour . . . and I want those old buggers alive, so none of your usual tricks. Now, sod off."

Nelly took a deep breath, and risked his life. "Boss, can I ask you something?"

"Oh, for God's sake—what?"

"Supposing the agents bring somebody to look at this house? Wouldn't we be better taking them to the usual . . ."

"What agents?" said Reg angrily. "Just mind your own bloody business and get on with it. You don't need a bloodhound to find two old men in their eighties,"

Shorty and Nelly backed out of the room, and then ran. When they were safely away from the waving gun, they stopped. "Which way, then?" said Nelly.

"Let me think," replied Shorty. "Best to start from

where they escaped, and then . . ." He tailed off, not having any real idea of where the men might have gone.

"Well, I know which way I'd go in their place," Nelly said, setting off down the hill towards Farnden.

"So do I, then," Shorty retorted, and the two set off in opposite directions.

After a few steps, Nelly stopped. "Hey!" he called. "Wait for me," and he ran back, puffing and blowing, to catch up with the brains of the duo.

Reg followed soon after. He was in a hurry.

THE DILAPIDATED COTTAGE WAS COLD AND DAMP, BUT Herbert and William had found mouse-damaged blankets in a relatively dry cupboard. They had slept fitfully, like Goldilocks, on each sagging bed in turn, until they found the most comfortable. As dawn came up, grey and reluctant, Herbert surfaced and for a moment could not think where he was. This wasn't the room where he had been confined for so long. Then he remembered, and sat up, looking round for his fellow refugee. The old man was hunched up under a dirty pink blanket which was riddled with holes, and for one horrible second Herbert thought he was dead. It had been touch and go whether William would make it on their slow progress towards the cottage. Then he saw a stirring, and William turned to face him.

"Where am I?" he said.

"With me," said Herbert. He had decided not to explain their whereabouts to William, in case this should prove foolish. He did not entirely trust him, remembering stories about the Cox family when he first moved to Long Farnden. He'd been told to steer clear of Cox's Farm and Woods, and had not done so. If Spot hadn't taken off after a rabbit that evening . . .

"Can't we go home now?" William was struggling to sit up, rubbing his eyes with a dirty hand.

Herbert shook his head. "Not yet," he said. "Remember what I said about them coming after us? We're a real threat to them now. We'll lie low here until the law comes looking for us. Then we'll get protection, and the whole thing will be sorted out."

"Not with that lot. They're slippery as snakes. There's good money to be made from what they're up to, and they've spent their lives evading the law. Like the fox, they vanish into the night."

"So you know them?" Herbert looked at Cox in surprise. William said nothing, and Herbert continued, "I only saw them once, in the woods. My Spot heard their terriers barking, and wouldn't come when I called. I followed him, and found that lot in the middle of torturing a badger. A big one, it was, and put up a good fight. I tried to run, but Spot's blood was up, and he wouldn't come. Then they saw us, and the rest you know."

"You're lucky they didn't rub you out straight away. Wouldn't be the first time with that lot."

"Why did they kidnap you? If you knew they were in your woods, you must have decided to let them get on with—"

"I'm not a brave man, Bert, and I am an old man. The way they work is enough to persuade me to do anything, more or less. I'd seen people sniffing round in the woods, and thought they might be police, so I told them to get out. Then they threatened my old Rosie . . ." He turned away and coughed. "And then, after what they did to her, I went berserk. That tall one bashed me, and I didn't come to until I was in that clinic, or whatever it was." He pulled the blanket up around his neck, and said pathetically, "I wouldn't mind a cup of tea. At least we were looked after back there. Food was good."

"Freedom's better," snapped Herbert, "and my name is *Her*bert." He stood up, rubbing his back. "I'll go down and see if the owners left any supplies."

"Won't they be back?"

Herbert explained that this dump had been bought as a holiday cottage by some Londoners, and they had most of one summer living here, with big plans for restoration. But folk said they'd run out of money, and it had been empty and unvisited for two or three years, continuing to deteriorate and slowly retiring into the undergrowth that surrounded it.

To his surprise, Herbert found that the gas stove still worked, fed from a Calor cylinder under the sink. He filled a cheap tin kettle and turned on the gas. Matches. No matches anywhere. They'd probably have been damp and useless, anyway. He turned off the gas. "Got any matches?" he yelled up the stairs.

"No, don't smoke," was the reply.

He looked at the top of the stove. Among the buttons was a small one with a lightning sign by it. Ah! He turned on the gas again, and pressed the button firmly. It sparked, and the gas ring was alight. "Done it!" he yelled.

A growling voice came back, "Clever bugger. Where's my tea, then?"

There were teabags in an airtight jar, and a tin of evaporated milk on a shelf. Herbert found a tin-opener and pierced a hole. He made the tea in two grimy mugs, and went slowly back up the stairs. His legs ached, and he had a blister on one heel. When he handed William his tea, the grey faced old man took a sip. "No sugar," he said.

"Downstairs," Herbert suggested, "there is probably sugar in a jar. Why don't you go and look?"

Cox shook his head. "I'll go without," he said, and made a face as he took another sip.

Silence fell between them, and Herbert tried to make some sense of the situation. He and this miserable old devil were condemned to each other's company for maybe more than a few days. Nothing could be gained from getting on badly. He knew William Cox was not likely to change, so decided he would have to hold his tongue and keep the peace. Then there was a vital need for food. When he'd had a splash with cold water in what passed for a bathroom, he would investigate the rest of the kitchen cupboards. The fridge had been empty and turned off. Just as well, he thought, if they haven't been back for years.

Suddenly William said, "Herbert . . . I've got an apology to make."

"No need."

"Yes, I've been stupid. You got us out of there, and found a hiding place, and thought it all out, while I just tagged along. Sorry, chum. I'll do my best to help."

Herbert's smile was relieved as well as forgiving. It would certainly make life a lot easier. "Come on then," he said. "Let's go down and see if cook has made our breakfast. Kippers, scrambled eggs, bacon and mushrooms, and nice hot coffee and toast."

"In your dreams," said William, but he smiled and began to get off the bed.

As Herbert was opening cupboards in the kitchen, he heard a familiar sound. "Sshh!" he said to William, who'd appeared behind him. The sound came again, a whimpering and scratching at the door. Herbert rushed to open it, and said, "Spot! Little Spotty!" He picked up the terrier and buried his face in the mud-splashed fur.

William stared, and then saw tears rolling down Herbert's stubbly cheeks. "Right," he said, "I'll make the next cup," and began to fill the kettle.

OUTSIDE THE COTTAGE, HIDDEN IN THE THICKET, REG Abthorpe watched. He had used that wreck of a house himself once or twice. But it was too far off the beaten track to be useful, and there was no way of getting a car down there. But on foot—and he guessed the old men would be walking—it was still just about reachable. He had released the terrier, and seen him follow the scent to the door. He saw the door open, and Herbert Everitt take his dog in, and the door close again. Reg smiled. It had worked, and those two idiots were probably still searching and calling. As his mother would say, if you want a job done properly, do it yourself.

FORTY-TWO

❦

SHORTY AND NELLY CONSIDERED DOING A RUNNER. They had not found the two old men, and had no idea where to look next. They knew only Cox's Wood and the farmhouse, and the rest was strange country to them. They'd worked for Reg on the baiting for a few years, and had taken on this kidnap job at his insistence. They weren't particularly sorry for the old men, but were fed up with the daily caring for them, having to disguise themselves each time they went in. It was quite a lark at first, but now they felt uncomfortable and not safe. They wished desperately they could get out of it and return to the straightforward sport of dogs and badgers. They knew all that inside out, but Reg and his plans were outside their experience. On top of that, he scared them witless.

"We could disappear," Nelly said.

"He'd find us, and then it'd be worse." Shorty squared his shoulders. "We'd better get back and tell him. He won't kill us," he added bravely. "Where would he put the bodies? Nah, he's all piss and wind. Come on, let's get it over."

Whistling in the dark, thought Nelly, but he followed obediently.

Reg was back in the farmhouse by the time they shuffled in. They had no reason to think he had been anywhere whilst they were away. Probably planning what to do to them if they failed in the search.

"Now then," he said to them, in that horrible whispery

voice. "Where are they? *Where the bloody hell are they?*"
His hand went into his pocket and produced the gun once
more. "Couldn't find them? Thought maybe they'd gone
home and you felt sorry for them? *Turn around. Both of
you!*" He waved the gun, and they both obediently faced
the wall. A wet patch spread down the front of Nelly's
trousers.

Then suddenly Shorty turned back to Reg, and raised
his fist. "If you pull that trigger, you're done for, Reg
Abthorpe. My missus knows where we are, and all about
you, and she's not frightened of nobody. She'd eat you
for breakfast." He laughed. It was a quavery laugh, but
Reg slowly put the gun back in his pocket.

"Right," he said, "here's what I've decided. You two
are *such* a valuable pair, I'll keep you on, and give you
more time to ferret about. But don't waste time going to
Everitt's house. He'll not go back there. He probably
knows I've got a lookout over the road. So concentrate on
outlying hiding places. Old barns, sheds, down in that
quarry on the Waltonby road. Oh, and walk. That way
you don't miss anything. Go on, bugger off."

Outside the farmhouse, Shorty looked Nelly up and
down. "I've heard of shit-scared," he said, "but grown
men don't pee themselves. For God's sake, grow up, and
we'll get out of this somehow."

"Couldn't help it," Nelly grunted. "Anyway," he
added, "I never heard you was married?"

"I'm not," Shorty said, and led the way back to the
road.

REG SAT FOR A LONG TIME, DEEP IN THOUGHT. THERE
was no chance of Nelly and Shorty finding the cottage
where the old men were holed up. The idiots were
Londoners, and knew nothing about the countryside
hereabouts. So what to do with Everitt and Cox? He considered leaving the old men until it was dark, and then
getting them back. It had all been working out well, and
he was near to success over the whole thing. He just

needed some signatures on paper, witnessed by Nelly and Shorty, and that should be easy once the old parties were once more under his control. Then would come the tragic accident. He brooded on how they had escaped. They should have been too dozy even to think of it. The pills were strong. Pills . . . that was it! Somehow they'd stopped taking them. Trust those idiots not to notice!

His mind churned on, until he came to a decision. He saw again the cottage, derelict and uninhabitable. He knew now what to do. Nothing, that's what he would do. Just leave them in a damp, cold place, with no food, fuel, and probably no water. Certainly no heating. And they'd be too weak to try to move on. Where could they go? No, they'd be hoping to be rescued. Some hopes! The cops were too busy looking for teenage louts who could have hung up those dead things. And that woman Meade had obviously taken the warning. On reflection, it was just as well he'd failed with the plan to get her in the house and frighten the knickers off her. No telling what her husband might have done.

So he'd leave the old blokes for as long as necessary. He and the two fools could take turns in keeping watch, in case Everitt decided to play hero. He and Cox would be only too pleased to sign anything by then. Perfect.

He locked up the farmhouse again, and walked to where he'd hidden his car. The actor playing estate agent in Tresham had said he was bored with the part, and anyway, had been offered a job in a theatre up north. Not worth paying the rent any longer. He'd wind that up, keep an eye on Mrs. New Brooms Meade, and make sure everything else went as smoothly and quickly as possible.

Lois was very far from being warned off. Now she had straightened things out with Derek, she felt happier. He had certainly been warmer towards her after their night of passion—she chuckled—but the excitement had quickly worn off and now he was polite but disapproving.

She hoped that this would wear off, too. She was sitting with Gran after lunch, drinking coffee and playing with Jeems. "She's still, a puppy, isn't she," she said. "Do you think she'll ever grow up?

Gran shrugged. "Some people don't," she said. "Don't know about dogs."

Lois recognized a snub when administered by her mother, and stood up. "I have to go to the shop," she said. "I'll take Jeems for a walk after that. Get a breath of fresh air before I tackle paperwork." She also needed some thinking time, and planned a walk across the meadows so that Jeems could have a good run. She picked up a chewed rubber ball and put it in her pocket. "Bye then, see you later."

Gran managed a grunt, and then rattled dishes as she began to clear the table.

Perhaps I should offer to help, thought Lois. But that would give Gran an opportunity to score another point. Still . . . "Do you need a hand with those?" she ventured.

"No more'n I ever do," Gran said. "You go off and enjoy yourself. I know my place."

"Oh, for God's sake!" Lois fixed the dog's lead and marched out, shutting the door firmly behind her.

The shop was busy, and Lois attached Jeems to a hook by the waste bin outside. A gang of small children, out early from school, were jostling by the sweets display, working out what they could get for coins clasped in hot hands. "Something you want, Mum?" Josie said over the tops of heads. "This lot'll be ages."

"Don't worry. I'll wait. Just wanted a word, that's all." Lois checked on Jeems through the shop window, and turned to inspect the greetings cards. Her eye was caught by "new baby" cards, and she selected one that would do for boy or girl. Always good to think ahead, she reckoned. Be prepared, as the scouts said. Thinking of scouts took her to speculating on Ben. So far, he had been fine, doing the work efficiently and upsetting none of his clients. Floss continued to be excellent. But this situation couldn't last. Both of them would probably move on soon, and then she'd have to be thinking about recruiting again . . .

"Penny for 'em, Mum." Josie was smiling at her, and she realized the children had gone.

"Ah, yes. I'll have this card for Rebecca. Nobody knows when that baby will arrive!" She paid, and then said, "I just wondered if I could ask you something. And no, don't joke. This is deadly serious. I don't mind what you answer, or even if you want to think about it. But here it is: you know I'm still feeding information to Cowgill. It's to do with Herbert Everitt, though I've still got to convince Cowgill there's anything wrong with the old boy disappearing. By the way, Dad knows all about it. The thing is, the meeting place Cowgill has used is lousy. I'm not going there any more. So I wondered if . . . ?"

"If you could come here? Not bloody likely! I can't think how you've got the nerve to ask," Josie said. "Anyway, you know it'd soon get around. Lois Meade is having an affair an' her daughter's in a conspiracy to hide it from poor old Derek."

Lois sighed. "I expected you'd say something like that," she said, "but I've thought it out carefully. Nobody'd think anything of my coming round to the back of the shop out of hours to see you. And Cowgill could come that back way through the old passage nobody uses. You're not overlooked at the back, so there'd be no danger of him being seen."

"Did he suggest this?" Josie's voice was hard and suspicious.

"No, it's my idea, and I haven't even told him. You can just say no, and we'll forget the whole thing now."

"Well," Josie replied slowly, "for the moment I'll say this. On condition that you tell Dad all about it, I'll consider it. I'll have to ask Rob, of course. You do your side of the bargain, and I'll try to sell it to Rob. I can't say it's the best plan you've ever proposed, but I'd like to help old Everitt. I hope I can trust you, Mum."

"Have I ever let you down?"

Josie shook her head. "No . . . Well," she added briskly, "there's sorting out to do in the stockroom, and that dog of yours is turning out the contents of the waste bin, so I'll say cheerio."

She went away, and Lois rushed out to repair the damage. She felt bad, and for two pins would have gone back to Josie and told her it was all off. She'd find somewhere else. Then she remembered the supermarket and her bladder weakness story. She couldn't do that again. But she had to see Cowgill in person and convince him that something was badly wrong with Herbert's prolonged absence. No one could contact the old boy, or even discover which nursing home he had been taken to. As for Cox, Lois didn't much care about him. She knew too much about his past. But the fact that two well-off old gents, neither with family who cared about them, had disappeared in a short time couldn't be dismissed. She unhooked Jeems, and headed towards the meadows.

THE PLEASURE OF THE WALK WAS NOT ENHANCED BY the smell of sewage borne on a warm wind, but Lois hurried past the gurgling mass and was soon out of range. Jeems was still on an extending lead, and Lois sat down on a tree stump by the old railway line, playing the little dog like a fish. She decided to sort out what she knew into a list, and prepare a case for police action next time she met Cowgill. She had only to telephone him, she knew, to fix the date.

First, Reg Abthorpe was the obvious central figure in what was going on—and what *was* going on? He came and went like the Red Shadow, and seemed to live nowhere. He had men working for him, and organized badger-baiting was one of his jolly games. But was this all? Lois suspected not. In fact, the baiting could be a cover for something else. Something connected with the two old men?

Secrets: Floss and Ben were hiding whatever had happened that night in the woods. Ellen Biggs was not revealing all she knew about William Cox, Lois was sure. Ivy Beasley probably doing the same thing. Frances Wallis hiding everything, but quite definitely connected with Reg Abthorpe in some way. Her brutish husband, too.

So what to tell Cowgill to convince him? Hard evidence was what he wanted. Lois reviewed what she had just listed in her mind. Ben and Floss were the most likely to be harbouring something useful. If she could get either of them to tell her exactly what had happened to frighten them into silence, she had a hunch things would get moving with Cowgill. She got up from the tree stump, and walked on. Right, next step was to talk to the youngsters. Separately, would be best. Maybe starting with Floss. Perhaps she'd arrange to call in at the Hall when Floss was working there. She could easily think of a convincing pretext.

"Good girl," she said absently, as Jeems squatted on the grass. Lois fumbled in her pocket for a scented pink nappy sack and concentrated on the job in hand.

FORTY-THREE

ॐ

NOW THAT SPOT WAS RESTORED TO HIM, HERBERT Everitt was a different man. Optimism oozed from every pore, and curmudgeonly old William's depression didn't bother him in the least. He had searched the entire house and discovered a number of useful things, including an ancient paraffin stove nearly full of fuel. During the day he opened all the windows to air the place, leaving Spot tied up outside to act as lookout. He found an undamaged blanket for William to drape around his shoulders to keep warm. In the early evening, he lit the paraffin stove and put it in the living room. "Quite cosy?" he said to William.

"Stinks," was the reply.

But Herbert could see that William was trying hard, and so they reached a kind of truce. When William found a stash of tins of food in a cupboard high above the sink, he actually laughed, and the two worked out carefully how long this would last them. They reckoned they could exist on iron rations for a week or ten days. By then, Herbert insisted, someone would come and rescue them.

"You're enjoying this, aren't you, Bert?" William said, as they sat at the rickety table drinking perfectly good pea soup.

"Always been my favourite, pea soup," Herbert replied. He had given up demanding William call him by his full name. Anyway, now he was getting used to it, Bert seemed more friendly.

"No, no . . . I meant enjoying all of it. It's all one big adventure to you. The Terrible Two go hiding in the thicket. Find a stash of food, and manage to keep going until Uncle and Auntie find them and take them home."

Herbert looked at him. "That's good, Bill," he said. "Very clever. But Uncle and Auntie are more likely to be Reg and his henchmen, so we'd better make a plan for what we'll do if they turn up before help comes."

He cleared the dishes, and put a damp notebook on the table. The pencil William had found on the floor in the small bedroom still worked. "Now," Herbert said. "First of all . . ."

"I said you were enjoying it," grumbled William, but he sat up straight and listened to what Herbert had to say.

At this point, Spot barked ferociously outside. "Hide!" said Herbert. "I'll take a look." He crept round to the window, keeping out of sight, and peered out. Spot was straining at his rope lead, and aiming his warning at a thick thorn bush very close to the back door. Herbert continued to watch. Then he thought he saw a shadow move and disappear. Spot stopped barking after a minute, and

Herbert went back to William. "You can come out now," he said, and William crawled from under the table. "We're unlikely to be bombed," Herbert said with a smile.

"What was it, then?"

"A rabbit, probably," Herbert replied. "No sign of human beings of any sort. "Right," he continued, "let's get on with the plan."

GRAN WAS IN A BETTER MOOD WHEN LOIS RETURNED home. She'd had a visit from Mrs. Pickering and they'd obviously enjoyed one another's company. "What did she come for?" said Lois, antennae waving.

"It was all to do with WI, and nothing to do with New Brooms," Gran said firmly. "Mrs. Pickering and me have agreed to do teas next month at the group meeting."

"Did she say anything about Floss?" Lois said casually.

Gran frowned at her. "Only that she really loved working for you, if that's what you want to hear."

"Well, it's nice to know, Mum. I like my team to be happy."

They moved on to the subject of whether Jeems had had her feet wiped after running about in those muddy fields. While Lois was obediently drying a wriggling dog, Gran said, "Oh, there was something that might interest you. Apparently Floss and Ben are getting engaged. Well, talking about it, anyway. Floss's parents are insisting that they wait at least two years before even thinking about getting married, but otherwise they've given their blessing."

"Floss hasn't said anything to me!" Lois felt quite hurt that Gran had known first.

"Maybe that's because you're so busy with other things," her mother answered. "Anyway, I should congratulate her as soon as possible, if I were you. Apparently they're talking about moving away soon, somewhere where Ben can get a proper job."

This bombshell galvanized Lois into action. She dialled Floss's mobile and waited. "Hello? Mrs. M here. Are you still at Mrs. T-J's?" Floss replied that yes, she would be there for a while, having found a message on the table that the mistress would be back soon and would like everywhere spick and span. The gardener, apparently, had a key and had left the message, together with muddy footprints and finger marks everywhere.

"I'll be over in ten minutes," Lois said. "Look out for me. No, nothing wrong, I just want to have a word. See you."

Lois was there in fifteen minutes. She sounded her horn to attract Floss's attention and went to the back door. "Thanks. Better lock it behind me," Lois said, walking into the kitchen. "Shall we go and sit in the drawing room? The sun shines in there in the afternoons, and we've got something pleasant to talk about, haven't we?"

Floss led the way, and they settled into comfortable chairs. Floss grinned broadly, and said, "I bet I know who told you. It was your mum, wasn't it. My mum told yours, and the cat was out of the bag. I was looking forward to telling you myself, but never mind."

"Go on, then, tell me," Lois said. "It'd be nice to hear it straight from you."

"Well, Ben and I are engaged. We haven't got a ring yet. We're going to look for one next Saturday. Can't be a diamond or anything expensive! Ben's not got much money yet, but one day he will have. Mum and Dad have agreed, and Ben's folks say they're delighted, though I'm not so sure about his mum."

"Mothers and sons," said Lois enigmatically. "Always difficult."

"So there we are, Mrs. M. I wish I could have told you first, but I hope you approve."

Lois stood up, walked over to Floss, and gave her a big hug. "Congratulations!" she said. "Nothing could be nicer. You'll be the first romance we've had in the New Brooms team. Will you be able to tell the rest on Monday?"

"Oh, yeah. Looking forward to it. I expect we'll get teased a bit, but they're a nice lot and I'm fond of them. Even Bill! Ben's a good friend of his now, so no jealousy there!"

"Bill and Ben, the Flowerpot Men," said Lois, and Floss looked puzzled. Not worth explaining, thought Lois, and said, "Come on, then, now I'm here I'll give you a hand. What's left to do?"

"Landings and stairs," Floss said. "I'll finish the kitchen. Thanks a lot."

Lois lugged the heavy old Hoover up the stairs and began cleaning the landings. The carpet was threadbare here and there, and she had to stop and disentangle bits of thread from the machine. When she straightened up, a shaft of sunlight had appeared through the window at the end of the corridor. She blinked. It couldn't have been!

"Floss!" she called.

"Yes?" The girl's voice came from downstairs.

Lois yelled back, "Nothing. Thought I heard you shout." She'd heard nothing, but had seen something. The swiftly crossing figure of a man, emerging from one door and disappearing into another, had passed through the sunlight. It was a familiar figure, and Lois's heart sank to her boots.

Should she go and look, or leave well alone? She had no desire to meet Reg Abthorpe again, particularly as she was on her own with not even a small dog to defend her. But . . . She grasped the Hoover, and with the motor running, pushed it to the end of the corridor. Leaving it switched on, she tried the handles of both doors in turn. Both were locked. How had he . . . ? Unwilling to consider the possibility of a ghost, Lois went back to the stairs and quickly finished her cleaning.

"All done, then," Floss said, and the two walked towards their cars.

Lois asked, "Ever seen anything in this place? Are there any stories of ghosts?"

Floss laughed. "Oh God, yes. I think I saw one myself once. Looked like a man flitting across the corridor upstairs. Saw him outlined against that window at the end. But he didn't stop to talk. Shame, really. Anyway, thanks for coming over and being so nice. Cheers, Mrs. M."

For a while after Floss had driven off, Lois sat in her car and thought. It was no ghost, she was sure. Was this a clue to where Reg Abthorpe was holed up? But surely Mrs. T-J wouldn't . . . wasn't . . . no, of course she wasn't. Lois drove off, narrowly missing a cock pheasant too tame to get out of the way.

FORTY-FOUR

FRANCES WALLIS STOOD BEHIND HER NET CURTAINS, keeping lookout in Blackberry Gardens. She had switched off all the lights in the house, as instructed. Reg should be back soon, and then she could draw the curtains, put on the lights, and let some normality back into her dark and dismal home. If only she could get out of this village, this country, even, and begin to live a quiet, unbothered life. Alone. She wouldn't care if she never saw her husband again, or Reg, come to that. It wasn't as if Reg was her real brother. He'd traced her after a long search, and broken the news that they both had the same father, but different mothers. "Spread it around, he did," Reg had said with a laugh. "I reckon I take after my mum. I don't know about you?"

"Not sure," Frances had said, carefully not telling him the identity of her mother, which he clearly wanted to know. Reg had stayed in touch, become very friendly with her husband, and then suggested they should work together at his little schemes. He said he'd found a really nice house for them in a lovely village. It had turned out to be this village, of all villages. Reg could be nice as pie, and then change in seconds to a cruel, unprincipled crook. If he took after his mother, then Frances hoped she would never meet her. He scarcely ever spoke of her, but when he did, it was with contempt and bitterness.

Now the back door slammed shut. Frances turned and heard Reg shout, "I'm back. Where's supper?"

Frances remembered the times when Reg's visits had concerned just foxes and badgers, baiting and fighting. But all that seemed to have stopped. Those horrible terriers hadn't been out for ages. They were bred for the job, and were difficult to control. Reg had been in court for badger-baiting once, and was forbidden to keep dogs. So he'd parked them on Frances, who kept them tied up most of the time. When they were freed and taken out by Reg, they went mad.

"Help me draw the curtains," she answered, and the two went round the house drawing all the curtains before switching on subdued lighting. "How much longer is all this going to take?" Frances said. "I'm fed up with living like a recluse."

"Like to join the Women's Institute, would you? Sing in the church choir?" Reg's smile was without warmth.

Frances shivered. "Well, as a matter of fact, yes, I would. But there's no chance as long as you and those villains of yours are creeping about."

"And what would hubby say? Have you mentioned it to him, maybe suggested he should join the Whist Club? I can guess what he would say. Would you like me to mention it to him?"

Frances looked at him with hatred. "Don't you dare!" she said. "Mind your own bloody business for once. And get going out of here as soon as bloody well possible!"

"Language!" Reg mocked. "I'll go as soon as I'm ready, sister dear, and not before," he said, and went upstairs whistling.

* * *

DEREK HAD RELUCTANTLY AGREED TO LOIS MEETING
Cowgill at the shop. "Only very occasionally, Lois," he'd
cautioned. "It's bad enough you doing this ferreting, but
I'm not having our Josie involved. Is that clear?" Lois
had nodded, and consulted Josie. Her partner had not
seemed to care much, apart from suggesting in jest that
they charged rent to the cops. Josie had said what a good
idea, and that it would stop Cowgill turning up at all
hours. "Of course, I'll warn you when he's coming," Lois
had said. "It won't be often, I can promise you that!"

She wondered if it would be worth arranging a meeting straight away, but she had nothing more in the way
of hard evidence to persuade him to take the disappearance of the old men more seriously . . . except her encounter at the farmhouse with Reg and his trusty
helpers. She was reluctant to tell him about that, as she
hadn't come out of it very well, especially having to be
rescued by Derek. Still, no ordinary estate agent, let
alone a posse of villains, would have chased her through
the woods if the offer to show her the house had been
genuine.

She went into her office and dialled Cowgill's private
number. He had given her permission to use it, and sometimes in the evenings he sat in his lonely sitting room,
bored with television, willing the phone to ring. So far, it
had never been Lois at the other end.

"Hello? It's me."

"Evening, Lois. How are you?"

"Fine. I'll make this short and sweet. I've fixed a new
place for us to meet." She told him about the shop, and he
said facetiously that he was glad she would have her
daughter as chaperone upstairs. "Now listen," said Lois,
irritated. "One foot put wrong, and you're out on your
ear."

Cowgill reflected that nobody ever spoke to him like
that any more, and how grateful he was to have Lois.
Well, in a manner of speaking. "So name the day," he
said.

"I'm warning you!" Lois said. "I can be there in the

room at the back of the shop tomorrow at six o'clock. And don't be early, otherwise Josie won't have closed up." She continued with instructions as to how he should arrive, and told him to park his car the other side of the village. "Leave it by the disused gravel pits," she said. "Nobody ever goes there, since a child drowned a few years ago. There's an old footpath from there."

"Right. Any further orders, Mrs. Meade?"

"Be your age, for goodness sake. I don't know which is worse—Cowgill the professional cop, or Cowgill the joker. No, there's nothing else."

"How about Cowgill the serious policeman, with a soft spot for one of his informers?"

"Not him, definitely. I'm going now. See you tomorrow."

In the house in the thicket, Herbert Everitt had found some mouldering books on a bedroom shelf, and had carried a few downstairs to see if there was anything interesting in them. "What've you got there, Bert?" Cox was dozing in a chair that Herbert had contrived to make more comfortable, with old blankets and a cushion or two he had dried out by the oil stove.

"Old books. They smell a bit. Gone mouldy, some of 'em. Still, here, take a look. There might be something interesting." Herbert handed over a small pile, and William took one and opened it.

"*On The Road*," he read, "by somebody called Jack Kerouac. Blimey, how do you pronounce that?" He read halfway down the first page and then shut it with a cloud of white dust. "Not my kind o' book," he said. "Nor yours either, I reckon, Bert."

Herbert opened another one, and said, "Here, this looks more like it. It's a book about wild animals."

"Afraid I couldn't care less about lions and tigers," William answered.

"Not those kind of wild animals. It's all in this country—rabbits and mice and voles and squirrels. All that."

William brightened. "Has it got badgers in it?" he said.

"Don't talk to me about badgers," Herbert said. "Badgers are responsible for me being in this mess."

"Not the badgers' fault, was it? Wasn't it your Spot led you into the woods, so you saw them crooks at the baiting?" Herbert had to admit that this was the case. He gave the book to William, who immediately looked up badgers and became totally absorbed.

The other books were mostly American novels, and Herbert was not interested. Then he found a thriller, set in Scotland, and put it to one side. "That'll do me," he said. "Take my mind off survival for an hour or two."

William looked at him for a few seconds, and then said, "I've been thinking, Bert."

"Always a dangerous occupation." Herbert grinned.

"No, seriously," William continued. "I've been thinking that we could walk out of here and go home, and once we'd told the police we'd not have to be afraid any longer. Doesn't that make sense?"

Herbert's smile faded. He sighed. "You could be right, Bill," he said. "It might work. But there's something I was keeping to myself. All the time we've been here, I felt we were being watched. Twice I've seen the shadow of a man disappearing back into the thicket. Spot barks furiously every time, and I suppose that lets him know we're still here."

William got painfully to his feet. "Why the hell didn't you call to him? It might have been someone looking for us, coming to rescue us! Oh God, why didn't you yell at him?" He sat down again and covered his face with his hands.

"Don't take on," Herbert said, and awkwardly patted William on the shoulder. "I didn't call to the man, because I recognized him. It was that Reg. The boss man. He has somehow found out where we are, and is keeping an eye on us. I dare say it suits him to have us holed up here. Costs him nothing, and keeps us out of the way until he finishes whatever wicked scheme he's got going."

"You mean it's not just the badgers?" William uncovered his face and stared at Herbert. "What else is he up to, then?"

"What else is there? What are all the likes of him up to? Money. That's what he's after, I'm sure. Though I'm not certain how he plans to get hold of it. You got any ideas?"

William looked shifty. He shook his head. "No idea," he said. "He came here from nowhere, and bullied me into allowing the badger-baiting. That was all. Never mentioned money." He turned away and studiously read his book. Herbert left the room and stood at the kitchen window, looking out at the dense thicket. He sighed again. William was lying, he knew for certain. But why?

FRANCES WALLIS HAD GONE EARLY TO BED. REG HAD stayed in his room, listening to his favourite music from the sixties. She had quite liked it at first, but quickly became bored with the same old songs over and over again. She pulled the covers over her head and tried to get to sleep. Her husband was away on a long driving trip, and she was alone in the house with Reg.

Sleep would not come, so she sat up and reached for a book. But she couldn't concentrate. Perhaps she would go down and make a cup of tea, but that would risk disturbing Reg, and she didn't want that. Her thoughts went round and round and she realized she had read the same page three times without taking in any of it.

Reg had told her only the bare details of what he wanted from her, and she had little idea of what he was up to. She'd had enough of it, and decided to make a plan. She was sick of being at his beck and call, of telling lies and acting like a gangster's moll—without the fun! No, it had to come to an end somehow, and an idea began to form in her head. She switched off the light, settled back under the covers, and began to think. First, she had to find out as much as she could about what was really happening. What were the secrets, the transparent lies, that he had told her? Where were the gaps in his stories? The two most obvious were, first, old Mr. Everitt's sudden decision to go into a home, when there was clearly no need for him to do so. Reg had spun her some tale about advancing senility and not safe to be living alone. But was that really so? Then, on one of her rare outings to Tresham, she had passed old Cox's Farm and it was up for sale. When she asked Reg what he would do, now that there would be a new owner, and very likely one that was opposed to the badger business, he had said that he would soon find another suitable farmer. Most of them with livestock were anxious to get rid of the diseased little buggers, spreading tuberculosis. His words. William Cox, he said, had finally accepted he was too old and disabled to run the farm, and decided to sell. He'd already gone off to sheltered accommodation. "Same place as Herbert Everitt?" she'd suggested.

"No business of yours," Reg had snapped.

So where *had* William Cox gone?

With a plan of action, and plenty to find out, Frances cheered up. She would begin tomorrow. Reg would find out that she could be equally devious. Perhaps it ran in the family, she thought, and smothered a chuckle. In no time at all she fell asleep.

FORTY-FIVE

⁂

LOIS WAS HAVING SECOND THOUGHTS. HAD SHE been wise to suggest the shop for meeting Cowgill? One of her reasons had been that Derek would no longer worry about the possibility that she might be having a bit of the other with the cop he so disliked. In spite of the fact that she had been working with Cowgill for years now, Derek was still suspicious, though he hid it successfully most of the time.

Now, as she checked the time on the kitchen clock and reached for her jacket, she was not so sure. Up to now, she had kept her ferretin' more or less separate from the family, but by fixing up the shop rendezvous she had brought it slap into the family's midst. Ah well, it was worth a try, and if it didn't work, they could easily find some other place.

"Just off to see Josie," she said to Gran. Only Josie and her partner, and Derek of course, were to know about the meetings. "Tell Gran, and you tell the whole village," Lois had said.

Once more, Derek was reluctant. "I'm not telling no lies for that bugger," he said.

"You won't have to," she had assured him. "You won't have to say anything."

The blinds were down on the shop windows, and Lois opened the side gate to walk round to the back. Cowgill stood there, and as he saw her his face lit up. "Ah, there you are, Lois. This seems like a good idea."

"Yes, well, we'll see," she said, and knocked lightly on the door. It was ajar, and she pushed it open. "Josie? It's Mum. OK for us to come in?"

Josie appeared, unsmiling. "There's a couple of chairs there. Give me a shout, Mum, when you're going, and I'll lock up after you. We have to shoot all the bolts. You never know when villains will break in." She looked pointedly at Cowgill, then turned around and disappeared, shutting the door with a bang.

"Ah," Cowgill said. "Do I gather your daughter does not altogether approve?"

"She's OK. Just wants us out of here as quickly as possible. But Derek approves, and nobody else knows. Now, shall I start?" Cowgill nodded. Lois did not know that he had had a word with Derek, and assured him that, contrary to appearances, this was part of his plan to wean Lois away from her work with the police. With him, specifically. Derek had grudgingly agreed. Cowgill sat down on one of the uncomfortable chairs Josie had provided.

Lois gave him all the details of her abortive inspection of William Cox's house and did not spare herself. "If it hadn't have been for Derek, I don't know what would have happened. I was an idiot to think I could spy without them looking around and seeing me."

"I wonder if you were a bit hasty, Lois," Cowgill said cautiously. "It could have been a perfectly genuine meeting, and the people with the estate agent were perhaps other clients looking at the house?"

"And they all decided to chase a woman innocently walking in the woods? Pull the other one, Cowgill."

He smiled at her, and said, "You know my name is Hunter."

"Bad luck for you, but I can't help that," Lois snapped. "So you don't believe me?" she added, standing up.

"Sit down, please, and listen," Cowgill said, and now his voice was gently authoritative. "Of course I believe you. I believe every word of your account of what happened. It is just that at moments when we are expecting something nasty to happen, we sometimes misinterpret what actually happens. They could have thought you were in trouble and needed help, or—"

Lois interrupted him sharply. "Oh, come on, Cowgill," she said. "I'm not stupid. I know when crooks mean business, and that lot certainly did."

"Right," he answered. "Let's leave that for the moment. I wanted to tell you that we are following up the sale of Cox's Farmhouse, and the whereabouts of Cox himself. We went to the estate agent's office, and it wasn't there. Empty. None of the surrounding neighbours knew anything about them, except that they had hardly arrived in the premises before they disappeared again. I then sent one of our lads to look at the property itself, and the For Sale sign had gone. Now, either the agent's business has gone bust, or they have sold the farmhouse and decided to move on to a more lucrative district. There was no sign of William Cox, so he's safely in an old folks' home somewhere. I don't think we need to worry about him."

"So what *are* we worrying about? Still not caught the serial rapist in Tresham? I bet you haven't given a thought to old Everitt. He's safely in another old folks' home, is he? And what about Reg Abthorpe? I am certain he was among that group of louts at the farm."

"We still have Mr. Abthorpe on file, and are proceeding with enquiries."

Lois groaned. "I think we're wasting time here," she said. "I don't know what it takes to convince you that much worse than badger-baiting is going on. By the way, have you been out trying to catch them at it?"

"No evidence of any baiting going on at the present time," Cowgill said. "Plenty of signs of past activity, but nothing new."

A gentle knock at the door interrupted them. "Come in, Josie," Lois said wearily.

"Are you nearly finished? I need to get some stock from the shelves."

"We're finished, thanks. I'll let you go first," she said to Cowgill, indicating the back door. Then she turned to Josie, and added, "I don't think we'll be needing this room again, love. But thanks anyway."

After both had gone, and the lights were out, a shadow moved along the overgrown footpath behind the shop. It was Reg Abthorpe, returning to Blackberry Gardens by an interconnecting network of footpaths that hadn't been used for years. He had watched the cop and that woman leaving separately, and could scarcely smother a laugh. My God, couldn't they do better than that? But there was a serious point here, he reminded himself. Mrs. New Brooms Meade was still ferreting, and reporting back to the cops. Something would have to be done about that.

*   *   *

"So how did it go?" Derek said, when they were alone in the sitting room. It was WI tonight, and Gran was a faithful member.

Lois shook her head. "Waste of bloody time," she said.

"Lois! It's not ladylike to swear."

"You do," she countered.

"I'm not a lady. But let's not get into an argument. Why was it a waste of time?"

"I just can't get it into his thick head that there's something wrong about Herbert Everitt and William Cox. I know it, but I can't get any help from him. He fobs me off with cops' replies."

"So you're giving up?" Derek was hopeful, but one look at Lois's face gave him his answer. She never gave up.

The speaker at the WI meeting in the village hall had been a good one. After the business of the meeting, including planning for entertainment at next month's group meeting, the president introduced a pleasant, friendly woman who would tell them the story of how she had become interested in quilting, bringing exquisite examples with her. There was a buzz of conversation as tea was prepared, and members clustered round the jewel-bright quilts, stroking them covetously.

Gran was impressed, but not being a needlewoman herself she made room for others and sat down to wait for tea. Ivy Beasley from Round Ringford was next to her, and sniffed when Gran asked politely after her health. "Could be better," she said.

Gran thought she looked hale and hearty, but was sympathetic. "It's old age with me, I'm afraid," she said. "Twinges and aches are constant companions. Specially first thing in the morning."

Miss Beasley did not want to hear about Gran's twinges, and turned the conversation back to herself. "But I have no help in the house," she said. "Not like you with a family around you."

Gran's hackles rose. "You do have one of Lois's cleaners coming in, don't you? Isn't it young Bill?"

Another sniff. "At present, yes," she said. "But I expect he'll be off for a better job once he's a father. Can't support a family on scrubbing floors."

"He has his vet work as well," Gran said. She decided to try a safer subject. "Did you see Cox's Farm is up for sale?" she ventured. "I wonder where the old man has gone. No family round here, I heard."

"I've already told your daughter that I know nothing about it," Ivy Beasley said firmly. "But I'll say this," she added, "William Cox pleaded poverty all his life, but if he is in a home you can be certain he's got the money to pay for it. You ask Ellen Biggs. She'll tell you." Ivy looked towards the kitchen. "Where's our tea, then? Ah, here it comes. Nab a piece of that chocolate sponge for me, will you? Good. Thanks." And that was that. Ivy's mouth was full of cake, and Gran heard no more.

When she got home, Gran relayed word-for-word what had happened at the meeting, what the speaker had said, and the president's vote of thanks, and her conversation with Ivy Beasley. Lois had been interested in her mother's description of an amazing quilt in black and gold, hung up like a shining banner on a frame. Then she heard Ivy Beasley's name, and pricked up her ears. So Ivy had told Gran to ask Ellen Biggs. Had Ivy been trying to pass on a hint to Lois? Something more about those early days when Ellen's sister was the unhappy bride of a faithless young farmer?

Lois did not need telling twice, and planned a visit to the hospital tomorrow morning.

FORTY-SIX

❧

"OH, I'M SORRY, MRS. MEADE," THE NURSE SAID. "I am glad you rang and saved yourself a wasted journey." Lois' heart missed a beat, but the nurse's next words reassured her. "Ellen went home yesterday. We shall be keeping a close eye on her from here, but she was so anxious to get back to her own home. She has good friends to look after her, and will be having plenty of help from Social Services."

And from me, Lois thought. She told Gran she would be out all morning, and decided to call on Miss Beasley before seeing Ellen Biggs. Ivy would certainly be up to date with any news about Ellen, and it was as well to be prepared. Bill should be there this morning, and Ivy would be in a good mood.

"D' you want to bet on it?" Gran said drily. "That woman's moods are a mystery to man and beast. Still, you might be lucky."

It was raining hard as Lois drove through the narrow lanes to Round Ringford. At intervals, the old ash trees had meshed their branches and formed a tunnel over the road. It was twilight gloom, and the heavy drops banged on the van's thin roof. Not a good day for someone living in a tiny lodge house with small windows and diamond panes. Light was always dim in Ellen's house, and Lois hoped she was not sitting miserably in the dark, saving electricity.

But first Ivy Beasley. Bill's car was outside Victoria Villa, and Lois touched the doorbell lightly. "Hi, Mrs.

M!" Bill sounded relieved to see her. Ivy *not* in a good mood, then.

"Is Miss Beasley in? Could I have a few words with her?"

Bill winked at her. "I'll just go and ask," he said. Lois heard a short conversation and then Bill reappeared. "Miss Beasley is willing to receive you," he said in a near whisper, so only Lois could possibly hear.

"That's quite enough of that!" Ivy's voice was loud and clear.

"Ooops!" said Bill, and led the way.

"Good morning, Miss Beasley," Lois said. "How are you this morning?"

"Never mind that," said Ivy. "Have you come to see Bill or me? And get on with it, because I've got things to do."

"I was on my way to call on Mrs. Biggs," Lois said firmly. "But I thought I would look in to see if you had any news of her that I should know before I go. You are her greatest friend, I believe?" Flattery will get you everywhere, Lois hoped.

"I don't know about that," Ivy replied, softening. "But I have known her a very long time. Yes, she's home, but frail. Quite a change since I last saw her. She'll need looking after, Mrs. Meade. Still the same obstinate old woman, though, and that should keep her going."

"Thank you," Lois said. "I'll be off then. I don't want to interrupt you when you're busy." She turned to go, but Miss Beasley put up her hand.

"Don't be in such a hurry!" she said. "I thought of something that would interest you, and now I can't call it to mind. Bill," she added, "make your boss a cup of coffee . . ." She turned to Lois and said, "That'll give me time to remember. Pull up a chair."

Crumbs, thought Lois, what did I do right? But she obediently sat down, hoping that Ivy's memory would concern William Cox. Time passed. Ten minutes later, they were still exchanging trivialities about village affairs, and Lois said, "I really must get round to see Ellen now. It's been nice talking to you."

"Hold on," said Ivy. "It's coming back to me. Yes . . . it was about that sister of Ellen's. Poor silly Martha. I remember it was the talk of the village at the time. When she died, I mean. They had a girl working for them at the farm, a cross between char and housekeeper. Martha was so useless, and spent a lot of time in Tresham, meeting old friends and spending William's money. So this girl was there several days a week. Lived in the village, at the pub. She was the daughter of the people running it at that time. There was talk, of course, everybody knowing William's reputation! Then she left suddenly, and disappeared. The pub people said she'd got a job in Essex, but we never saw her again. Shortly after that, Martha began to sicken, and it wasn't long before we were following her coffin to the church. Thought you'd like to know," she added, "because I wasn't born yesterday, Mrs. Meade, and I know what you're still up to. Right. Tell Ellen I'll be down with Doris to see her later. Bill! Show Mrs. Meade out, there's a good lad."

At the door, Lois couldn't resist. "Bye, my good lad," she said, and walked swiftly down the path.

She sat in her car for a few minutes, thinking over what Ivy had just said. A girl from the pub. That publican and his family would have gone long since. But Ellen might remember them. Lois started her engine and drove slowly round the corner and up the lane to The Lodge.

"So what is it this time?" Ivy said to Bill. "She's much too nosey, your Mrs. Meade. Still, if it helps solve some unpleasant mystery, then I'm prepared to help. I know it's to do with William Cox and his poor wife, but what exactly?"

Bill shook his head. "No idea, Miss Beasley," he said truthfully. "Mrs. Meade doesn't confide in me about private matters like that."

"Nonsense!" Ivy actually grinned. "I know New Brooms' team are all on the snoop. Ideally placed, in and out of people's houses. Still, I won't ask you again. I'll mind my own business, as always." This, coming from Ringford's arch-gossip, was rich, and Bill went back to finish the little bathroom with a smile on his face.

By the time Lois had parked in the entrance to a field, bumping over the ruts and hoping her van would stand up to it, the rain had eased off. There was a fine drizzle now, and she stepped smartly over to the Lodge, avoiding puddles and heaps of horse manure. More horses than people in Ringford, she knew, and not too particular where they dropped their dollops. She reached the arched front door, and before she could knock, Ellen stood there, smiling broadly. "I thought it was you, making a fist of parking over there," she said.

"Is that all the thanks I get for turning out in the storm to come and see you?" Lois was smiling too. Ellen laughed her fruity laugh, and, taking Lois by the hand, drew her into the dark little sitting room. Lois lowered her into a chair. "Now, you sit down, Ellen, and I'll make us a cup of tea."

"Coffee for me, please," said Ellen, and relaxed in her usual armchair. Lois knew that she could not be feeling quite herself, otherwise she would have objected violently to anyone using her kitchen. "There's cake in the tins!" Ellen shouted. "People have been and brought me so much cake I could set up a stall at the Bring and Buy all by myself!"

Lois returned in a few minutes with coffee and cake, and sat down. "So, you've had visitors. That's nice, isn't it?"

"It's nice when Doris Ashbourne comes," Ellen said, "but not so good when Ivy hobbles down with her. That woman could fill the cemetery single-handed. Talk about depressed! If you weren't suicidal before she arrived, you certainly would be by the time she went!"

"I've just been to see her," Lois said. "She and Doris are coming down later to see you're all right. Something to look forward to . . ."

Ellen grimaced. "Thanks for the good news," she said. "But let's forget them. How are you, me dear, and that lovely family of yours. How's your Josie getting on in the shop?"

"Fine. She loves it, and my mother helps out a lot. It's the gossip that *she* loves. Still, it means Josie can go off to the warehouse, and do some deliveries. It's hard work, running a shop. And with the post office too, she never has a minute to herself." Lois paused, and Ellen nodded but didn't speak. Another sign that she was still not quite tickety-boo. "But Josie doesn't seem to mind. I must say, I like a girl who's not afraid of hard work. They're a bit rare these days, not like old times when all the family had to buckle to and bring in some money."

"Well, I certainly did," Ellen said, following Lois's trail. "I was a kitchen maid at fourteen. Lowest of the low, dealing with anything from spilled soup to cockroaches. Now, my sister, she was altogether different. Martha got this idea she was a lady, and wouldn't soil 'er lily-white hands! She wasn't the slave she let people think she was."

"But on the farm she must have helped?"

Ellen laughed. "Hated the smell of cows and getting 'er feet wet. And she was forever telling the men to leave their muddy boots outside. Well, you know what farmers are, and William Cox was no different. They 'ad row after row, and Martha would go to what she called her 'sewing room,' though she never did any sewing, and sit and sulk. Eventually they got a girl from the pub to help out, but that made things worse, 'im bein' what he was."

"What happened to the girl?"

"God knows," Ellen said. "She was no better than she should be, and worked in the bar at the pub in the evenings. Got what she deserved, I dare say."

"And what was that?" said Lois, holding her breath.

"What they all get," Ellen said. "A bun in the oven. And served her right. Her mum and dad were respectable people, and they sent her away. Never saw her again, though they missed her in the bar! The men did, anyway."

"Do you remember her name? Do her parents still live in the village?"

Ellen shook her head. "No, they moved away when they retired. It's a while ago now, and I can't remember the name. I wasn't one for going to the pub . . . I wouldn't have minded, but girls didn't go to the pub at all in those days." She frowned, in an effort to recall the publican and his wife. "I tell you who might know," she said, brightening. "Doris Ashbourne. She's got a memory like an elephant. Ankles like one, too!"

Ellen's roars of laughter gladdened Lois's heart, and she remembered what she had primarily come for. "Now then, Ellen," she said. "I've been thinking, and for a few weeks I've arranged for Sheila Stratford—you know her well—to come in an extra couple of mornings a week to tidy you up and do any jobs you need doing. Just 'til you're better," she added, seeing thunderclouds gather.

"Don't be ridiculous. I can't afford that, and you know it. I shall manage very well with them women from Social Services, and our Doris and Ivy. They come for free!"

"And so will Sheila," Lois said firmly, rising to her feet. "No arguments, Ellen. Sheila's looking forward to it You two'll have lots of memories of the villagers to talk about. No, don't get up. I'll rinse these through, and then I'm off. I'll pop in again soon, and see whether you're being good."

Ellen opened her mouth to object, but then it turned into a yawn, and she realized she was tired. It was very nice of Lois, and she might as well give way, for once. "By the way," she said in a sleepy voice, "if you see William Cox, ask *him* the name of that girl. He'll remember all right."

FORTY-SEVEN

৯১

WILLIAM COX HAD WOKEN UP AT DAWN, AND IN the clear light looked sleepily around the room, seeing the familiar cobwebs on the ceiling, the patches of damp destroying the wallpaper. One of the patches was in the shape of a pig's head . . . no, it was more like a badger, with its piggy snout and long face. He wondered what was happening in his woods. Was Reg still operating his nice little earner, taking fees from bloodthirsty lowlife who wanted a bit of sport? Funny how most of them came from towns and cities. Their idea of country life, maybe? No, they just liked killing, seeing animals fighting, tortured and suffering.

His eyes wandered on round the room, but suddenly he looked back at the badger's head. Now he was not seeing the damp, but under the buckled wallpaper the outline of a door. He got out of bed and went over to the corner where he ran his hands over the unmistakeable outline of a door. The floor was cold, and he returned to pull on his grubby, now smelly, clothes and shoes. He looked around the room. It was too early to rouse Bert. On the rickety table under the window he found one of the pencils Bert had unearthed. With the sharpened end, he pushed it round the door outline, cutting easily through the sodden wallpaper, and tore away soggy strips to reveal, as he'd hoped, a door. His heart sank when he saw a keyhole with no key. But when he turned the handle it opened immediately. A blast of musty air hit him, and he backed away.

After a few gulps, he returned and peered in. It was pitch dark, and he could see nothing.

"Bill?" It was Bert, walking bleary-eyed into the room. "I heard you moving . . . what the hell is that?"

"What it looks like. Another room. But it was papered over. I've looked in, but can see bugger-all."

Herbert put his head inside the musty darkness, and stayed there for a few minutes until his eyes adjusted. "There's a window over there," he said. "At least, I can see a window frame, but it's been bricked up. We'd better find a light."

William didn't move. "I know what it is," he said. "My grandmother used to have a room like this in her old house. The dark chamber, they used to call it. Been bricked up at the time of the window tax. They used to put all kinds of junk in there, and when she died we found things from a hundred or more years ago.

"Right," said Herbert, unimpressed. "Well, if we're going to find hidden treasure, we'd better find a light. Come on. No good standing there shivering."

They went downstairs fast, too fast for William, who slipped and ended up on the bottom step on his rump. He struggled painfully to his feet, and Bert took one look at him and walked over to put on the kettle. "We'll have a spot of breakfast first," he said. "Plenty of time. That's the one thing we *have* got plenty of."

OUTSIDE IN THE THICKET, EYES WATCHED THE FIGURE at the window. It was very early, and Reg had not expected the old codgers to be about. The dog was not out yet, either. This could be a good thing, he reckoned, stroking the cool metal of the gun in his pocket. He had decided it was time they were back under his care, after all. That old Everitt was too resourceful, and might even have spotted him. He had planned to take them by surprise when they were still in bed, but this could be a better way. Once he saw that Everitt was dressed, he could grab them and force them back to their luxury apartments at gun point. Nobody would be about at this hour, and they'd be up and ready to go without hanging about.

Half an hour passed, and he reckoned it was safe to move.

FRANCES WALLIS WAS ALSO UP EARLY. SHE HAD HEARD Reg leaving the house at least an hour ago, and although it was only a chilly dawn light, she had been unable to get back to sleep. She'd tried the bedside radio, very low so that she could hardly hear it. This usually did the trick, especially if it was some boring programme about world economics. Radio 4 did not kick in until five thirty, and up until then the BBC World Service brought news to and from far-away places. Fine for people on night shifts, and excellent for insomniacs.

Downstairs in the kitchen there were no traces of Reg. He must have gone out without so much as a cup of tea. What was it this time? Some nasty, secret errand. God, how she disliked him, even if he was her half-brother! She put on the kettle and turned to find milk in the fridge. The doorbell rang, and she froze. Who on earth? She put out all the lights, and then crept into the dining room to peer from behind the net curtains. It was Shorty. She didn't know his real name, and didn't want to. Backing quickly out of sight, her heart beating fast, she retreated to the stairs. Reg had locked up securely, she was sure of that. All she needed to do was get back into bed, and Shorty would go away.

He didn't. He rang the bell and kept his finger on it. Frances put her fingers in her ears and pulled the bed covers over her head. The shrill bell penetrated, even so. Well, the battery would run out sooner or later. Then it stopped, and she heard Shorty's footsteps on the gravelled drive. But he was only going round to the back of the house, and she heard banging and crunching as he pulled a ladder out of the garden shed.

That's enough, Frances decided. She got out of bed and marched to the back bedroom. Flinging open the window, she shouted, "What the bloody hell do you think you're doing!"

Shorty looked up, smiling. "Ah, Frances," he said. "Can't y' sleep?"

"Don't try being funny! Just bugger off."

He shook his head. "Let me in, Frances," he said, now unsmiling. "I want to talk t' you about Reg. Me and Nelly have decided to do somethin' about him. He's bloody mad, and we're getting out. But he owes us a lot o' money. We reckon you can help us."

"I've got no money, so get out of here before I call the police."

"Reg wouldn't like that, Frances," Shorty warned. "Anyway, we don't want *your* money. We want t' get him somewhere safe, wivout his gun, and persuade him to pay up. We're good at persuadin'." His upturned face was white in the early morning light, and his grin more evil than usual.

Frances was silent, thinking. If those two idiots could pull it off, with her help they might be able to get rid of Reg Abthorpe for good. She had nothing to lose. Yesterday's post had brought a card from her husband saying he would not be back for a while, as he had to stay out of the country. He sent his love, which she did not want, and she put the card in the bin. Nothing to lose, then. She leaned out of the window, and said in a whisper, "Hey, Romeo, wait there and I'll let you in. And no funny stuff, because Reg is not the only one with a gun."

"We'll sit in the kitchen," she said, pulling Shorty inside. Before she could shut the door, Nelly appeared from nowhere and squeezed in behind. "Don't put the light on!" Frances snapped. "My neighbours are a nosey lot."

"They'll not be up at this hour," said Shorty.

"Doesn't matter. Just do as I say." Frances pulled up the blinds, and the kitchen was dimly lit by the lightening day.

"What's the plan, then?" Frances had no great hopes

for imaginative strategy from these two, but had decided
to listen to what they'd got to say.

Nelly opened his mouth, and shut it again as Shorty
glared at him. "I'll do the talking. Well, it's like this. We
know Reg is living with you—"

"*Lodging* with me," Frances snapped.

"And so we need your help. We got a great place to
take him, where we can give him a goin' over. But we got
to get him there."

"Is that it?" Frances said incredulously. "Your great
plan? Sounds more like wishful thinking to me. Where is
this place, anyway?"

Nelly said, "It's up the . . ." Shorty dug him in the
upper arm with his elbow, and the other winced. "Sorry,
mate," he said.

Shorty turned back to Frances. "We can't tell you now.
Security, an' that. But if you agree to help, we'll give you
the details later."

Frances laughed. "D' you think I was born yesterday?" she said. "Now, straight up, if you don't tell me the
place, you can get out now and don't come back."

She opened the kitchen drawer, which she knew held
nothing more dangerous than wooden spoons, but they
both chorused at once, "All right. We'll tell you!"

Shorty continued, "No need to be hasty. I know we
can trust you." He didn't, but he had no alternative.

"So where is it?" said Frances, her hand still hidden in
the drawer.

"Up at the farm," Shorty said tersely. "A barn at the
back. Nobody knows about it, but Reg's made it into a
lock-up garage for his car, and space for a camp bed.
Nelly's had a spare key cut. Knows a bloke what done it
for us on the nod."

"Does Reg know you know?" Frances was almost
persuaded, and shut the drawer. Reg was clever in his
twisted way, and a barn out of sight at an empty farmhouse, with dark woods creeping up to it, was a great hiding place. She knew something had gone wrong with the
trap for the Meade woman.

Shorty nodded. "Yes. But we don't get asked up there often, and we don't go without bein' asked. Unless we're sure he's not there."

"So, when are you planning to do this?" Frances looked at the kitchen clock, and began to worry that Reg might be back soon.

"Well, that's it. We got to make a date OK with you. You'd have to slip stuff into his goodnight cocoa, and then give us the signal."

"Ain't you forgotten somethink?" Nelly said.

"What?"

"The gun. She'd need to find that and put it where he couldn't find it. He'll be dopey, but not uncon . . . uncon . . . scious."

"Right," said Frances. "You two can get going now. Reg might be back any minute. How can I contact you?"

"Tie a dog lead to the gate. I'll be watching," said Shorty. "Reg won't suspect nothin'. You can say you dropped it and somebody brought it back. I'll come when he's out. No need to say anything except the day and time." He grabbed Nelly's arm, and the fat man winced. It was where Shorty had thumped him. In seconds they were out of the door and disappeared.

Frances sat for another ten minutes, thinking over what her visitors proposed. It could work, she decided. It was worth a try at anything to get rid of Reg. She opened the fridge and took out milk and juice. Helping herself to a generous portion of muesli, she drowned it in milk and began to eat hungrily. A good start to the morning. She prayed that the rest of it would go equally well.

Forty-Eight

ॐ

Reg Abthorpe was uncomfortable. He had been standing motionless for about twenty minutes and had cramp in his foot. He carefully shifted his weight and looked at his watch. There had been no signs of either of the old men in the kitchen. They were probably getting dressed. A good time to strike! He was about to emerge from the thicket when the back door opened. It was Herbert Everitt, and he had his terrier by the collar. He bent down to tie the dog up, but it lifted its head, stared straight at the thicket hiding Reg, and began to bark hysterically.

Herbert looked across in alarm, and the dog pulled away from him, rushing towards Reg. It disappeared into the thicket and there was sudden shouting and growling and more furious barking. Herbert instinctively ran towards his dog, desperate to rescue him, but almost immediately there was a shout of "Get off, y' bugger!" and then the sound of a shot, followed by dead silence.

For one terrifying moment, Herbert was shocked into immobility. Then he turned and scuttled back into the house, slamming and locking the door. Reg followed, limping and cursing, but he was too late. The house was still, with no sounds. Reg consoled himself that he had only to wait. Everitt would not be able to resist coming out again to look for the dog. Best to hide again, this time in a different place, and wait. He limped back and hid behind a thick thorn bush, scratching himself deeply on his arm. He was close to crying. His ankle hurt like hell where the dog had sunk in its teeth, and he knew he should have it treated. But to give up now was to waste time. He would have to start all over again. And anyway, the old men knew he was around now, and would do all they could to keep him out. No, it had to be today. He crouched down and took a look at the ankle. Blood was oozing out fast. He folded up a cleanish handkerchief and bound it round the wound. That would have to do for now.

HERBERT SAT UPSTAIRS ON WILLIE'S BED, HIS HEAD IN his hands, his shoulders heaving.

"Oh, Bert, how could anybody do that?" Willie said, his arm around Herbert's shoulder. "I can only think of one thing to say that might help."

Herbert sniffed hard, and said, "What's that, then?"

"It would've been quick, Bert. Like the fox—a good shot in the head is far kinder than being torn apart by hounds. I never used to think that, but I do now."

Herbert lowered his hands and stared at William. "What if it's not a good shot? Supposing Spot is lying out there in the bushes only half dead, in agony? I'm going to find him," he added, and stood up.

"No, you're not, Bert," William said, pulling him down again. "Just listen to me. If Spot is still alive, and hurt, he'd be whining and calling you. Listen . . ." They were both quiet for a couple of seconds. No sounds from outside. "See? The old boy's in dogs' paradise by now. Special supper of his favourite meat, an' a dog choc to follow. Oh, shit," he added, muttering to himself and rubbing his eyes.

They sat in silence for five or so minutes, and then both spoke at once. "We've got to think now," William said, and Herbert reluctantly suggested they should both make the house as secure as possible and then find a hiding place. Together they stood up, and looked across at the open door leading to the dark chamber.

"That's it, boy," said Herbert. "Everything's locked up

downstairs. He can crash through the windows, o' course. But I reckon Spot had a good go at him, got his jaws round his leg, before he . . . well, until he . . . you know. No, let's get in there and move some of that stuff up against the door. There's heavy trunks in there, and Abthorpe looks a bit of a weed."

"And no windows in there," William said. "Couldn't be better. D' you reckon we should get some water and food?"

Herbert shook his head. "Better stay up here now. I've got water by my bed, and you have, too. Bring that."

William looked embarrassed. "I've got some choco-late biscuits, too. They were in that cupboard over the sink. Gone off a bit, but still edible. I'll get 'em." They collected up these meager supplies and went quickly into the dark chamber, pulling the door shut behind them.

Reg, listening intently from outside, could hear faint sounds of bumping and scraping, and then all was quiet. He decided it was now or never. He'd have to get help with his ankle soon. He emerged from his hiding place into the back yard once more, and limped over to the door. He could hardly put his foot to the ground, but he tried to forget it. The door was locked, of course. He threw his weight against it, but it didn't budge, and he had difficulty in suppressing a scream from the intense pain.

The windows, then. He limped round the house, but all windows were shut and the catches rusty and fixed. He could break the glass, but how would he climb through with his dodgy ankle? He slid down on to his haunches, his back against the wall. Think, Reg, think. He felt dizzy, and after a minute or two of being totally unable to think of anything except the pain, he decided he would have to get back somehow to the farm, and rest up until he could think clearly again. He'd have to ask the two idiots to get some dressings or something similar from the shop. If they had any. Antiseptic cream would be better than nothing. He knew that driving his car was out of the question.

He fell forward on to all fours, and began to crawl across the yard. How are the mighty fallen! he said to himself and went doggedly on, stopping now and again to take deep breaths.

Inside the dark chamber, Herbert and William sat on a box, side by side, eating a stale chocolate biscuit and drinking rationed amounts of water. "If we ever get out of this," Herbert said slowly, "I've been thinking of making a suggestion."

William looked at him. "No good proposing," he said, with a brave effort at a smile. "I'm spoken for already."

Herbert bit his lip. "Close," he said. "My proposal was that you come and live with me in Blackberry Gardens. There's plenty of room for us to keep out of each other's way when necessary. But it'd be companionship. Maybe watch telly together in the evenings. That sort of thing . . ." He tailed off, looking anxiously at William.

"It's a deal, Bert." William replied. "Here," he added, holding out another biscuit. "Half each to clinch it."

FORTY-NINE

ɜ

FRANCES HAD GONE BACK TO BED AFTER HER EARLY morning snack, but she did not sleep. She was thinking hard, and had come up with an idea which, if it worked, would solve all her problems at once. She was not stupid, and knew that Shorty and Nelly had not told her everything. Once Reg was out of the way, they would be back with one thing on their minds. Blackmail. But she could be one step ahead. They were not, after all, the brightest of crooks. She got out of bed and looked at the clock. No sounds of Reg's return, but that meant nothing.

He came and went like a pale shadow, and never told her where he was going or when he would be back.

It would be a good time to make the call, she decided, and picked up the telephone.

LOIS HAD JUST WAVED OFF DEREK ON HIS WAY TO Tresham when the telephone rang. She rushed back into the house, thinking as usual that it must be one of her grown-up children in trouble. Derek was always reminding her they were no longer children, but she couldn't kick the habit.

"Hello? Who's that?" she said.

"Mrs. Meade? Oh, good. It's Frances Wallis here. Blackberry Gardens."

Lois sighed with relief. "Good morning, Mrs. Wallis. What can I do for you?" It would not be a cleaning job, she was pretty sure of that. So what else?

"Well," said Frances, "I'm not sure, but I think I may be able to do something for you. Could you meet me somewhere? Not here, and not at your place. Could we meet by chance across the fields this afternoon?"

Lois was for once taken off balance, and stuttered, "Um, y-y-yes. of course. I won't ask why. Yes, well, fine," she added, regaining confidence. "I shall be out with Jeems at half past two, across the fields, past the sewage works—sorry about that—and along by the river. There's a couple of willow trees where the river bends. I'll wait for you there, but if you are first, don't go away. I shall definitely be there." She was still thinking of Frances as a timid soul, easily frightened off.

"Don't be too late, then," Frances said. "It's very important that I'm not seen talking to you. Must go now." There was a click, and she was gone.

Frances had heard a noise outside, and was sure it was Reg returning. But when she looked out, there was nothing there . . . except a parcel leaning against the back door. She knew the postman had not been. It could only come from one person—or maybe two. She looked at it closely, then touched it with her foot. It was not going to explode. Those idiots were too dim to play the terrorist. She decided to open it, and knew she was right. A dead chicken, headless and ripe, fell out on to the step. There was a note, misspelt and badly written: "Do not blabb! Wotch it." Frances rewrapped the mouldy mess and dumped it in the bin. She went back into the house, laughing derisively.

Reg had managed to make his secret way back to the farm, crawling where possible and limping painfully the rest of the way. It took him a long time, and the last stretch, across a neglected footpath full of stones thrown up by years of ploughing, nearly broke his resolve. He was tempted to lie down and die. But he knew that it would take a long time for a bitten ankle to finish him off, and had staggered on. His two useless henchmen were due to meet him this afternoon, and he meant to be there. As he'd dragged himself along, he made a plan. It would be foolish to stay long in the farm bolt-hole. Sooner or later, probably as a result of betrayal by his faithful pair, the police would arrive. No, he had to think of somewhere else to go, and exactly the right place had come to mind. After dark, Shorty and Nelly could drive him, and nobody need know. First a farewell call on Frances, who knew too much, and then safe seclusion. And how appropriate! Where else would a man in trouble go, but home to Mum . . .

In the dark chamber, Herbert peered at his watch. They were rationing themselves on candlelight, but it took only a second to see that it was noon. "Not really midday in here, is it, Willie," he said.

"Well, I dunno," was the answer, "I think my stomach knows. I could just do with a nice plate of juicy fish and crispy chips."

"Don't!" groaned Herbert. "Don't talk about food. I

reckon if my stomach could speak, it'd be swearing blue murder at us."

Silence. "You know what you just said," William said.

"What?"

"Blue murder."

"Well, what of it? It's just a saying, isn't it?"

William slowly shook his head. "Not to me, Bert," he said. "Not to me."

Herbert wished he could see the other's face. He'd never thought before of how much he could read in people's faces. "You're not going to suggest we finish off that Reg?" He kept his voice light.

"No, not him, though he deserves it. No, I'd better tell you. I've never told anybody else, not all these years."

Herbert was not sure he wanted confidences along these lines, but made encouraging noises. After all, it would pass the time.

"You know I was married once? No? Well, she was a lovely girl. Lived in the village. There were just two of them, two sisters. You'd know the other one. Old Ellen Biggs, her that lives in The Lodge at Ringford."

"No, don't know her. I haven't got around much," Herbert said. "Did she work at the Hall?"

"Ellen worked her way up to cook," William said, "but my Martha was too ladylike for servants' work. Anyway, she was young when I married her. Hadn't had a chance to do much, except snare the handsomest young farmer for miles around."

"You, I suppose?" Herbert laughed, but Wiilliam did not join in.

"We were happy at first," he continued. "I'd have given her whatever she wanted. And did! But after a while, she seemed discontented, always wanting to go out, on shopping trips an' that. And then . . . well, you'll understand . . . she withdrew her favours, if you know what I mean."

"Oh dear," said Herbert, beginning to dread what might be coming next.

"Yes, well, I was a normal bloke with normal appetites. So I had to look elsewhere. I suppose that was the beginning of it—or maybe the end. Of our marriage, anyway."

"She found out?"

"Oh God, yes. The nosey women of the village made sure of that. I don't know why she was so surprised. I should've thought she'd expect it. But she was hit hard. It was a terrible blow to her vanity, I suppose. She'd always been the prettiest girl in the village, you see."

"So were you divorced?"

"No. I offered, but she wouldn't have it. Never had divorce in her family, she said. It would be a disgrace, and she wouldn't consider it. So we soldiered on, living more or less separate lives. I let her get on with it, and she began to lose weight. Her sister tried to get her to eat more, and to go out together, like they used to. But she became practically a recluse. We had the doctor, but he couldn't help. In the end, she just faded away. Faded away, Bert, and I reckon there was only one person who could have stopped it."

"Who?" Herbert spoke very quietly. He could hear that the old man was near to tears.

"Me. I was her husband, and I should've been able to do it."

Herbert said nothing, and after a few minutes William said, "But to get back to murder, the rumour went around the village that I'd done her in. Poison was the favourite weapon with the gossips."

"My God!" said Herbert. "What did you do?"

"Nothing. The more you say, the worse it gets. So I just laid low and said nothing. They forgot it eventually. Ellen Biggs has never forgiven me. She hated my guts anyway. But some of the old biddies are dead, and others are ga-ga. There's always new scandals to gossip about, and the village has left me alone."

They were so quiet, Herbert could hear a blackbird singing from a tree outside. He had no idea what to say, so he said nothing. William blew his nose, and then began to speak.

"I reckon it's lunchtime, Bert," he said. "How about a delicious chocolate biscuit and a drink of water? And then we'd better think what we do next."

FIFTY

~

"Lois," Gran said at lunchtime, "I've offered to look after the shop this afternoon and give Josie time off. The post office is shut anyway. She's worked so hard lately. Beginning to look a bit peaky. I expect you've noticed it, being her mother . . ."

Lois recognized this as criticism, and bristled. "She's a busy woman and so am I," she said. "We don't need to be in one another's pockets to be close."

Gran grinned, knowing she'd hit a bull's eye. "Good," she said. "Well, if you're taking the dog for a walk this afternoon, you could ask Josie if she'd like to come with you."

Lois said nothing, but started washing the dishes. Her mother was a genius at messing things up. She was a wonder and a tower of strength, a brilliant cook and a good grandmother, thoroughly reliable . . . But . . . She could not resist adding her four penn'orth most days, and sometimes it was infuriating.

Gran pushed her to one side, telling her washing-up was her job, and she should go off and telephone Josie. There was nothing for it but to hope that Josie could not come. Lois dialled her number.

"Hello, Mum. What can I do for you?" Lois obediently asked if she would like a walk with Jeems this afternoon. "Thanks, but no," Josie said. "I've seen enough of the soggy fields round Farnden, and I'm off to

Tresham to buy some new clothes. I seem to have been slopping around in these for ever. As Gran said, 'you'll lose your man unless you smarten up.'" Realizing that they had both been manipulated, they hung up in good spirits.

Trudging across the marshy field where shining yellow marsh marigolds flowered in summer, Lois thought of Josie's "soggy fields" and remembered how it had been when they first moved to the village from Tresham. She had felt it was alien country, and it was a while before the slow pace of life and long periods of empty streets seemed anything but dull. But now she grumbled along with everyone else about the rumbling modern farm machinery, shaking the foundations of all the houses. Some people, she knew, never adjusted to country life and had to have regular doses of noisy supermarkets and crowded town centres. Perhaps Josie was going to be one of those.

She was speculating about the rest of her family, and did not realize she had come to the willows. "Here I am," said Frances, popping out from behind one of the trees. She looked around, up and down the river and over to the spinney at the edge of the next field. "I'll make it quick," she said. "Hope you don't mind, but it *is* important."

Jeems sat down on the wet grass. Lois nodded and said, "Carry on." She could not help noticing that Frances seemed like a different woman. There was an air of authority about her. She spoke with confidence, and Lois listened carefully.

"There are things I can't talk about," Frances began. "Just believe me when I say I know what's going on, and I know about your part in it. Now, these are the facts you need to know, and I hope you'll act on them."

Lois said, "Fine," and the other continued.

"Reg Abthorpe is behind it all. The two old men are still alive and in hiding. Two brainless crooks from London work for Reg. They are fed up with him and plan to get rid of him. I shall help. Then the crooks will turn on me. To stop that, I want you to get them. I shall get in touch and at the time and place I tell you, be there with your cop friend. I'll leave the rest to you."

Lois marvelled at how much this woman knew about everything. She saw that Frances was again looking around apprehensively, and said quickly, "When will it be?"

"Can't tell you that, but be ready."

Lois and Frances both saw a figure approaching in the distance. "I'm off," Frances said, and walked away in the opposite direction. Lois loitered, and then had a dog's ball-game to allow the figure to catch up.

"Hi, Josie," she said, "that was a quick shopping trip!"

"Didn't go," Josie said. "I felt bad about turning you down, and decided to come after all."

Lois impulsively gave her a hug, and Jeems barked. "I'm really glad to see you, Josie," she said, and then looked down at her daughter's smart shoes, soaking wet. "Mind you," she added, "you'd have done better to put on your wellies."

"Yes, Mum," Josie said humbly, and as Frances disappeared from sight, Lois made sure they took another route home.

THE CONFERENCE IN THE DARK CHAMBER WAS NOT going well. Neither William nor Herbert could think of anything sensible to do. They suspected that Spot had slowed up Reg, but had no idea of the extent of the injury. They did not even know if Reg was still out there, patiently waiting until they should be forced out by hunger or desperation.

"It'll be hunger, won't it," William said. "I reckon both of us are strong enough to stay here until Reg gets fed up and moves in. Probably with help from his trusty helpers. But after these biscuits are finished and the water gone, we'll have to go down and find something else. Maybe at night, when we'll be pretty sure nobody will be around."

"Reg will expect that." Herbert's voice was dismal. "No, he'll post a watch night and day. Except, o' course," he added, brightening, "so long as we don't have any light, we can probably creep down and get food without him or his crew knowing."

"So shall we try tonight?" William sounded keen. "I don't mind going. I'm used to keeping quiet, stalking animals an' that. You townies haven't got a clue."

Herbert let that pass, and said William was welcome to try. One of them had to go, and the other would have an emergency plan at the ready.

"What emergency plan?" William asked.

"Haven't thought of one yet. Give me time. You can have a little snooze while I think."

"No chance," said William. "I couldn't sleep now, not if I had the best feather bed and a good hot-water bottle. No, I'll shut up while you think."

Several minutes elapsed, and Herbert was amused to hear from William's breathing that he had in fact dozed off. As he listened to the birds outside, he tried hard to imagine normal life going on not a couple of miles from where they were holed up. Blackberry Gardens would be quiet. Nothing much happened there between the rush to work in the mornings and the return home in the evenings. Young Ben opposite would be looking for work and irritating his mother. That strange woman with the terriers would skulk about, peeping from behind net curtains. And those dogs! He had disliked them intensely, hated their barking which set off Spot . . . oh Lord, Spot . . . His eyes filled with tears, and he sniffed hard.

"You all right, Bert?" William had woken up, and heard sounds of distress.

"I'm all right. Still thinking, though."

"Right-o. Tell me when I can speak."

Herbert concentrated on the emergency plan, but his mind returned to the Gardens, and he wondered what had become of his house. It would be full of spiders and mice by now. Probably eaten everything edible. Which meant most things to mice. His fridge would be crawling. Still, nothing that couldn't be put right when he got home. If he got home.

The emergency plan. Well, what was likely to happen? If Willy went down at night in pitch darkness it was unlikely that the watcher, or watchers, would spot him. Spot. There'd be no Spot to bark. He forced his mind back, and imagined the look of the cottage from a watcher's point of view. If they—it would probably be them in the middle of the night—had a torch, they could shine it in at the windows. But they'd only do that if they suspected something. If Willy was as good a stalker as he said, he should get back upstairs safely. The most likely hiccup would be if Willy crashed into something in the dark, or slipped and fell. He might yell involuntarily. Those villains could break in easily, the two of them. So then what?

Herbert was sure that they'd have instructions to capture and not kill, and would force him and Willy back to wherever it was they'd been captive, and then Reg would carry out whatever he had in store for them. What was it, for God's sake? The longer he kept them around Farnden, the more likely he was to be discovered. He had to ask Willy some difficult questions.

"You awake, Willy?"

"O' course I am. Have you come up with anything?"

"Not yet. I need to know a bit more about things. D' you mind if I ask you something a bit personal?"

"I told you most of it already. Still, fire away."

"It's about Reg Abthorpe. Where did he come from, and what does he really want with us?"

There was a long silence, and Herbert wondered if he'd gone too far. But he knew he was on the right track. This was the nub of it all. What was it between Willy and Reg?

"Willy?" There was no answer. Then a long sigh, and William began to speak. "It's been kept quiet all these years," he said. "Martha helped. It must have been like a knife in the back for her. Bert . . . promise you'll never tell?"

"You can trust me, Willy. You know that."

Willy coughed, then cleared his throat, and said in a

flat voice, "Reg is my son. His real name is Cox. And he's after my money."

"What! Your son? Then who was his mother?"

"I'll never tell anyone that. And don't try to guess. It's my secret and it'll go to the grave with me."

Herbert's thoughts were whizzing around. That certainly explained why Reg wanted Willy in his grasp; but why him, Herbert Everitt, innocent widower retired to the country? As if reading his thoughts, William said, "And not just my money. He'll have his eye on yours. Blackmail, it'll be. Co-operate, or we make you disappear for ever."

"Just because I saw the badger-killers?"

"That'd have been the start of it. With me, he claims he is entitled to his inheritance. Wants me to change my will. I've stuck out so far, but I expect he'll get my signature in the end. I've really ceased to care, Bert. Your idea of sharing your house, coasting peacefully to our end, seems fine to me. I've no other heirs that I know of, so he might as well have it."

"No! Willy, no! He's a crook! You have no idea what kind of crimes he's responsible for. Don't let him get away with it, for God's sake! There's two of us in this, and we'll beat him yet." Herbert had no idea how, but he had to keep Willy propped up at all costs, if there was any hope of either of them seeing Blackberry Gardens again.

FIFTY-ONE

❧

WHERE ON EARTH WAS REG? FRANCES WAS BEGIN-
ning to worry. Not on Reg's behalf, but her own.
Much as she hated him, she felt safer when he was in the
house than when he was out of her sight, plotting and
scheming with his crooked helpers. She did not trust any
of them. It was getting dark, and she looked out of the
front window, still from behind the net curtains, though
since she had talked to Lois Meade she felt a little more
confident. At least she wasn't bearing the whole weight
herself.

At first she thought the figure hurrying down the
Gardens was him. But then she recognized the stooping,
lanky figure. It was Shorty. He came straight into the
driveway and round the back of the house. She went
quickly to make sure the door was locked.

"Let me in, for Christ's sake!" Shorty hissed through
the keyhole. "There's been a hitch!"

Frances reluctantly opened the door and let him in. He
was pale and trembling. "There's been an accident," he
said, slumping down on a kitchen chair.

"That'll save us a deal of trouble, then," said Frances
calmly.

"No, he's not dead! It was Everitt's dog. Reg knows
where the old men are, and we were guarding them in
turns. It suits Reg to keep them there. He was watching
on his own, and the dog got him on the ankle. A very
nasty bite. He can hardly walk."

"And the dog?" Frances knew the answer.

"Shot him, o' course. Bloody little terrier. They're the worst." Shorty looked longingly at a whiskey bottle on the kitchen worktop.

"Forget it," Frances said. "Where is he now?"

Shorty hesitated. He had little to lose now, and he was desperate that the plan should still succeed. "He's at the farm, holed up in that barn he's made into a garage. We told you. He made a good job of it. Nobody'd know."

But I do, thought Frances. "Is he staying there?" she asked.

"No. He's not too good. Needs proper looking after."

"So he's coming here? Suits us, doesn't it?"

"He's not coming to you," Shorty said, shaking his head. "Doesn't trust you, now he's crippled. He's got a place to go. Back to Mother. But don't ask me any more. I've sworn to keep it secret, especially from you, Reg said."

"It's never stopped you blabbing before, and don't forget I've still got the stuff." Frances said. Shorty knew when he was over a barrel, and looked fearfully around the kitchen. He whispered a couple of words to her. She nodded, and said, "So you'd better take it and leave me out of it. You can get his gun when he's conked-out there, and then carry on. What about his mother?"

"We'll take care of her," Shorty said carelessly.

Frances gave him the packet, opened the door and half-shoved him out of it. "Good luck, and I don't want to see you again. Ever."

It was completely dark now, except for a single street light in the Gardens, and after a while, Frances drew the curtains across, shutting out the night. Had she not, she would have seen a figure limping painfully along the Gardens in the direction of her house. As it was, she relaxed, and, looking forward to an evening of uninterrupted telly, she went towards the telephone to ring Lois Meade. But the terriers began to bark frantically, and then were suddenly quiet. Better take a look. As she opened the door of the outhouse where they were confined, the limping man came round the corner of the house and before she could scream he had his clammy hand over her mouth.

FIFTY-TWO

BEN CULLEN HEARD A SINGLE SHOT. HE RAN DOWN-stairs to where his parents were watching television, but they said they'd heard nothing. He looked at the screen and saw cowboys racing across a sandy landscape, shooting as they went. That was probably it, then. His father turned down the sound, and they all listened. Silence, except for a randy cat on the prowl.

"It could have been one of those rook-scarers, Ben," his mother said.

"Or a firework," his father added. "Kids let them off all the year round these days. Any excuse, and it sounds like an air raid."

"You're too young to know what an air raid sounded like," Ben scoffed. "Still, I expect you're right. I'm off out. Meeting Floss." His father turned up the sound, and was once more engrossed in the movie.

REG LIMPED ALONG TOWARDS THE HILL LEADING TO the farmhouse. The pain in his ankle was agony. Shorty had dropped him off to go to Frances' house, and they'd arranged to meet on the corner. Nelly would catch them up there. He hoped to God that the two idiots would be waiting, and had not decided to betray him after all. He'd had to cross their palms with more than silver to persuade them to help him. Now that he was so lame, they thought they had the upper hand. Reg caressed the gun in his pocket. They'd soon find out how wrong they were.

A flashing light signalled that they were there. At least, one was. Shorty was on his own, and whispered, "Get in quickly, Reg. Nelly had a quick job to do. He'll meet us there, where we're going."

"How?" Reg was irritated. He intended to finish the relationship once and for all, with both of them.

"Borrowed a bike. Won't take him long." Shorty helped Reg into the front seat, and shut the door. "We'll go a different way round," he said. "Just in case."

"In case of what?" Reg said. He was sure they were up to something. Still, they were unlikely to turn down the large sum of money he had promised them at the end of the job. And the info he had on them still gave him power over them.

At last, after negotiating twisting lanes that Reg could have sworn he'd never seen before, they drew up outside his destination. "We'll wait outside until Nelly gets here," he said. That should fix them.

Shorty began to disagree, but felt the gun hard against his ribs. "Right, Reg," he said, "you're the boss."

They waited in silence and darkness for a while, and then Shorty said, "Is your mother expecting you?"

"Shut up and don't be so bloody ridiculous," Reg said fiercely.

At this moment, Nelly arrived. He leaned into the car, and said to Shorty, "Job done."

Reg said, "Get in the back, both of you." Nelly began to splutter, until he saw the outline of Reg's gun waving at him. He hopped quickly into the back seat, and Shorty followed him. His feeling of dread was justified. Nelly's last thought was a prayer that someone would come from somewhere and rescue them. But nobody came.

IVY BEASLEY LIFTED HER TELEPHONE AND DIALLED Ellen Biggs. She had formed a habit of calling the old lady around bedtime, just to make sure she was all right and did not need any help. Not that Ivy herself would dream of turning out, but she could alert Doris, who was always ready for anything.

There was no reply. Ivy tried again, in case she had di-alled the wrong number. Still no reply. The old thing was deaf as a post, but she usually heard the telephone. She would not have gone to bed so early. She was quite a late bird, saying she did nothing all day to get tired. Ivy shook the telephone receiver in irritation. She dialled Doris, but there was no reply from her either. Then she remem-bered. Saturday was whist night, and they often stayed at the village hall until half past ten, gossiping and drinking tea. A wicked waste of time, in Ivy's opinion. What should she do, then? She dialled again.

Lois was in her office, catching up on paperwork while Derek was at the pub, and answered the telephone immediately. "Miss Beasley! Is something the matter? Are you ill?"

"Calm down, Mrs. Meade," Ivy replied. "Nothing wrong with me. No, it's Ellen Biggs. I can't get any reply from her. I always ring her about this time, just to check the silly old thing hasn't fallen over and can't get up. I tried Doris too, but she's playing whist instead of staying at home like she should."

"So you want me to do something?" Lois was not keen. She was tired, and was sure that Ellen had gone to bed early. Maybe getting a cold, or just feeling like an early night.

"Indeed I do," Ivy said. "I want you down at The Lodge as soon as possible. I've got a feeling in my bones that something's up."

Lois suddenly remembered Frances. Was this her sign? "You haven't been talking to Mrs. Wallis, have you?" she asked.

Ivy's caustic reply convinced her that it was not the sign. "Who's she when she's at home? Don't talk rub-bish! Get over here, and bring your cop with you," Ivy said firmly, and hung up.

Oh my God, Lois thought. It must be something to do

with Reg. Frances had said he was behind the whole thing. And Ivy knew more than she'd ever told about the Coxes and the Biggses. She was sure of that. She dialled Cowgill, and thanked God that he answered. He could not believe his luck when he heard Lois's voice. "Listen, Cowgill," she said urgently. "No backchat, just do as I ask. Please."

He listened carefully, told her to do nothing until he got there. "Do *not* try to enter the lodge," he said. "That's an order, Lois."

But Lois had put down the telephone and was pulling on her coat. "Got to go out for half an hour!" she yelled to Gran in the sitting room, and was in the van and on her way to Ringford before Gran could get to the door to stop her.

Now Lois was certain Ellen was in danger. She had no idea why, unless William Cox had escaped from wherever he and Herbert Everitt were being held. Cox might have gone to Ellen's cottage to threaten her. But why? He had no reason to. At least, not unless it was connected with Ellen's poor sister. It had begun to rain, and the roads were slippery with mud deposited from huge tractor tracks. Skidding on a bend, Lois realized she was driving too fast, and slowed down. The familiar journey seemed to be taking hours.

There was a car parked outside The Lodge, and Lois drew up behind it. She didn't recognize it, and could see nobody inside. Probably a courting couple indulging in a bit of the other in the back seat, she thought, and didn't look too closely. She walked up Ellen's garden path and knocked at the door. There were no lights, and her alarm grew. She told herself that, of course, the old lady had gone to bed. She was probably snoring happily and dreaming of chocolate cake.

She was about to turn and go back to her car, when the door opened slowly. She could see a dark figure and knew that it was not Ellen. "Get in here quickly," said a voice, and she began to back away. A hand came out and grabbed her arm. "This is a gun, Mrs. Meade, and I shall not hesitate to use it."

A quavering voice called out from the sitting room, "Do as he says, Lois! Please do!"

Looking hopefully back into the road, and seeing no sign of Cowgill, Lois reluctantly did as she was told. Once inside, she saw in the dim light of a dying fire that Ellen was tied up in a chair, pale as a ghost and her face wet with tears. Lois rushed across and tried to untie the narrow string that was cutting into Ellen's wrists.

"Get back!" snapped Reg. "If you both do what you're told, she'll be free in a while. Matricide has so far been against my principles," he said, and laughed.

He's lost it, thought Lois, mad as a bloody hatter. What does he mean, anyway? Matricide? Then the penny dropped. Ellen is Reg's mother. And his father? She looked at him, and the resemblance was clear. An unholy alliance, since it was her sister Martha, and not Ellen, who had married William Cox. She looked from one to the other, and Reg laughed again.

"You've twigged, have you, Mrs. Meade? Not the quickest off the mark, are you? Fancy yourself as a bit of a detective, I hear. Well, look where it's got you. A nice old lady tied up and in tears, a desperate, wounded man, and yourself looking into the barrel of his gun. Not what you'd call an unqualified success. Of course, if I'd known about your little hobby, I'd not have asked you to clean Everitt's house, would I?"

"You mean your uncle?" Lois said sourly, sitting down heavily on a chair next to Ellen. The pointing gun did not frighten Lois much. It wasn't the first that had been aimed at her over the years, and she hoped she would be warned when Reg was about to use it. If she had known she was number four on the list for tonight, she might not have been so confident.

"What uncle?" Ellen said, sniffing away tears. "He ain't got no uncle. There was just Martha and me, and Cox didn't have no brother. Not that I know of, anyway. Now just you listen to me, Reg," she said, gathering her strength. "This is the wrong way to go about things. You'll come off worst, and that's a fact. You stay here with me until you're better, then go. I'll not say a word."

"Too late to try mothering," Reg said, all smiles gone. "You couldn't get rid of me fast enough when I was born, could you? Sent to an orphanage, and good riddance. And Auntie Martha?" There was venom in his voice now. "Did she know that her own sister had bunked up with her husband? With yours truly as the result?"

"O' course she did. Organized sending me away before it showed. A job in service, she told everybody. Then you come along, and she was ready with the orphanage. She weren't having me in competition with her! No, she did it all. Took you away, a few days old, and I never saw you again until recently. Then I come back to the village, spinning a tale about not liking the job."

Good old Ellen, thought Lois. She's keeping it going, hoping I've got Cowgill following on close behind. But where the hell is he?

FIFTY-THREE

❧

FLOSS PICKERING HAD AGREED TO GO BACK WITH Ben to his house for a coffee. "I expect the folks will have gone to bed, but if they haven't, they'll be pleased to see you," he said encouragingly. As they walked down Blackberry Gardens, Ben remembered the sound he'd heard. "It was like a shot," he said, telling Floss. "But Mum and Dad said they'd not heard it, and I was late for meeting you, so I forgot about it."

"Where did it come from? Which direction?" Floss was curious.

"Next door—the Wallises. The bloke's been away quite a while. Probably in the nick. But the wife's there. Name's Frances, I think. D' you think we should take a look? I'm still a bit worried . . ."

"Can't see any lights," Floss said apprehensively, but she agreed to go in with him up to the door. They knocked lightly. "We can always say we were just being neighbourly, checking that she's OK."

It was raining, and a leaking gutter dripped steadily on to the stone path which led to the back of the house. There was nothing stirring in the house.

"Come on," Ben said, taking Floss's hand. "Let's just check the other door."

Floss pulled back. "She's probably asleep. She won't thank us for waking her up." But Ben insisted, and when they tried the back-door handle, they found it reluctant to open. With a couple of shoves, it gave way.

"Yoo hoo!" called Ben. Silence.

"Ben, please, let's get out of here," Floss said urgently. "I don't like it. There's a bad feeling."

"Nonsense! It's just dark. We'll tip-toe into the sitting room, and if there's no sign of her, we'll tip-toe out again. I'll be satisfied she's asleep, and no harm done. You can wait here if you like. It's funny she didn't lock up properly, though," he added.

Floss said she was not staying on her own, and would go with Ben wherever he went. He chuckled softly, and they went quietly through the hall and into the sitting room. Floss stopped dead. "Ben! Look on the sofa! It's her, isn't it?" There was something odd about the way she was sitting, slumped to one side and head down.

"She's asleep," said Ben. "We'd better go."

He turned, but Floss grabbed his hand again. "No, she's not. Put on the light, Ben. I think I'm going to scream . . ."

Ben flicked the switch, but Floss did not scream. She saw a trail of dark patches on the carpet. "Oh my God," she said, perfectly calm. "She's dead, isn't she. Best get the police."

DEREK WAS BACK FROM THE PUB EARLIER THAN USUAL. "Hi, Gran," he said, taking off his wet jacket. "Where's Lois?" As Gran told him what had happened, he rapidly put on his jacket again and left the house, shouting back that he was going to Ringford to put a stop to this nonsense, once and for all.

He put his foot down, and careered along the narrow lanes, skidding dangerously on the bends. No bugger's going to be out in this weather, he reassured himself, as he rounded a corner. He was wrong. Standing hard on his brakes, he slid into a high grassy bank and stopped just short of a car. In the middle of the road, and with hazard lights flashing, a man was fumbling with the offside front tyre.

"What the bloody hell are you doing?" Derek said, getting out and standing over the huddled figure.

"Good evening, Derek," said a familiar voice. "I seem to have a flat tyre. Perhaps you could help. I expect we're on our way to the same place." He stood up, and was then taller than Derek. "Hunter Cowgill," he said. "Shall we get stuck in?"

"RIGHT," REG SAID, AFTER THE WHOLE SORRY STORY of his birth and childhood had been thoroughly aired. "On your feet, Mrs. Meade. We have to leave now. Sorry, Mother," he sneered. "We'd love to stay, but you'll be fine. Have a snooze, and someone will soon be along. In fact, Mrs. Meade, we should hurry now." He motioned Lois to her feet with the gun, and took a car key from his pocket. "Our carriage awaits," he said, smiling crazily.

Humour him, thought Lois. At least if we're out of here, Ellen will be all right. She went ahead of him, feeling the gun at her back, out of the cottage and down the garden path.

"Not your van," he said, as she turned towards it. "We have a limo over there. Here's the key. You drive and I'll navigate."

As she opened the door, she glanced into the back seat. What had happened to the lovers? She felt an urgent desire to vomit, but choked it back. "Take no notice of them," he whispered in her ear. "They have gone to a far, far better place. Now, get in and no tricks."

FIFTY-FOUR

ॐ

Lois's hands on the steering wheel were shaking, but she gripped hard and tried desperately to think of something to say, anything to interrupt the sound of Reg's quick, nervous breathing. He shifted in his seat from time to time, wincing with pain.

"I think I know where we're going," she said, and immediately regretted it.

But Reg nodded. "Good girl," he said. "I'm glad you've been doing your homework. Not so stupid as I thought, heh?"

"I hear things," said Lois, with an effort. "In my line of business, all kinds of gossip goes around. Some of the clients don't like it, of course," she struggled on, "and I have to tell my girls to be discreet."

"I know one of your clients who wouldn't like it," said Reg. "No, turn left here. Looks like you don't know where we're going after all. No, your Mrs. Tollervey-Jones is very much against gossip. And with reason, of course," he added, looking sideways at Lois.

He wants me to ask why, she thought. Right, then. "Why is that? She seems a very respectable lady."

"And so she is . . . now," he replied. "Don't slow down," he added, nudging her with the gun. "None of your delaying tactics!"

Lois quickened up. "Can't go too fast on these roads," she said. "So what's the old dragon done in the past?"

"You'll find out when we get there," he said, his mood changing abruptly, "so shut up and keep going."

As they approached Farnden Hall gates, Reg ordered her to turn in. "There's nobody there," said Lois. "She's still away, isn't she?"

"Shut up!" Reg said again. "Round to the back, by the stables. You know the way now. I've seen you there often enough."

So the shadow in the corridor had not been a ghost, Lois thought. She had a sinking feeling that time was running out. Cowgill would have arrived at The Lodge, and Ellen would have no idea where they'd gone. He'd probably go up to the farm next, and then God alone knew how long it would take anyone to find her. She thought of Derek, and bit her lip. He'd probably just be leaving the pub. No help there, then.

"Get out!" Reg was beside her in the stable yard, and she walked towards the back door of the Hall. "No, no," he said. "Not there. Over here, and be quick about it." He opened one of the stable doors, and shoved her inside. Then he shut the door behind her and in the inky-black darkness she heard him fumble for the switch. The light revealed a strange scene. In one corner there was a narrow bed, and against the wall stood a table with a chair pushed under it. Another more comfortable chair was beside the bed. One of the corners had been curtained off. It was a bare room, but the walls had been plastered and painted white, and there were large rugs on the floor. It was habitable, and nothing like the long-neglected stable Lois had expected.

Reg pulled the chair out, and told her to sit down. "Desirable one-roomed flat," he said, in his now feverish voice. "Empty and to let. There's another similar one next door. Reasonable rent, and all mod con. Well, nearly all. Warden controlled, and delicious food available. Previous tenants now resident elsewhere and in good hands."

Lois swallowed hard. "Food from where?" she said. "I'm very particular what I eat."

"Oh, you'll like this," he said. "Gourmet menu, straight from Dallyn Hall Restaurant. By courtesy of the lovely manageress. Piping hot, and fresh veg every day."

He's completely barking, Lois thought sadly. Was it here, then, that the two old men had been held? But where were they now? And who was giving them good care?

"I'm afraid I have to leave you now," Reg said. "Some rubbish to be disposed of." His colour was high, and his limp very pronounced. "You'll be quite safe. Locks have been recently renewed. Back soon!" he said with a mad wave, and was gone.

Lois looked around. A new, efficient-looking lock would be no help at all. She put her ear to the keyhole, and heard a car door open and Reg grunting and cursing. He was heaving those unfortunates out of the back of the car. What on earth was he going to do with them? Then she heard a lock turning. She backed away from the door, but it wasn't hers. Must be the desirable residence next door. That must be where he's putting them. He would soon be returning, then. After more of Reg swearing and cursing, she heard the car door slam shut, and quickly switched off the light. She stationed herself so that she would be behind the door when he came in. With any luck, he would be surprised by the darkness and hesitate for a few seconds. Please God, let it be enough time, prayed Lois.

Hours seemed to go by. Then Lois heard Reg's footsteps on the cobbled yard, and braced herself. The door opened slowly, inch by inch, cautious Reg, ever watchful. Finally he stepped forward, saying, "Wherever you are, don't—"

Lois put out her foot, at the same time grabbing his arm and forcing him into the stable. It went like clockwork. He sprawled at her feet, yelling with pain and rage. He still held the gun, but had dropped the door key. For one moment she wanted desperately to run. But somehow she stayed to pick up the key, watching as Reg began to pull himself up and bring his gun round towards her. Then she was out, and a shot just missed her as she locked the door behind her and pocketed the key.

She realized Reg had taken out the car key, and began to run, faster and faster, down the long drive away from the Hall. Suddenly she was blinded by headlights, and then more lights following on behind. Dazzled, she stepped off the drive and on to the grass, waving her hand.

"Lois Meade! Get into this car at once and no sodding arguments!" It was Derek, of course, in his van, but next to him . . . ? Good God, it was Cowgill, looking equally stern.

Lois hesitated. "Who are those others?" she said, and then Derek got out of the car, lifted her up bodily and dumped her on the floor of his van. "Sit there and say nothing," he said. "I'm doing all the talking from now on."

Cowgill said nothing, but Lois could see in the driving mirror that he had a small, chilly smile. "Where do we go, Lois?" he said, and Derek looked angrily at him. Cowgill shrugged. "Well, Derek, we need to clear this up quickly. You said so yourself."

"The stables," Lois said. "Reg Abthorpe is locked in there, and he's got a gun. He's behind it all, and Ellen what about Ellen?" she added anxiously.

"Behind us, in the next vehicle," said Cowgill, "and behind them we have Mr. Cox and Mr. Everitt, all of them keen to see Mr. Abthorpe-cum-Cox."

Lois began to speak, but choked, and Derek said in a kinder voice, "Don't worry, me duck, we'll explain it all later. Now, here we are. Over to you, Inspector bloody Cowgill." Raised eyebrows were his reply, and Cowgill disappeared to talk to his boys in the following cars. Then the tottery figure of Ellen came towards them, and Derek helped her into the passenger seat, then joined the others.

"Stay here," ordered Cowgill, and a posse of police approached the stable door.

"Ellen! Are you all right?" Lois said, from her uncomfortable crouching position in the back. "Never mind about that," Ellen said. "If those cops get anywhere near him, he'll shoot himself. I've got to get there first. Quick, Lois, help me out. They won't dare to stop me. Not an old bag like me."

"Now what am I going to do?" Lois said under her breath. She thought of calling Derek, but in the end she struggled from the back of the van, and quietly helped Ellen out into the yard. All car lights were off, and a deadly quiet prevailed.

"Let go, dear," whispered Ellen, and Lois reluctantly watched the hunched old lady softly approach the men. Just as Cowgill stepped forward, about to hail his quarry, Ellen said, "Wait! Let me talk to him first. Please . . . he's my son . . ."

As Lois watched, fingers crossed on both hands, a torch shone on the stable door, and she saw Ellen approach. Her voice was suddenly strong and authoritative. "Reg! It's y' mother! I know, not much of a one, but I'm all you've got. And I'm old and cold, and I want to help. Let me in, dear, and we'll have a little talk." Now she sounded like a mother talking to a naughty little child. Silence followed, and the tension in the night air was palpable.

Then a grating voice came from inside the stable. "Can't let you in. Haven't got the key."

Lois rushed forward and gave Ellen the key. She inserted it and turned. "Unlocked now, dear. Let Mother in, there's a dear." Now there was the sound of agonized sobbing, and Lois put her hand to her mouth.

"For God's sake be careful, Ellen!" she whispered. Cowgill came forward and took Lois by the arm. Slowly he edged her back to join the others. Now there was nothing but the sound of Reg's despair, louder as he approached the door. It began to open, light shone out, and Ellen walked in.

Immediately, there was a police semi-circle at the ready, guarding the open door. Reg had switched on the light, and a gun could be seen in his hand, hanging loosely at his side.

"Now then," said Ellen in the same soothing voice, "let's have some sense in this silly nonsense. I'm your mother, and you must do what I say. Just for once." Lois could see inside from where she had retreated into the yard, and couldn't believe that Ellen had a warm smile on her old face. "Better start by giving me that thing," she heard Ellen say. Just as Reg's arm was stretching out to give her the gun, a figure hobbled silently across from the cars and plunged straight through the police and into the stable.

In the sudden chaos, there was a shot, and as Lois cried out, "No, no, not Ellen!", she saw that the intruder was William Cox, and he was being carried out, his face covered, by a couple of policemen.

With order restored quickly, Reg Abthorpe was escorted yelling and screaming with pain into one of the police cars. Derek was by Lois's side, and ordered her into the van. "That's enough," he said. "Satisfied, are you? Old Cox dead, his son a raving lunatic, and Ellen a collapsed old woman. A good night's work, would you call it?"

Lois ignored him, and lowered the van window, shouting loudly, "Cowgill! Where's Ellen?"

He came over, and said that Ellen was fine, just shaken up, and was in the care of a very nice policewoman. "Go home now, Lois," he said. "And listen to what Derek has to say. It's for you to decide."

FIFTY-FIVE

❧

Lois and Derek were greeted by Gran with a broad smile on her face. "Guess what!" she said.

"You won the Lottery," Lois answered wearily.

"If only," said Gran. "No, something nicer. Bill phoned. Rebecca's had the baby, and they're calling her Louisa! She's quite small, but fine, and Bill wants you to go with him to see her tomorrow, Lois. Lois and Louisa! I think there's a compliment in there somewhere!"

Lois, exhausted and confused, burst into tears. Derek put his arm around her and led her out of the kitchen and into the sitting room. "Sit there, me duck," he said, "an' Gran will make us a nice cup of tea."

"What did I say?" Gran said, as Derek came back.

"Oh, it's not you," he said. "We've had a lousy evening. Let's all have some tea, and then I've got something to say to Lois and I suppose it'd better be in private."

Gran sniffed. "You don't have to tell me. I know when I'm not wanted. I'll take my tea up to my room and watch telly up there. You go back to Lois and I'll bring the tea."

Derek sighed. He joined Lois on the sofa, and put his arm around her. She sat stiffly, not yielding. "So what have I got to listen to?" she said.

"You know, don't you?" Derek began. "But this time I'm deadly serious. If you want to keep this family together . . ."

"You mean you and me?"

"Yes, I do. If you want us to stay together, you have to promise me you'll have nothing more to do with Cowgill, give up all these dopey ideas of bein' a private detective, and concentrate on your business and us. It's that simple, Lois. As Cowgill said, it's for you to decide."

Lois was silent for a couple of minutes, then she said, "Can I decide later? Can't think straight at the moment. Tomorrow? Will that do?"

Derek withdrew his arm. "Yep," he said sadly. "That'll do."

NEXT MORNING, VERY SOON AFTER BREAKFAST, THERE was a telephone call for Lois. It was Ellen Biggs, sounding jaunty. "Lois? Can you come over this afternoon and have a cup of tea with me? I'm planning on makin' a cake to a new recipe, and I want a second opinion before I try it on old Ivy. And," she added more quietly, "I got somethin' to tell you. All right, then? Good. See y' later."

Five minutes later, there was another call. It was Ben, and his voice was strained. "Mrs. M," he said, "would it be all right if I did Floss's job tomorrow? She's a bit off-colour." Then he told her why, and she sat down hard on her office chair.

"Poor Frances," she said, and then, "All right, Ben. Sounds like both of you'd better take the day off. We'll manage."

He said it was kind of her, but he'd rather be doing something. "See you at the meeting," he said.

Of course, she thought, it would be Monday tomorrow. Back to business.

But before she could pick up her diary, a third call came in. This time she almost put down the phone, but didn't. "Hello? Lois, are you there?" It was Cowgill. "How are you this morning?"

"What do you want?" Lois couldn't believe he wouldn't give her a day or two to recover. "I'm very busy this morning."

"Ah, that's a pity."

"Why?" Lois was aware of Gran, lurking out in the hall, and kept her voice low.

"It's just that Herbert Everitt is very keen to get back to his house straight away. We found him a nice place to sleep last night, but he's determined to go back to Blackberry Gardens this morning. I was hoping you might be able to help. Maybe put some flowers, a few supplies, that kind of thing." He paused, waiting for Lois to speak.

"You don't have to ask," she said finally. "I'll be glad to help the old boy. What time?"

They arranged for Lois to be in the house half an hour before Herbert arrived, to make sure he got a good welcome. By the time Lois got there, half the village was waiting on the pavement with flowers and streamers. How on earth had the news got round? Oh well, Lois thought, as she went up to the house and let herself in, I should know by now that villages are full of mystery.

A cheer went up, and she opened the front door. Tears were in her eyes as she saw Cowgill helping Herbert out of the car. She saw the old man shake off Cowgill's arm, and walk unaided to the reception on the pavement. After a few minutes of greetings, he turned towards the house. "Blackberry Gardens, here I come!" he shouted, and made his sprightly way up to the door.

"Now," said Lois. "You two sit down, and I'll bring in the coffee."

She handed it to the two men, and then Cowgill said, "Sit down, Lois. Herbert has something to say."

It was very embarrassing for Lois, and she tried to deny that her part in it was in any way important. "Oh yes, my dear," he said. "I shall never forget. But there is one more thing. I wonder if you would take me over to the kennels at Waltonby next week? We need to choose a dog." He hesitated, then continued, "I can't replace Spot, but I've always fancied a Cairn. There's a breeder there, and they've got some pups. Would you mind?"

"Delighted!" said Lois. "We'll fix it up."

Cowgill rose to his feet. "And there is one more job for me to do," he said. "I must get your freezer open,

Herbert. I need to see inside. Have you got a key to the padlock?"

"What padlock?" Herbert shook his head.

"Ah, right," Cowgill said. "I'll ask you to stay here and talk to Lois while I go and open it." He disappeared, and loud metallic noises floated through to the sitting room.

Herbert rose to his feet. "I'd better go and help," he said, and before Lois could stop him, he set off. She followed closely behind, and then they stood staring at the opened freezer. Cowgill tried to shut the lid, but Herbert stopped him. "It's all right. I've seen worse," he said.

The freezer was full to the top with carcasses in plastic bags. There were badgers, foxes, game birds, and some unidentifiable furry bodies. Herbert spoke first. "Seems I've got my own private slaughterhouse, kindly donated by Reg," he said. "If I had my way, there'd be another corpse in there." Then he turned and walked back to the hall. He touched the flowers that Lois had arranged. "Thank you, my dear," he said. "And now I'll just go up-stairs and have a little rest, if you don't mind. You have no idea how wonderful it is to be home."

FIFTY-SIX

༄

ELLEN'S COTTAGE WAS NEAT AND TIDY, WITH A BRIGHT fire in the hearth. "Sit down, dear," she said. "You're lookin' a bit peaky this afternoon."

Lois smiled. "*You're* looking very well," she said.

"Nothing like a few problems solved to buck you up," Ellen said, and handed Lois a cup of coffee and slice of airy-looking sponge, filled with jam and cream. "Get that into you," she added, "while I let you into a few things.

Probably should've told you months ago, but there it is."
Lois said nothing, and waited. Ellen settled herself in her
armchair, and began.

"About Reg, first of all. You know he was taken away
from me after he were born. Then, after all these years,
he turned up a month or two ago, told me who he was,
and asked to come in. He said he knew William Cox was
his dad, and he'd come to collect what was owing to him.
Little did he know that most of that farm belongs to the
college! I tried to tell him, but he wouldn't listen. Said
my mind was wanderin'."

"Nothing wrong with your mind! " Lois exploded.

Ellen smiled, and continued, "He needed a place to
stay now and then, and where better, he said, than with
his old Mum. I weren't keen, but he didn't give me much
choice. He were into that badger-baiting game. An' all
that stuffin' trophies an' that. An' he charged Londoners
to come down here and 'ave a bit of excitement with the
baitin' an' that."

Lois had a quick mental picture of the contents of
Herbert's freezer. "Did he ever threaten you at all?" she
said.

"Not in so many words," Ellen said. "Mind you, I
think it was why I landed up in 'ospital. The worry of it.
It were just that sometimes he could be really nice, and I
wished I'd known him years ago. But other times, he was
not nice, in a cruel, hard way. Said some awful things.
An' I must admit I were a bit afraid of 'im."

"But where did he stay in this cottage? There's only
this room and your bedroom?"

"Oh, he could kip down anywhere. I reckon he'd led a
dodgy life, skipping from one place to another. Very good
at disappearing, were my Reg. I just wanted you to know
this, Lois, because you can't turn against your own flesh
and blood. In the end, I thought I could mebbe help him.
But it were too late."

Ellen was staring into space, and her cup began to
slide off the saucer. Lois leaned forward, steadied it, and

patted Ellen's arm. "You've got nothing to regret, Ellen. It was your sister's fault, taking the baby away."

"Not really," Ellen said. "Everythin' that's happened is down to William Cox in the end. If he'd bin a proper husband to Martha . . . But he were like a randy dog. All round the village, he went. Even her up at the Hall. When she were young, she were a good-looking girl. Hard to believe now, I know! Still, she fell for William's charms, head over heels. Her family put a stop to that, but Reg found out about it and now he's got her over a barrel. She'd do anything, he said, to stop him spreadin' the story. That's how he got them stables to do up. I suppose he thought it would be a good place to go when he needed to keep out of the way, or for them two crooks working for 'im. Then, o' course, they came in useful for the old men."

"But did he tell you about it?"

Ellen nodded. "Yep. I knew where to send the cops last night. He's boastful, is Reg. Couldn't resist telling me how clever he is. An' it didn't take him long to find 'em, after they escaped. They hid up in that old ruined cottage in Farnden thicket. Most people don't know it's there, but Reg did. I must say the cops were quickly on to that, once I told 'em where to go. O' course, Reg didn't think I'd ever tell. But there's always a final straw, ain't there? You were it, Lois. I wasn't 'avin' him hurt you."

"You saved my life, Ellen," Lois said seriously. There was a silence, and then she said, "Did you talk to Mr. Everitt at all, after William Cox was killed?"

Ellen sighed. "Yes, Herbert Everitt were in the car with me and the policewoman. He were blubbin' his heart out. God knows why! I don't like to see a man cry, d' you Lois? Not manly, somehow . . . Still, if my Reg had done a bit more cryin' when he were a kid in that home, maybe they'd've let me 'ave 'im."

"Oh, Ellen! And you've known all along what Reg was up to, and kept it to yourself?"

Ellen looked straight at Lois, and her lip trembled. "Wouldn't you, Lois, if it was your Jamie, or your

Douglas? I really thought I could help him. But he got in with the manageress at Dallyn Hall. Nasty piece of work, that one. He got her under his thumb, and there were no stoppin' him then."

There was nothing Lois could say to that, and seeing Ellen on the verge of tears, she changed the subject. "This cake," she said, "is the best sponge I have ever eaten in the whole of my life. It's too good for Ivy Beasley!"

With a sniff and a weak smile, Ellen replied that nothing was too good for Ivy. At least, that's what Ivy thought.

When Lois had judged it safe to leave, she said, "Thanks a lot, Ellen. Now, are you going to be all right here on your own."

"I'll be fine," the old lady answered. "Plenty of friends, and no more surprise visitors, I hope." She paused, and then took Lois's hand. "What d' you think'll happen to 'im, Lois?"

"Broadmoor, I should think," Lois said. "Taken care of for the rest of his life, Ellen. Nothing more for him to worry about." Though I hope I'm wrong about that, Lois added to herself. I know what I'd do with him.

On her way home, she thought again of Derek's ultimatum. Perhaps he'd give her more time. After all, later on she was going with Bill to see the new baby. Another day wouldn't make much difference, surely? She loved Derek dearly. Wasn't that the most important thing? Well, it was Sunday today, not a day for big decisions. Nothing much happens on a Sunday, does it?